The Runaway Rock Star

ROCK STAR KISSES, BOOK ONE

Veronica Blade

PUBLISHING

Gardnerville, Nevada

The Runaway Rock Star

Crush Publishing, Inc
Gardnerville, NV 89460
www.CrushPublishing.com

Crush Publishing, Inc name and logo are trademarks of Crush Publishing, Inc and
are used only with its permission.

The places, characters and events portrayed in this book are fictitious. Any simi-
larity to real persons, living or dead, is coincidental and not intended by author.

ISBN 978-0-9910756-7-6

Cover design and layout by Rose Nomura

Printed in the United States of America

The Runaway Rock Star

ROCK STAR KISSES, BOOK ONE

EXCERPT

As Liam slid his palm around the nape of my neck and slowly inched toward me, I knew I should push him away. Kissing him was a bad idea. But since seconds ago when he'd admitted to wanting me, all I could think about was feeling him against me. Maybe I needed to get the kiss out of the way so my brain would start working properly again.

He paused with his mouth hovering over mine, as if asking for my blessing.

Oh, to hell with it. I dropped my purse on the seat, raised my chin, and slipped my fingers though the belt loops of his jeans. He moved in closer, and I inhaled sharply before his lips brushed my own. He moved his mouth over mine, lingering, teasing, then grazed my bottom lip with his teeth just before he withdrew. Shivers danced over my arms, and my stomach dipped.

I barely caught my breath before his mouth came crashing down on mine again. I opened for him, and our tongues tangled, causing tingles to spread out from my belly. He took the kiss deeper. As dizziness swept through me, a small moan escaped my lips, and I gripped his arms to keep my balance.

Abruptly, Liam muttered a soft curse, stepped away,

and ran his hands over his head. "I promised myself I wouldn't molest you. What the hell is wrong with me?" He dropped his arms and stepped back.

Nothing was wrong with him. Absolutely nothing.

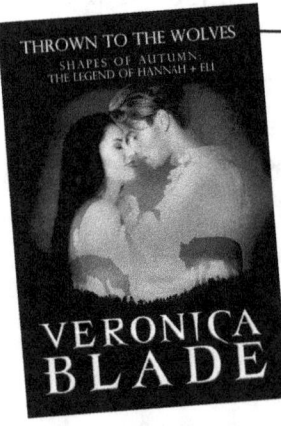

For Zayne Lily Blade

I'm so happy you came into my life. You drive me crazy, but I love that you're mine.

CHAPTER ONE
★ *Liam* ★

I burst into my Hollywood Hills mansion, slamming the garage door behind me. Red-hot fury wrapped itself around my brain like tentacles as I drove my f¬¬¬ist into the drywall. White chunks skittered along the wall and settled on the dark maple floors.

"Damn you, Faith!" I clenched my throbbing fist and stumbled to the bathroom. At that moment, I hated my older sister more than anyone else in the entire universe.

I rooted through the drawers for my clippers. Anger festering into a frenzied rage, I set the length for number five and sheared strips across my scalp until dark brown hair littered the floor. Then I decimated my trademark goatee.

Since I'd graduated high school six years ago and decided to skip college to pursue a music career—much to my stepfather's disappointment—I'd always had long hair and hadn't exposed my chin in ages. Totally worked for my rocker image and the girls seemed to love it. Right now though, I wasn't in the market for a hookup and couldn't risk the tabloid attention. I just needed to slip past my gates unrecognized.

After cramming enough clothes into a suitcase to get me through the next week or so, I locked up. Inside the garage, I stalked past the Audi R8 and the Viper, then halted in front of my newest acquisition: a fully restored 1968 Shelby Cobra convertible. I'd been too busy touring to test-drive it, and only my manager knew I'd bought it. Which meant no one would be expecting me to be in it.

Least of all my sister. The mere thought of her made acid rise up into my throat, and I white-knuckled the steering wheel. I needed to put some miles between me and Los Angeles, take some time to think. Preferably without the photographers all over me. For just a few days, I'd have privacy to lick my wounds.

I used to crave media attention — until my sister Faith turned it into a problem.

Late autumn's frigid fog wove through the streets like spider webs as I rolled my car through the gate, checked both directions for paparazzi, and cut out onto the street. All good. A couple of blocks later, I stopped for a red light, stared down at my raw, bruised knuckles, and winced. Smashing my fist into the wall wasn't the smartest thing I'd ever done. Then again, neither was providing the perfect photo op last night.

The green sign overhead pointed the way to the freeway entrance; time to figure out which way to go. Heading south toward San Diego might lead to Tijuana. I didn't need that kind of temptation while Faith was still pissed at me. I couldn't go west since that would dead-end at the Pacific Ocean. No doubt Las Vegas would also be a big mistake, which meant I wouldn't be traveling east either.

Full Throttle had had a gig in Reno about four years ago before we got signed, when we were desperate enough to drive seven hours to play our music for anyone who'd listen. Maybe I'd end up in Lake Tahoe or something. Enjoy the fresh air and mountains until this crap with Faith blew over.

I cruised onto the 101 freeway north, a dull ache welling in my chest. The last thing I wanted to do was leave my nephew Xander. Since the moment he'd come into the world, I'd been hooked. I'd already been away on tour for three months straight without seeing him. I'd missed the little guy so much that I'd taken an earlier flight home because I didn't want to wait another day. He was the reason I'd woken extra early this morning and sped over to Faith's.

But she'd made it clear I wouldn't be hanging out with him anytime soon. If I stuck close and waited until she came around, I'd go nuts knowing Xander was only miles away and I couldn't do a damn thing about it. So what was the point in staying?

I drove for hours, passing deserts, forests, and lakes, and the farther north I went, the longer the stretches between cities. Since I had nothing better to do and no place to be, I pulled over occasionally for a quick hike or to sit by the edge of a lake and relax to the gentle ripples of ducks swimming.

Mile by mile, the tension eased from my limbs. The

hollow in my chest gradually filled with images of the mountains, the scent of pine, and crisp country air. Yeah, getting away had been a good idea.

By the time I took the exit into Gardnerville hours later for a bite to eat, the sun had dipped low behind the Sierra Nevada. The tallest building in the small town was five stories high, and the streetlights ended abruptly a couple of miles ahead, opening up to a residential neighborhood.

I hoped they had a real restaurant. After eating drive-thru on the road all day, I'd reached my limit of crap food.

I slowed the Shelby toward a huge rustic building that could've been mistaken for a log cabin if not for the neon in the windows and the sign over the roof that said The Wagon Wheel Saloon. As I veered into the gravel parking lot, the people inside came into view. They were eating at tables, milling about, or at the bar waiting for a drink. Looked promising.

Climbing out of the car, I plucked my leather jacket from the seat and stepped into the chilly fall air toward the entrance. I inhaled the familiar scent of smoke and beer, along with fried chicken, and I picked up my pace, barreling through the door. I'd missed these kinds of bars since I'd begun playing at bigger venues.

Peanut shells crunched beneath my boots as I approached a slender podium to the left of the entrance. I scanned the large room, noting the dim lighting beneath the high ceilings, the shuffleboard near the jukebox, and washed-out black-and-white photographs hanging on wood-paneled walls alongside old tin ad signs. And judging by the skinny redheaded guy singing on stage without a band, it was karaoke night.

I stopped to check in with a petite brunette who greeted me with a friendly smile as she took a menu from a slot on the podium.

"One?" she asked.

I paused, half expecting her to recognize me. But like everyone else along the road so far, she didn't. "Yes, please."

She cast a quick glance over her shoulder for available seating. "Probably a ten-minute wait for a table, or you can sit at the bar and order right away."

I wanted to eat sooner rather than later and didn't need a whole table to myself. "Bar's fine. Thanks."

I took the offered menu and, avoiding eye contact with anyone, claimed the last stool on the end against the far wall. The opening to the bar was on my other side, which meant no one would be sitting next to me and I wouldn't be trapped in conversation. This position also gave most of the restaurant occupants a great view of the back of my head. I wouldn't be recognized that way.

"What can I get you?" A cute blonde with soft brown eyes crinkled her brows, and a small square napkin skimmed the bar top and landed in front of me.

The thought of having even one beer smothered me with guilt. Faith certainly wouldn't approve. But she wasn't around, and no one here knew me. "Whatever you have on draft is fine."

"Coming right up." She spun, giving me her profile,

and reached down for a cold glass, then positioned it under a spout. As she raised an arm to grip the lever, skin peeked out from under the red halter top. She had a flat, firm belly and a trim waist but still had enough shape where she needed it. I liked how the miniskirt showed off her curves. And from where I sat, I easily got lost in her every move. Not that I planned to spend the whole time leering.

Slanting toward me and giving me a stunning eyeful of creamy skin and the edge of the pink lace of her bra, she set a full glass in front of me. She noted the menu still in my hand and said, "Be right back."

She twisted around, and her straight gold hair swished past her shoulders as she sashayed down the bar. She served the next drink, and I got a perfect view of her legs. Damn, they were nice. Something to contemplate rather than fuming over my sister's judgy rant earlier.

Despite the blonde's rockin' body, she managed to give off a girl-next-door vibe. Tempting—if I went for girls who were barely old enough to drink.

Oh, who was I kidding? So long as they were over eighteen, I'd never cared.

I swiped my temple with my knuckle and caught a bead of sweat. The heat in this place explained why the bartender wore so little. I shrugged off my leather, slipped off the stool and covered it with my jacket. Seated again, I unconsciously located the bartender.

As she poured a Jägermeister into a shot glass, she chatted up a tall, lanky guy with a mustache. I couldn't hear what they were saying, but she beamed and desire ignited in my gut. I wanted to be the one causing her eyes to sparkle that way.

My stomach growled again, so I willed my focus back to the menu. When something brushed my shoulder, I craned my neck to see a cop standing next to me.

"Hey, Emma, can I get a coffee?" he asked her.

Cop. Great. They were trained to spot anything suspicious. For instance, people who were trying to hide their identity. I hunched over and sipped from my glass.

Emma returned with a steaming mug and slid it past me across the bar. "How's Maggie?"

"Beautiful as ever."

She grinned. "And India?"

His eyes lit up. "Said her first word yesterday."

She gave a wistful sigh. "That's the cutest age. Give her a kiss for me."

"I will." He drifted away with his drink.

Emma leaned a hip against the liquor shelf, one side of her mouth lifting. "Don't worry, you slid under his radar." She pivoted and sailed down the aisle, checking glasses to see who needed a refill.

The cop hadn't noticed my clumsy attempt at hiding, but she had. And I couldn't give her an excuse now because she was already in a conversation with a woman farther down the bar. I twitched and squashed the urge to enlighten her. I reminded myself I'd be gone soon and it didn't matter what she thought of me.

My gaze fixed on Emma's legs again, then her hips,

and as she rotated to get a bottle from a shelf behind her, my eyes clung to her butt. I'd been wrong about her being *cute*. She was gorgeous. Every inch of her.

She cleared her throat, and I realized I'd been staring at her boobs, my mouth parted. Yep, leering. Great. Thankfully, I'd be well fed soon and on the road again.

My phone vibrated, and I reached into my pocket to glance at the text.

I'm sorry. Come over tonight and we'll talk.

My muscles went rigid, undoing all the effort I'd put toward lightening my mental load. What did Faith want to talk about anyway? I knew my sister too well; she thought things through before speaking. Even if she was open to talking it out, that didn't mean she would change her mind about allowing me anywhere near Xander. I paid his preschool tuition, but apparently that didn't give me the right to spend my vacation with him.

Can't. Out of town. Will contact you when I get back, I replied.

When?

I don't know. Maybe getting some food into my belly would dull the fury.

Maybe not.

Okay, I had to admit Faith wasn't completely wrong. I should've stopped drinking last night when I couldn't count how many tequila shots I'd had. But someone had handed me another, and I forgot to care. I'd been licking salt off the neck of a half-dressed girl when a camera flashed and the moment had been immortalized.

Yeah, being caught bleary-eyed and wasted wasn't

my finest hour.

But my sister wasn't exactly a nun or anything. She'd done her fair share of drinking. In fact, she'd turned twenty-one two years before me and had bought beer for my friends and me. So who the hell was she to monitor my behavior or keep me from my nephew?

Just like I'd promised, I'd shown up early that morning, and my sister didn't even invite me in. All I could see through the door was her dark pixie-cut hair and part of a toned shoulder. She'd thrust the lit screen of her cell at me, displaying a picture from yesterday's binge. Then, as if she hadn't already made her point, she held up last week's issue of *Exposed!* and suggested I take a break from her kid. Hadn't I been doing that while I'd been away on tour?

Damn it. For weeks I'd looked forward to spending the next month with my nephew before rehearsals started up for our second CD. And because of a stupid photo in some gossip rag, Faith had changed her mind. Granted, this morning's news piece didn't help my case. But so what? I wasn't hurting anyone.

She'd even had the balls to ask, "If you had a son, would you want him to grow up to be like you?"

"Oh, you mean would I want him to follow his dream and be successful? Hell, yeah," I'd barked.

"So it's fine to do time? You'd have no problem with him making a court appearance or two?" Faith folded her arms over her chest, scowling up at me.

"I was exonerated." I frowned, wondering why

she was blowing a series of tiny incidents way out of proportion. "Why are you dredging up ancient history?"

"It was only two months ago, Liam." Faith blew a few strands of spiky bangs from her eyes and lifted her chin. "If you hadn't made bad choices and been playing around with morons, you wouldn't have been arrested in the first place."

"Who cares? No harm done and we got free publicity." I blew out a frustrated breath. "That translates into sales."

"I know how it works. The problem is that you're setting an example for millions of kids, including mine. Xander's three now, so he's processing information differently and asking questions. He looks up to you. One day he's going to be able to read the tabloids, and I don't want him to think it's cool to beat up a homeless guy because *you* did it."

"Faith, that wasn't me!" I gritted my teeth. "It was Theo. And the homeless guy started it." Granted, my bandmate enjoyed beating on things besides his drums. But the homeless guy *did* swing first.

"You keep making headlines, yet somehow it's never your fault." She reached behind the door where I couldn't see — since I was still stuck on her front porch — and produced another magazine that read "Saint Nick Spreading Fear to the Less Fortunate."

God, I hated that nickname. I'd decided early in my music career not to use my legal name, Liam Nicholas Blackwell, figuring the day might come when I'd want some privacy. For the stage, I had shortened it to Nick Black. Our lead guitarist, Sebastian, was always ribbing me for not partaking in *all* their misadventures — something which my sister didn't seem to be aware of at all. They'd dubbed me "Saint Nick," and the media had a little too much fun demonstrating why the nickname was such a joke.

She pinched the bridge of her nose. "Theo fights as well as you. He could've easily dodged the guy and nobody would've gotten hurt, but he had to show off. And you went along with it like you always do."

I had no idea what crawled up my sister's ass, but I sure wished it would crawl back down. "Always? You know half those stories aren't true."

Her voice held a hard edge. "It's the other half I'm worried about."

"Faith —"

"Please don't tell me this is the best you can do." She pressed her lips into a flat line while she paused. "How about expecting more from your friends, demanding that they be better? Maybe speak up when they get out of hand and you won't be guilty by association."

"Faith, c'mon." I groaned. "Why are you making such a big deal about this?" And why now, when I had plans with Xander?

"Because you're better than this." She expelled a breath then squeezed her eyes shut before her next cheap shot. "Because I want my little brother back, the way you used to be."

I scoffed, remembering the old me who had to

scrounge for loose change just to buy a pad of paper to jot down lyrics. "Oh, you mean when I was poor?"

"You know that's not what I mean. I love your music and people are willing to pay a lot of money to hear you sing it. I'm thrilled for you. My issue is with how you're handling this new fame. And I can't have Xander subjected to that lifestyle." She'd shook her head as if I was a huge disappointment, then followed it up with, "Maybe this will give you some time to reflect, think about where you're going in life and the kind of person you want to be."

And then she'd closed the door in my face.

I needed to reflect, huh? Think about who I wanted to be? I was twenty-four years old with a gold record, a Grammy win for Best Rock Album, and more money than I could spend. I was able to give her and Xander anything they needed and more, yet she was worried about a picture of me on the cover of some rag?

It had taken all my strength not to beat down the door and shout at her. I'd burned rubber to get home and ground my teeth the entire drive. The only thought in my head was to get the hell out of town, be someone else for a while. Just vanish.

And I'd be back on the road again, on my way to deeper anonymity, as soon as I got some food in me.

As I took another sip from my glass, I flinched at a shrill scream and liquid sloshed out the top of my mug. I wiped the drops of beer off my cheek and whirled around, searching for the crazed Full Throttle fan I'd need to dodge.

A tall blond guy wearing a yellow shirt that read

The Wagon Wheel Saloon Staff hovered near the stage. By the size of him, I guessed he was a bouncer. When I saw a girl to his left jumping up and down in front of another girl — oblivious to my existence — I realized my cover hadn't been blown. I commanded my muscles to unwind, and they complied.

Emma bent over the bar toward me, and I struggled to keep my gaze above her neck. "I didn't peg you for the type who scared easily."

Now I came off as if I was afraid of squealing women. *Great.* The urge consumed me to prove to Emma that very little scared me. Certainly not her. And I definitely didn't hate the idea of hanging around overnight to show her a few other things, like how I'd explore every inch of that incredible body. "Startled me is all. Didn't expect it to be so noisy."

Her gaze swept the room, then met mine again, her brow lifting. "In a place this busy?"

Good point. I nodded toward a customer several stools away. "He needs another drink."

She waited a beat, her eyes riveting to my arm. "Well, if you decide you want a change of atmosphere, there's a biker bar a couple of miles up."

Okay, so she wasn't into me. Whatever. "Once I've eaten, I'm gone."

She gave me one last glance, then moved to the white-haired guy on the next stool over. "Doing all right, Frank? Can I get you another?"

I examined the menu again but got distracted by my knuckles in my peripheral vision. They were still bloody from punching the wall earlier. Blood, tattoos, paranoia around the cops, and jumpy in general. She probably thought I was some kind of thug. Now her biker-bar recommendation made sense.

My eyes fixed on her backside again, and I forced myself to stop gawking. I'd left Hollywood to escape for a few days and figure out how to get Xander back into my life, not get mesmerized by a pretty blonde with spectacular legs. I needed to eat and get the hell out of there.

CHAPTER TWO
★ *Emma* ★

I scolded my stomach for fluttering over a customer, especially someone who looked that dangerous and was just passing through anyway. What was it about a hot man in leather and tattoos that made me all squishy inside? From his strong, square jaw and clear, smooth skin to his deep green eyes and straight nose, he was stunning. All six-feet-something of him. Standing probably nine inches taller than me, he didn't have an ounce of fat around those sinewy arms. If it weren't for the scar lying vertically over his left eyebrow, he'd be damn near perfect.

And then there was his cocky, I-know-you-want-me attitude that reeled women in. I'd fallen for that type before. No way did I intend to repeat that mistake. I'd vowed to hold out for a good man who treated me with respect, not get sucked in by a pair of pretty green eyes and a wicked smile.

Actually, scratch that. I didn't want my head filled with *any* guy. Not right now. I had a degree to get, a car to save up for, and a child to raise. Right now, squeaking an extra hour out of my day, much less a whole evening for a date, was near impossible. A man would only derail me. Especially an extremely jumpy bad boy. This one was pure trouble.

But, Lord, he sure was pretty. When he'd first walked through the door, I couldn't help but take note of his black motorcycle boots and muscular thighs clad in faded jeans. His super-short dark brown hair emphasized his strong jaw, and the snug black T-shirt showed off wide shoulders and a flat abdomen. Oh, yeah, I'd noticed him.

Hot.

That particular kind of hot was dangerous though. My taste had been flawed with every guy I'd ever dated, and until I could trust my own judgment, men were off limits. Especially this one. There was something about the stranger, the way he'd slid into the corner and kept to himself. He'd been a little twitchy, which made me wonder if he was running from something. Too bad my attempt to get rid of him hadn't worked. I consoled myself with his promise to leave soon.

While I waited to hear if Frank wanted a refill, I convinced my eyes not to stray to the bad boy just a few feet away.

"Hey, Emma," Frank began as he twirled the glass in his hands. "You know, we should go out for a drink sometime."

Considering he was probably twenty-five years my senior and wore a wedding ring, the last thing I'd expected from him was a pickup line. I gave him my most innocent smile. "Yeah, we should hang out. I've been wanting to meet your wife." I laid on the sugar. "You should bring the kids too."

The beautiful stranger at the end of the bar chuckled, and my pulse accelerated. *Damn it.* The last thing I wanted was to attract his attention. And, God, the way he'd been watching me earlier made me want to yank him into the storage closet and get tangled up in him.

"What can I get you?" I asked a small group who had just arrived.

For the next few minutes, I resolved to concentrate on taking orders, making up drinks, and collecting payments. That's it. No sneaking glimpses of the pretty stranger. But when I swung around to add a bill to the tip jar, my eyes betrayed me. Rather than let on how intensely aware I was of him, I made my way to the end of the bar as if I'd been planning on going there anyway. I reached to take his menu. "Did you decide what you wanted?"

He slanted his head to one side, lips pursed as he contemplated my question. After a beat, he asked. "What's good?"

"No matter what you have here, you won't be disappointed." I cringed when I realized how that sounded. I reined in my natural tendency to be friendly so he wouldn't think I'd just flirted with him.

He eyed me a moment, and his lip twitched before saying, "Cheeseburger and fries, no onions."

"Gotcha," I said, my head bent as I scribbled on the order pad.

Breanna bellied up to the bar and set down her tray. "Emma, can I get eight tequilas for Smith Construction?" After a quick appraisal of the stranger, her eyes glinted. Though Breanna was particular about whom she dated, when she set her sights on a man, she usually got her way. I couldn't blame her for targeting this one. "You're new."

For someone acting like he didn't want to be noticed, he sure was making a splash. I poured tequila into shot glasses, not even trying to smother the inclination to eavesdrop or peer up at them on the sly.

His eyes traveled over her black wavy hair, took in her voluptuous figure, then landed on her full lips. "Yeah, fresh from LA."

I rolled my eyes and hustled to the kitchen to put in his order. I came back to find him and Breanna still chatting. I sensed an imminent hookup and wondered if he'd give her his number or stay until she finished her shift. My stomach pinched, and I reminded myself I didn't plan on dating him. Unable to resist though, I snuck frequent glances at them as I poured another drink.

"What brings you to town?" Breanna asked as I set out eight glasses for the tequilas.

Somehow managing to snap himself out of his boob-induced trance, he switched his attention to the drink in front of him. "Had to stop for food."

Breanna tossed her hair over her shoulder. "On your way to...?"

"Don't know yet. Might head to Lake Tahoe for a few days, or maybe I'll keep going and land in Oregon.

Or I could cut east and head to Montana."

I finished pouring all eight shots in time to see her shoot him a flirty smile as she picked up her tray full of fresh drinks. "Let me know if you need any help deciding," Breanna said.

"I'll do that." He angled his neck, and his eyes followed her as she swished away, his cheek bunching up in a grin. But he didn't make a move to go after her. Abruptly, his eyes met mine, catching me staring.

My cheeks heated, and I circled around to check the clock. The kitchen would be closed soon, and everyone would fill up on drinks. And any minute, the after-dinner crowd would rush me, and help hadn't yet arrived.

My gaze cemented to the sexy stranger again, and I chastised myself for getting sucked in. Thankfully, he hadn't seen me look this time. He was too busy on his phone.

A few minutes later, a ding sounded from the kitchen, and I slipped past him to retrieve his burger from the cook. I dropped it off in front of him, stifling the urge to peek over his shoulder and see who he was texting. Probably a girl.

By the time I'd made my way down the bar, handling all the refills as I went, the line waiting for drinks was two-deep. Crap, where was Duke? He should've arrived a half hour ago. I couldn't work the bar alone on a Friday night.

I hastily slid a glass toward another customer. As I pried a cap off a beer, I noticed the bar owner. "Jesus, Rocko, where is he? I'm dying back here."

His jaw tightened as he typed into his phone. "Can't reach him." As if willing a reply to appear, he stared down at his cell, his shaggy light-brown hair falling out of the baseball cap.

"What about Stephen? Can he fill in?" I asked, ringing up the cash register.

"Already tried him." Rocko glared at his phone. "Stephen's out of town until Monday."

Rocko had recently inherited the restaurant only a few months ago and didn't have a lot of experience running it. I didn't want to order my boss around, but his lack of progress told me he needed a reminder of what was at stake. "I can't keep this up all night. If you don't want to be behind the bar with me, you need to find someone else." I snatched a shaker and strainer for a martini, praying I'd get help soon.

CHAPTER THREE
★ *Liam* ★

After devouring the last bite of my burger, I briefly considered pulling the flirty dark-haired waitress into my lap. Under normal circumstances, I would've just done it. A one-nighter with a pretty local wasn't staying under the radar though, and I couldn't risk my escapades ending up on TMZ. Not only that, my eyes wouldn't stay off the blond bartender long enough to take any other girl too seriously.

The guy on the other side of the waitress was doing a little more than admiring. She swatted his hand, but instead of backing off, he smirked.

Disgusting. Not much pissed me off more than a guy who treated women like whores. I glanced around the room for the bouncer I'd seen earlier and spotted him by the stage talking to the bar owner. He was too far away to do anything about this guy, and I'd feel like an ass for summoning help when the idiot hadn't done anything seriously pervy yet.

His eyes devoured her chest, and he raised his hand toward her cleavage. No time to wait for the bouncer. I nudged her aside, stretching up until I was eye to eye with him. "Touch her and lose a hand," I growled.

The guy glared at me, but I ignored him.

"Thank you," she mouthed, then dashed off.

"Who the hell are you?" he asked, rising off the bar stool. "Why don't we finish this outside, shit chute?"

I twisted toward him, taking another swig of my beer while keeping my gaze locked on his. "I'm ready anytime you are." Hopefully, I'd get to finish my drink first.

He sneered. "Right now, sweetheart."

If I got into it with this guy, I'd probably end up in jail. My cover would be blown, and the trip would be over. Definitely further from ever seeing Xander again. Faith's words echoed through my head; I could handle myself without getting into a fight or hurting anyone. Still, backing down just wasn't in me.

After a few seconds mulling over how to handle the perv, I was about to slam my palms on the bar and take him on. But he'd already assumed the worst.

"Chicken." He snickered.

As I took a deep breath, prepared to kick his ass all the way to the exit, a pretty redhead greeted him with a warm hug. He draped an arm around her waist, and without another glance at me, they left the bar area. They huddled around the pool table, and I decided he'd probably be too busy with her the rest of the evening to mess with the waitress. Or me.

So far, my attempt at invisibility was an epic fail. And the longer I stayed, the more trouble would find me. I needed to pay my bill and get the hell out. No conversations. No brawls. No more admiring pretty girls.

When Emma bent toward a customer and her body became partially concealed by the cooler, I took a moment to scan the restaurant. The place had become even busier in the couple of minutes since I'd finished eating. More people crowded the entrance in hopes of getting a table, and I spotted several more waiting to give their order to Emma.

"Can I get my check?" I asked as soon as she headed my way again. But she'd already peeled off when someone shouted their order and drowned me out. Resigning myself to a few more minutes there, I concentrated on the guy on stage who was doing a pretty decent job with a George Strait song.

The manager was hovering again, casting frequent glances at Emma who was mixing several drinks at a time. She slid a glass toward a waiting customer, then poured some red goop in another before tossing in a straw and handing it over. Dirty glasses piled up in front of me. If they didn't get washed and put away soon, I wouldn't be able to see Emma's legs. That would be a damn shame.

Whatever. It was time to go anyway.

"How much do I owe you?" I yelled over the karaoke singer, but once again, Emma didn't hear me.

On the next stool over, a guy pounded his fist on the bar top. "Emma, get that tight little ass over here and bring me a beer. Right now, woman!"

What the hell? Apparently, that nearby stool was a magnet for jackasses. What was the deal with men who thought they had a right to be rude to women? I'd seen too many waitresses and bartenders get the worst of it—as if working in food service gave men license to treat them like prostitutes. Douche bags.

I looked toward the voice to see a huge redheaded guy with camouflage pants and a black tank top. I was six one, and this guy had more than a couple of inches on me. His size didn't necessarily mean anything though. I could probably take him.

When I'd hit my thirteenth birthday, my stepdad had decided it was time for me to man up and bought me jujitsu lessons. I hadn't practiced as often as I'd wanted to since the record label signed me three years ago, but my black belt usually held up against most guys.

"Hold up, Bobby," Emma shouted. "Got several people ahead of you."

"Get that lead out of your ass and take care of your customers. That's all you gotta do, honey."

I shot off the stool. "Watch your tone with her or we're going to have a problem."

"Who the hell are you?" He sprung off the stool and bumped my shoulder with his knuckles. "You sure you wanna do this with me, runt?"

I wanted to beat this guy's ass for being a douche, but I didn't want to end up in jail because a couple of imbeciles frequented this place. I reined in my temper, muscling through the adrenaline rush that begged me to take this moron down.

"I got this," Emma told me, then waited until she had the guy's attention. "You ever talk to me that way again, Bobby, and your days of drinking here are over. You got it?"

Bobby's jaws clenched. "You're a bartender, and I'm a customer. Now get me my damn drink!"

She lifted her chin. "No."

"I'm not gonna tell you again. Get me my goddamn drink, bitch!"

Where was the damn bouncer when we needed him? A quick survey of the room told me he was probably in the bathroom. Taking in a deep breath, I laid a hand on Bobby's shoulder. "Sit down and wait your turn or go somewhere else."

He shrugged off my hand and got up in my face. "Get out of my way, asswipe, before I hurt you."

"Last chance, buddy." I moved my stool aside. Man, he was big. "Shut your hole, or I'll shut it for you."

With a meaty fist, he swiped the counter. Glasses exploded, shards flying in all directions.

Ah, hell.

I intercepted his arm with one hand and maneuvered him into a headlock with the other. The stench of garage grease and stale beer stung my nose. Backing up, I dragged him struggling alongside me. The room grew silent as the karaoke singer on stage stopped singing and all movement in the place ceased. The crowd parted, and someone pushed the glass door open for us.

Just before I tossed Bobby onto the asphalt, I growled, "If I see you here again tonight, it's because you're apologizing to Emma." And out he went, stumbling to the ground.

I shut the door and noticed several other guys flanking me. Bobby was grossly outnumbered, which led me to believe he'd go away and stay that way. Assuming he had half a brain, when the alcohol wore off, he'd come to his senses and see what an ass he was. Hopefully, he'd be embarrassed rather than attempt revenge on me. He might not be so easy to take down if he were sober. I wouldn't be around anyway.

As expected, he glowered at us, then shuffled away. When I passed over the threshold and into the bar, nearly everyone in the place was staring. Oh, yeah, way to be invisible. If I didn't need to pay my bill, I would've fled right then.

As I approached the bar, the guy who'd perved on the waitress earlier gave me a man-nod and took a step back. Emma stood still, her gaze riveted. Oh, crap, did she realize who I was? I scanned the crowd, but no one had their cell phones up to video me.

A moment later, the noise level rose as everyone returned to whatever they'd been doing before the ruckus. Emma resumed pouring drinks.

By the look of the three-deep mob of people waiting, I wasn't going to get my bill anytime soon. Whatever. I didn't need the check. I could leave some cash on the counter and go. But as I slid off the stool, I glanced between Emma and a group of people who had just arrived. Sighing, I collected my jacket and joined her behind the bar.

She circled back toward me. "What are you doing?"

"You're short a bartender, aren't you? I don't know

how to make the fancy drinks, but I can pour a draft and wash glasses. You keep all the tips."

Her eyes shifted doubtfully before coming back to me. "What's your name?"

"Liam Blackwell."

"Well, Liam, Rocko's might show up any minute and kick you out, citing insurance liabilities and crap. Until then, I'd appreciate the help. Thank you." She gave me a shy smile before spinning around and dispensing more drinks.

I stowed my leather jacket on a lower shelf, and by the time I stood again, she was in front of me. Her gaze glided over my raw knuckles and the tattoos covering my forearms, and she retreated just a hair. "Not exactly the boy next door, are you?"

If she only knew. "Not so much."

Without further comment, she went back to the customers. For the next hour, Emma and I barely kept up with the orders. No time to admire those mesmerizing legs.

I was pouring a pitcher of draft when Rocko shouted, "What's he doing behind the bar?"

Emma didn't miss a beat as she continued slinging drinks. "I needed help, and Liam was here."

The flirty dark-haired waitress sidled up beside him. "Bobby showed up belligerent and was rude to Emma. Broke some glass and made a mess. Liam threw his ass out."

I shot Rocko a quick glance and shrugged. "If your other bartender shows up, I'll take a hike. Wasn't planning on sticking around anyway."

Rocko seemed to mull that over. "Can you sing?"

Millions of fans thought so, but I didn't want them to know what I did for a living. In my peripheral view, a thin, balding man jiggled an empty glass at me. I didn't have time to ponder why Rocko wanted to know about my singing abilities. "Uh... a little, I guess," I replied, snapping up a bottle from the well and refilling the man's glass.

"You're hired. I'll be back to set you up with the other register. When you get a minute, find me and we'll get your paperwork filled out." He turned on his heel and disappeared into the crowd.

Emma rewarded me with a smile while she strained clear liquid from the shaker into a martini glass. I grinned back, and warmth radiated through my chest. Damn, she sure was pretty.

The clock on the wall behind me said eight o'clock. If it stayed this busy until closing and the real bartender never showed, I wouldn't be bailing early. Last call wouldn't be for another six hours. And I'd be drained by then. Seemed I'd be staying the night in Gardnerville — if I found a hotel.

Hanging around might not be so bad though. I was in beautiful country, and being an average guy was a nice change. Didn't realize how much I'd missed being normal until now. Working side by side with Emma made it even better. I liked the way she moved and the way she flipped her long golden hair out of her way. I especially liked how she didn't take crap from idiot guys.

But I couldn't let myself view her as anything other than just a girl who needed help. I'd stay as long as she wanted me there, then I'd hit the road. The end.

The waitress slithered up to the bar, carrying her tray. "Welcome aboard, handsome. I need a pitcher of light draft and four glasses." She dipped her head toward the cooler at my waist.

I slid open the cover, reached in and pulled out a pitcher, then started filling it up.

"You got a girl back home?" She raised one brow.

A grin escaped me. "Nope."

She tilted her head, giving me a mischievous smile. "We're taking bets on which team you play for. You gonna make me fifty dollars richer?"

I laughed and grabbed four glasses, setting them on the tray with the pitcher. "Only if you bet that I love women."

"You're so pretty, figured you couldn't be straight. Should've followed my gut." She wrinkled her nose and left.

I chuckled and wiped a rag across the bar. The rush had passed, and I didn't see anyone who wasn't already taken care of.

"You're on," Rocko shouted to Emma.

"What's he talking about?" I asked her.

"Karaoke. I'm up next. You know, to keep it rolling until the band goes on. Think you can handle a few minutes without me?"

I shook my head. "Probably not."

"Lightweight." Emma rolled her eyes, but the corners of her mouth tugged upward. An instant later, she'd planted herself right in front of me.

She didn't wear much makeup, which was probably for the best since her natural beauty was already casting a spell on me. I couldn't imagine what would happen if she put more work into it. Not that she needed any help. And though she was slim, she wasn't skinny like so many girls in Hollywood. Her curves were refreshing. And very hot.

She looked up at me, and I had an urge to close the distance. I only needed to ease forward a few inches to feel her mouth against mine. That probably wouldn't be enough. Maybe I'd trap her against the cash register and nibble on her lip while I ran my hands up and down those shapely thighs. Or lift her up and lay her across the counter and...

Emma's cheeks flushed as she peered up at me from under her lashes. "Um, I need to get by."

"Right." I'd been drooling like a teenage boy. Tingles of embarrassment swept over the back of my neck, and I stepped aside out of her way.

That was my wake-up call. She didn't seem the type to go for a one-night stand, and I didn't do relationships. Indulging in a fantasy involving her was as far as I would ever go.

I snagged a bottle of beer from the cooler, removed the cap, and set it on the bar as Emma whispered to the stagehand, then took the microphone.

The music cued, and I recognized the tune within

the first few notes. "Blood is Gonna Spill" was one of mine, a song with lyrics too wild for a girl like her. I'd written it after binge-watching a few too many episodes of *Sons of Anarchy* and presented it to the record label as punishment for trying to get me to do a more mainstream number. They wanted to appeal to a larger demographic. I wanted to make music I was passionate about. Turned out they loved the song and asked me to write more like it.

This was the first time I'd heard someone other than me sing it. Her performing my song stirred something in me. Something that was best ignored. The rasp in her voice was outrageously sexy, and I loved the way she moved. Subtle, like she knew how to work her body but didn't feel the need to show it.

Her confidence in herself only intrigued me more. And my eyes weren't the only ones glued to her. With a wave of her hand, the audience joined in, stomping and clapping. Before I knew it, she was on the last chorus.

"This time I won't stand still. Your blood is gonna spill. Will overflow onto the road, until you've paid what's owed."

I grinned until she replaced the microphone.

An older, heavyset woman sitting a few feet down the bar pushed her empty glass toward me. "Hope you can sing, honey, because Rocko might be calling you up soon."

I froze. "What?"

She lifted a magenta, polyester-clad shoulder. "Prerequisite to working here. Didn't he ask you if you could sing? He asks everyone before he hires them."

Yeah, I vaguely remembered him asking, but I'd shrugged it off. "The place is packed. Why does he have the employees sing when plenty of people are probably waiting their turn?"

"It's been a tradition since the place opened twenty years ago. Part of its charm." Her bright pink lips curved up. "Doubt you'll be able to squirm out of it."

My mouth gaped and my mind raced as I tried to think of a song they might have which wouldn't make me sound suspiciously like Nick Black. Rap?

Oh, God.

"Liam, you ready?" Rocko shouted from the other end of the bar.

My eyes bulged as I scooped up the woman's glass and strode toward Rocko. "Uh, not quite. How about a list of the songs?" *Please have some rap where I could talk my way through it.*

He pressed his lips together as he handed me a sheet of paper. I refilled the glass, then quickly scanned the songs and landed on something that might work. Not the type of music I usually did, but that was the point. The fact that I wasn't sure if I remembered how the song went would make everyone think I was a total rookie. Exactly what I needed. Of course, it would be better if I didn't get up on that stage at all.

"You're going to make me sing on my first night?" Which would be my last.

Rocko snickered. "Do you want to keep the job?"

Not particularly. But I didn't want to make a scene, and I certainly didn't want to get thrown out when it was still hours before closing. What if Emma got slammed again and I wasn't around to help her? Or worse, what if another creep popped up and harassed her?

I narrowed my eyes at Rocko as I delivered the drink. "It's not funny." In my peripheral vision, a guy scooted a ten-dollar bill toward me. I checked the price list so I knew how much to charge, and headed back to the cash register.

"It's a little bit funny." Rocko snorted. "You got five minutes."

"Fine. I'll do 'You Can't Hide' by Sunny Raze." I shoved the sheet back at him and started to go.

"Wait." Rocko stared at the sheet. "Isn't that rap?"

"It ain't country." I grinned and fled to the other end of the bar toward Emma. "You were great out there."

"Thanks." She slanted me a smile, making me completely forget about karaoke. When a guy bellied up to the bar and called out his order, Emma elbowed me. "I'll get that. You're almost on."

I groaned and weaved through the bodies toward the stage. The emcee shrugged when I gave him my song choice. "If you insist," he said, barely holding back a laugh. Apparently, rap was a rare occasion in this place.

The bouncer passed me the microphone, and a moment later, the emcee cued the music. Forcing my arms straight and locking my knees—because moving and actually attempting to entertain the audience was not the way to stay incognito—I spoke the words scrolling on the monitor.

After the first couple of lines, all the lyrics came back to me as if I'd never forgotten them. But I pretended to have no idea what was coming so I'd appear like a newbie stuttering during my performance.

During the first chorus though, I made the mistake of closing my eyes and letting the music fill me. I lost track of where I was and inched the microphone closer to my mouth as the words flowed out. While I paced across the stage, I rapped to the audience and pumped my fist. When I got to the chorus, the crowd joined in, snapping me right into Nick Black mode without me realizing it.

When the music stopped, the lights flickered, and I was tossed back into the Wagon Wheel. I blinked, surprised that the music had thrown me so completely and I had almost given myself away. Thankfully, that song hadn't required actual singing, or the crowd would've figured it out and my sabbatical would've been over.

I searched the faces of the room for Emma, who was clapping enthusiastically. Leaving the stage, I checked for signs that I'd been recognized. No one aiming their cell at me. All I saw was encouragement, like it was a big deal I'd had the balls to get up there and sing — along with surprise that I hadn't sucked.

Anxious to resume working with Emma, I weaved through the throng of customers.

"Oh, my God, that was crazy." She laughed, grasping my forearm, then stepped back. "That wasn't your first time."

"I've *never* done karaoke before." Which was the truth.

"No singing experience?"

Uh-oh. "Sometimes I sing in the shower." Beyond Emma, a customer waved to me and pointed at his empty glass. *Saved!* I jerked my head toward the guy. "I'll get his refill."

That had been a close call and, sooner or later, I'd give myself away. The smart thing would be to leave after taking care of this guy's drink. Emma would have to deal somehow. Or Rocko could chip in. Whatever. It wasn't my problem.

I made the customer a fresh scotch and soda, rang him up, then spun around to Emma. I had to tell her she was on her own. "So..."

Emma's lips parted, her eyes wide as she waited for me to finish. When I tried to form the words to break it to her, my tongue refused to cooperate.

"Something wrong?" she asked.

About fifteen people burst through the door. Emma would need help handling them. I sighed, knowing I wasn't the kind of guy who could bail on a damsel in distress. "Nope. All good."

"Bowling alley's only open till ten. After they close, everyone comes here for the live music." She motioned toward the stage where several guys were setting up equipment. "The band just arrived. It's about to get crazy." She patted my arm and squeezed past me.

Why wouldn't a bowling alley stay open later than ten on a Friday night? Oh, right. I was in a very small town. But not so small that this place didn't have live bands.

My eyes found their way back to Emma, and a part of me was grateful for the excuse to stay.

CHAPTER FOUR
★ Emma ★

Cursing under my breath, I served yet another drink while Liam bounced questions off me — like what went in which drink and how much they cost. He had experience tending bar, that was obvious. But judging by all his questions, it had been a while and he was rusty. I wondered what he'd been doing before he took this job. And how long he would stay.

He had badass written all over him, and it bothered me that I'd swooned when he'd manhandled Bobby. I especially disliked the desire that curled in my stomach every time I caught him staring at me. Not that he'd go for a nice girl like me. Breanna seemed more his type. But if I was wrong and he tried to hook up with me, I couldn't take a chance he'd be anything like Kyle.

Even knowing a relationship with this guy would be impossible, my curiosity triumphed. "Where'd you tend bar before this?" I shouted over the band that had just begun a country rock song.

He glanced up at me from the cash register. "Nowhere."

"Then how'd you learn to do it?"

"Friend of mine. I used to throw a lot of parties." A wicked grin spread over his face.

Tattoos, almost bar fights, and he knew how to tend bar, but only because he threw so many parties. He was quite the catch.

Not.

Yet I lacked the willpower to stop staring at him. Oh, God, why couldn't I get pathetically drawn to a guy who'd love me forever without becoming over-possessive or becoming a heroin addict? I was a hot mess, for sure. This time though, I wouldn't give in. Liam was off limits.

While we slung drinks together the next couple of hours, I avoided eye contact with him and concentrated on serving my customers. That was easy since Liam had become all business. He'd barely looked my way except to ask a question.

Time ticked by, and the older crowd cleared out, replaced by younger ones who I didn't recognize, probably band followers.

"Will it stay this busy until closing?" Liam focused on drying glasses and stacking them behind the bar with the others.

"Usually, yes. Then there's cleanup."

He put away another glass. "Ever find out what happened to the missing bartender?"

"Heard he was in the hospital, but didn't get the details." I pressed my lips together.

Rocko slapped the bar with his palm, appearing out of nowhere. More likely, he'd been around but I hadn't noticed because we'd been so busy. "Heard from his wife. He's out of surgery," he said, his voice barely carrying over the band's drums.

Liam frowned. "What was wrong with him?"

"Appendix. He'll be out of commission for a few days, I think." Rocko answered, resting his elbows on the bar top. "You two worked well together tonight. Band's playing tomorrow, too, and it'll probably be even busier. Then Sunday is girls' night, two-dollar drinks until closing. A lot of women come in, and they attract a ton of men. We'll be really busy. You'll be here, right?" he asked Liam.

"Well..." Liam looked unsure, possibly trying to think of a way out.

"You have somewhere else you need to be?" Rocko's eyes thinned. "Cops looking for you?"

Liam squirmed under Rocko's gaze. And considering Liam's reaction to Dave in uniform earlier when he'd ordered coffee, being wanted by the police probably wasn't much of a stretch. Knowing my track record with men, I fully expected to be wildly attracted to someone with a warrant for his arrest.

"Liam was only helping out tonight. He never intended to stay." I tried not to care that once he left I'd probably never see him again — even if he was a fugitive. "Right?"

A quick bob of his head answered my question. "I was taking a break from my life, not looking to start a new one."

Of course he wasn't looking for a new life, especially

not a quiet one in Gardnerville with a girl he barely knew. On the other hand, wasn't it a good sign that he wanted to get back to his life? That probably meant he wasn't on the run. Not that it mattered either way since he was only passing through.

Rocko cocked his head, studying Liam. "How long is your break?"

Liam lifted one shoulder. "I have a few weeks before I have to get back, I guess. But—"

"Perfect. Stay one week, and you'll still have plenty of time to do whatever else you want. You start at six thirty tomorrow, and we're kicking it off with karaoke again. Don't sing rap next time." Rocko hopped off his stool and slipped into his office, leaving Liam with his mouth open and words stuck in this throat.

I chuckled. Rocko was sometimes a softie, especially while he'd been learning the ropes and settling into the bar, but he knew how to get what he wanted from his staff. A few minutes later Rocko returned with a bucket of ice and handed it to Liam.

Breanna rested both elbows on the bar, and I suspected her boobs might burst from her top at any moment. Liam's gazed dropped, and I sighed. Typical male.

"So you're sticking around after all," Breanna purred.

"Seems that way." He averted his gaze and bent down to restock the ice bin. "Didn't hear you singing earlier."

"You just didn't notice. I followed Emma with 'Stay' by Rihanna." Her lips formed a pout.

Liam froze, worry lines etched between his brows. "Uh, I was kind of busy."

She blew out a breath. "I must be losing my touch."

He hit her with a cocky grin. "You're definitely not losing your touch."

Breanna squinted and tapped her lip with a long pink fingernail. "But it doesn't work on *you*. I'm going back to my original theory."

He laughed as he scooped up another load of ice, his arm muscles flexing as he dumped the pile into the freezer. "I'm straight. Trust me on that."

Why did I feel that Breanna was encroaching on my territory? He didn't belong to either of us. And if we competed, she'd probably win. Breanna wasn't exactly promiscuous, but she had no problem with an occasional fling when she wanted one. And she obviously wanted Liam. Irritation lapped at the nape of my neck, like an ocean hungering to swallow me.

"Hmm." She seemed to mull that over. "When was the last time you had sex? With a *woman*."

Liam laughed louder this time. "Last night."

Breanna's eyebrows flew up as if they were trying to connect with her hairline. "Didn't you tell me earlier that you were single?"

"Yeah," he answered with a shrug.

Which meant that the girl had been a one-night stand. Lovely. That reaffirmed my faith in the male species, for sure.

"Uh, yeah..." His body went rigid, and he set the scoop on top the freezer, his eyes oscillating between Breanna and me as if he'd been caught with his hand in his pants.

The conversation had taken an ugly turn. I couldn't save him from his blunder, but a change in subject might de-awkward the moment. After glancing up and down the bar, I concluded I could handle the drink load for a few minutes. "Would you mind helping me restock the coolers?"

He smiled, his shoulders loosening up. "Sure."

Breanna had vanished, which was fine by me. She'd become my closest friend since Rocko had hired me several months before, but tonight I wasn't feeling so friendly. I seriously needed to get over it, because even if I wanted to forget my standards, that didn't mean he'd go for it.

Not that I had low self-esteem; I knew my strengths. But most guys — especially smokin' hot guys who had sex with someone that wasn't their girlfriend and then left town — didn't usually care about morals when it came to women and sex. I wasn't a prude by any means. Prudes didn't become the biggest cliché in teenage history by getting pregnant on prom night. But I had morals *now*.

It was all a moot point anyway, since any weak moments on Liam's part would probably be to Breanna's benefit. That was just as well since I had no intention of being his next one-night stand. Or anyone's one-nighter. Breanna could have him.

Between making drinks, I did a quick inventory, made a list, and directed Liam to the storage closet.

While Liam was off stacking cases, Breanna returned and rested a hip against the stool. "At least he's honest."

I rolled my eyes. "End up with that kind of guy and years from now, when you're tired of his crap, all you're left with is whatever respect you had for him to begin with. If you never had any, you've got nothing." I set an empty bottle down a little too hard. "C'mon. If you don't expect more than that from a relationship, you're selling yourself short."

"Who says I want a relationship? I tried standing on principle, and all it got me was a broken heart. I'd rather be happy." She tossed a wink over her shoulder.

I stared after Breanna, my heart heavy for her. I hoped she found love one day, the right kind. With my luck and my taste in men, she'd be happily married long before I settled down.

Two more hours until last call, and it couldn't come soon enough. I needed to go home, give my snuggle-bug a kiss, get a good night's rest, and forget about Liam. He'd probably be long gone tomorrow anyway.

CHAPTER FIVE
★ Liam ★

What kind of idiot blurted out the awful truth to any woman who asked? Answers that would send most girls running and screaming in the opposite direction? Me. I was that idiot.

I'd never been a good liar, because the process of selling someone on something untrue and betraying their trust never came easily for me. Even if they bought the lie, I'd have to remember it. And lying required planning to make sure all aspects of the story were covered. Too much work. And anytime I'd ever attempted it, I always ended up too nervous about getting caught to enjoy the benefits. I was all kinds of things to my fans—immoral, crazy, outrageous—but my parents raised me to value truth.

But, God, couldn't I have come up with an answer without actually answering? Maybe toss her a smile and say, "Wouldn't you like to know?" Nope. I had to lay it all out. What a loser.

Whatever. I wouldn't be taking either of them home tonight, because I'd leave before closing and be checked into a hotel before they finished their shift for the night. Not that I had a room reserved, much less found a hotel. But as soon as the crowd died down, I'd get one. Alone.

Breanna was beautiful, but I barely saw her with Emma around. I didn't know what it was about Emma, but the whole package intrigued me. I adored her voice and the way she tossed her golden hair before she served a drink. I loved her confident efficiency as she worked and how she didn't allow her strength to overpower her sweet nature. Plus she had a fantastic body.

Didn't plan on going there though. For one thing, she didn't seem interested in me. No doubt I'd pique her curiosity eventually, but I didn't have time to grow roots in Gardnerville. So why did it matter what she thought of me if she didn't even know who I really was?

Taking a deep breath, I rolled the loaded dolly out of the storage closet and wheeled it behind the bar. Emma looked at me askance as if my confession had rattled her, then mumbled her thanks.

"Hey, Em?" What excuse could I offer? That the one-night stand had been justified because the girl wasn't married? Because she'd wanted the same thing? Because I purposely stuck with flings since relationships always ended anyway? Because this way I was in control rather than being ambushed later? Yeah, sure, any one of those explanations would go over beautifully. Yep. "Uh... forget it."

She scrutinized me as she made another cocktail. "Something on your mind?"

Knowing I had no defense she would ever buy, I

abandoned all thoughts of providing an explanation and opened the top box on the dolly. "Yeah, where do these go?"

She waved a thumb toward one of the coolers and started another cocktail. "Don't forget to rotate them with the warm ones at the bottom."

Emma went out of her way to avoid me the next hour, and once she gave last call, we were too busy with final drinks to make small talk. And then it was all about closing up.

Twenty minutes later, we were the last of the staff to leave, and Emma handed me a wad of cash. "Your half."

I backed away, palms up. "Keep it."

Scowling, she thrust the money toward me. "I can't keep any of this because it doesn't belong to me. *You* earned it."

I shook my head. By this time, I was moving backward and weaving to avoid chairs so the cash couldn't stick to me. "Didn't do it for the money."

Unable to catch up with me, she slumped in defeat. "I can't take something that isn't mine."

"I'm giving it to you. Now it's yours. Problem solved."

She huffed out a breath. "Let's get out of here," she muttered.

In a matter of minutes, she would drive away and I'd never get a chance to change her low opinion of me. But that's what I wanted, right?

I waited outside while she set the alarm. The lot was empty except for two cars — mine and a four-door maroon Honda Civic.

She checked the door to make sure it was locked,

then rolled around to me. "Thanks for your help tonight."

I shoved my hands into my pockets when what I really wanted to do was press her against the door, lift her up by her hips and feel those incredible legs wrap around me. Since I was still in town and too tired to do any serious driving, I wasn't going anywhere. Wouldn't hurt to see if I could get somewhere with Emma, maybe go back to her apartment. I wouldn't have to scrounge for a hotel room or take a cold shower. "Need a ride?"

"I have my car, but thanks." She jingled her keys against her thigh, before tipping her head to one side. "You'll be doing the bar with me tomorrow?"

Hell no. The longer I stayed, the higher the risk someone was going to realize who I was. I'd call Rocko in the morning and give him a heads-up. Saying the words out loud to Emma though would make never seeing her again too real. "Rocko's expecting me, I guess."

"Then I'll see you later." She hesitated a moment before gifting me with one last smile and heading toward the Civic. "Cool ride," she called out and opened the driver's side of her own.

I strolled toward the far end of the lot to my Shelby, then stopped to salute her as she climbed behind the wheel. The lights came on in her cab and, a moment later, the Honda's engine turned over then fizzled. She tried again, but it didn't start. I waited while she tried a few more times before finally flinging the door open and ejecting herself from it.

I was already making my way toward her. Maybe I'd

get my wish after all. "Change your mind about that ride?"

Her fingertips circled her temples a moment before she blew out a breath and headed in my direction. "I'd appreciate it."

"Where do you live?" I opened the passenger door for her.

"A few blocks away." She slid into the seat and dropped her head against the window. You?"

"Just passing through." I closed the door, then skirted around and got behind the wheel. "Which way?"

"Make a right. About six blocks, hang a left." She swiveled in my direction. "I meant where's your hotel or wherever you're staying? If you come back to work tomorrow, you'll have to sleep somewhere."

"I hadn't intended to stay the night, so I didn't make arrangements." I signaled just before changing lanes and turning left.

"After the second stop sign, third house on the right."

We drove in silence a couple of minutes until she pointed to a house just ahead. The structure wasn't anything special, with gray stucco covering its plain lines. But the flower beds under the windows and the thick, green lawn gave the impression of someone doing their best to make it a home.

In a moment, I'd stop the car, then Emma would go inside. If she didn't ask me in, I'd never see her again. Why the hell did my gut pinch at the thought? I reminded myself that I only needed one thing from her, and she didn't seem the type to give it to me after knowing me for only a few hours.

"Damn it, what's he doing here?" Emma threw the

door open and jumped out before the car completely stopped. She marched toward a big man sitting on the front step. The redheaded guy I'd thrown out of the bar earlier.

I climbed out of the car and approached with caution.

"What are you doing here, Bobby?" Emma planted her hands on her hips. I couldn't see her expression, but by her stance, I'd say she was furious.

Bobby swayed as he took a step forward to stand in front of her. "I came to apologize, Emma."

"Mm-hm. And what are you sorry for?" Her tone said she wasn't anywhere close to forgiving him. "Because I'm guessing you drank more after you left. Whatever you want to say, you need to put it off for another time when you're sober."

He gave her a sheepish look. "Yeah, but... I took something from your car. Uh, so it wouldn't start."

"You did *what?*" She moved forward, and I grabbed her arm to pull her back.

"Well, yeah. So I could drive you home."

"Even if I was stupid enough to get into a car with you after you've been drinking, epic fail for not being there when I closed up."

Bobby's brows furrowed, and he blinked hard. "Oh, I didn't think of that."

"Obviously. If Liam hadn't been there, I would've been stranded," she growled.

He noticed me then, his eyes fiery. "What the hell is

he doing here? Jesus, Emma, I've been trying to get you to go out with me again for months. This guy shows up, and you take him home the first night?"

"You moron, I wasn't taking him home! I needed a ride because you messed with my car." She lunged at him again, and I nudged her aside, stepping between them.

"Get your hands off her." His fist came flying at me, and I caught his hand, then landed a punch in the gut. He doubled over, and I wrenched his arm around, throwing him facedown into the grass.

"Here's the way this is gonna go down." I pressed my knee into his back, and he grunted. "You're gonna call a cab, and you're going to take the ride. You will apologize to Emma, but you'll do it another day when you're sober. Got it?"

He nodded, his cheek grinding into the ground.

"Emma, make the call." I couldn't see her with the house behind me, but I heard the screen door bang.

"You don't have to hold me down. I promise to leave," he mumbled.

I released his arm and eased off his back. "No blood or broken bones this time. I see you again tonight, and that's gonna change."

He slowly staggered away. Without taking my eyes off him, I reached the porch and jumped the steps.

Emma stood on the other side of the door, a phone to her ear as she opened the screen door for me to come in. "They put me on hold."

"Forget it." I paused in the doorway. "He's walking. He could use the fresh air anyway."

She hung up the phone and tossed it onto a bright red fuzzy couch. "Thanks for getting rid of him."

"No problem." My eyes scanned the place. Over to my right was a small dining room with a blue table in the center surrounded by a variety of colored chairs. Her house was filled with light and a thousand different hues, but somehow they all seemed to work.

I needed to go, but Emma wasn't closing the door on me. If she wanted me to leave, wouldn't she be showing me the door and saying good night? I wondered how she would react if I crossed the threshold and kissed her. Would she go for it and give me what I've been wanting since the first moment I saw her, or would she slap me? Somehow, I didn't picture Emma behaving like the groupies who tried to get into our hotel rooms after a show. She probably didn't kiss on the first date, and we hadn't even had that. And we wouldn't.

"Uh, you don't need me anymore." As I lifted my heel to take a step backward, a girl came into view. She looked around eighteen. Emma's younger sister? Except the girl had long dark hair and olive skin — nothing at all like Emma.

"Everything okay?" The girl's eyes strained against the light, making me think she'd just woken up.

"It is now." Emma shot me a grateful smile, then reached into her purse on the coffee table. She dug out some cash, counted it, and handed it to the girl. "Thanks, Lily. I'll see you tomorrow same time. Were there any problems tonight?"

"The usual. She wanted a bedtime story, then a

glass of milk and a snack. Finally fell asleep around eight thirty, I think." Lily yawned as she took the cash. "Thanks."

Rather than backing out, I moved farther into the house to get out of her way. "You don't need a ride?" I asked the girl.

Her eyes widened, as if she'd only just noticed me. "I have my car. Thank you though." She ducked past me. I followed her to the door and kept an eye on her until the car disappeared.

Childlike sobs came from the darkened hallway. "Mommy."

Emma dashed to a little girl and embraced her. "It's okay, baby. I'm here."

So Emma had a kid. Single mom? If the kid's dad were in the picture, wouldn't he be here and not a babysitter? Whatever. As soon as I had Emma's attention again, I'd say good-bye and never look back. Emma might have been smokin' hot, but the baby baggage changed *everything*.

A tear slid down the little girl's cheek "There's a monster at the window."

At the window... inside or outside? Didn't matter. According to Xander, I was a professional monster hunter. I had a job to do. "I'm on it."

I slipped past Emma and the little girl to check the first room then the closet and the room nearby. After inspecting a bathroom on the way, I scanned the hallway cupboards, making lots of noise so the kid would know I was looking. Once I was sure the house was safe, I returned to the living room to find her curled up on the sofa, Emma stroking her back.

Now that I was sure the house was safe, it was time to go. Get in my car and drive. Call Rocko from the road tomorrow and tell him to find someone else to cover Duke's shift.

"It's all clear. You must have scared away the monster," I told the little girl, knowing I needed to get going. Instead, I got mesmerized by her hair. I inched closer until I could almost bend down and touch the soft, sunny blond curls. When I met Emma's gaze, I knew I wasn't going anywhere yet. Kid or no kid, I wanted to stay until she demanded I leave.

"Thank you." Emma gave me a meaningful look. "Scarlet, this is Liam."

"Great to meet you, Scarlet," I said. Jesus, she was adorable. Looked a year or so older than Xander, but the opposite of his almost-black hair and brown eyes.

Without the smell of stale liquor, grease, and sweat from the bar, Emma's own scent of soap and flowers came through loud and clear. I took a step back, hoping to get far enough away so her sweet fragrance couldn't reel me in. "You should lock the door behind me."

She whispered something in the girl's ear, then rose and followed me. At the door, she lowered her voice. "The thing is..." She licked her lips, her eyes wavering to the girl for a moment. "For all I know, there really was a monster looking in through the window. Maybe it was Bobby, and what if he comes back?"

I scrubbed my hands over my face, trying to crush

the desire to hunt Bobby down and beat his ass so he'd know what it felt like to be scared that way. "What do you want me to do? Call the police?"

"No." Emma glanced over her shoulder at the kid, then leaned in. "That would probably scare her more. I was thinking... I can pay you back for all your help and the tip money you wouldn't take. If you stayed here — given that you're *not* a mass murderer" — she paused to give me a stern look — "you'd save on hotel expenses."

Oh, hell, this was not happening. I averted my gaze so I couldn't see her and be tempted to drag her into one of those bedrooms and show her why it was such a bad idea to stay under the same roof together. "Uh..."

"You'd have the guest room, of course. It's a converted garage, actually, down the driveway. It'll be like your own little house." She sucked her bottom lip into her mouth, and I wanted to suck it back out.

God, being only a building away would drive me crazy. I'd probably be up all night thinking about her and that phenomenal ass. But if I deserted Emma and her kid, I'd only worry. If Bobby really had been lurking around the house, and if he came back and hurt either of them, I'd never forgive myself for bailing. I'd very likely track down Bobby and get myself into a world of trouble. "Okay."

Her breath whooshed out. "Great. Let me get her back to bed, and then I'll make sure your room is ready. Why don't you bring your things in?"

A few minutes later, I returned with my bag to an empty living room. I locked up the front, then checked the back door and all the windows. Not knowing what to do with myself while I waited, I poked around her kitchen. Childlike sketches were stuck on the refrigerator, and a plaster imprint of a baby-sized hand hung on the wall above the counter. The whole place was filled with mementos and handcrafted knickknacks that made it feel warm and friendly.

As beautiful and luxurious as my own house was, it seemed cold and sterile in comparison. I made my way back to the living room as Emma tiptoed from the dim hallway and into the light.

"She's asleep," she said. "I'll go fix up your room and be right back."

After she vanished through a door at the back of the kitchen, I wandered around the living room, looking at photos of Emma and Scarlet in homemade frames. When the wood floor creaked, I spun around. "Hey, uh, thought you were sleeping."

"I keep waking up," she said. Even her high voice was cute as hell.

"I see that." I snatched the remote control off the coffee table and flopped down on the sofa, tapping the spot next to me. "Maybe we should check out what's on TV."

Her gold curls bounced as she pattered over to me and climbed onto the couch.

"So how old are you?" I asked, clicking the remote until I hit the History Channel. That should put her to sleep.

"Four." She held up the corresponding number of chubby fingers.

What was I supposed to do with her? I'd babysat

Xander quite a bit, but I hadn't been around other children. I didn't know anything about Scarlet, and I had no clue how to relate to little girls.

She snuggled against me, and I stopped worrying about what to do, slipping my arm around her tiny shoulders. Her soft, little body reminded me of Xander when he spent the night at my house and how we'd fall asleep cuddling in front of the TV. Scarlet wasn't Xander, but she was doing a pretty good job of filling the void. My chest ached from missing him.

I'd gotten up extra early that morning to get Xander, planning to spend the day with him. That was over twenty hours ago, and my lids scratched against my dry eyes. Sensing Scarlet was slowing down, I remained inanimate until her breathing steadied. Her head slid down until her cheek rested on my elbow. Xander had done the same thing last time I'd had seen him a few weeks ago. My insides turned to mush.

After shutting off the TV, I carefully lifted my feet onto the coffee table and scooted sideways until my head reached the arm of the sofa. The day had been too long, and my eyelids drooped.

CHAPTER SIX
★ *Emma* ★

I made the bed in the converted garage and thought of Liam. By Lily's flushed cheeks, I easily guessed what was going through her head when she'd laid eyes on him. I couldn't blame her. Liam was dreamy.

I set a washcloth and a couple of fresh towels on the bathroom counter, then sprinted up the driveway and through the back door into the main house to check on Scarlet. From the back of the kitchen, I slipped into the hallway that led directly to her room. The moon sneaking between the curtains cast a glow over her empty bed.

My heart pounded against my ribs.

Where was she, and why was the house so quiet? What was I thinking to leave a near stranger in my house unsupervised, someone who might really be a mass murderer?

Guilt and fear whirled in my head like a cyclone as I sped into the hallway before poking my head into my bedroom. No one. Finally, I looked in the bathroom. She wasn't anywhere. And it was too damn quiet. Except for the adrenaline shooting through my veins.

Air wheezed through my frozen lungs as I tore

down the hallway. Where was my daughter? Where was Liam? I charged into the living room toward the front door, tears stinging my eyes. I passed the sofa, and my breath caught in my throat when I spotted Scarlet sprawled over Liam.

"Oh," I whispered through a quick sob.

Scarlet was totally conked, and they looked so natural together I couldn't decide whether I should carry my baby to bed or leave her with Liam. The former was out since I didn't want to risk waking her. The latter was unthinkable since I barely knew Liam.

Rushing into my room, I didn't bother turning on the light as I threw on some sweats and a T-shirt, then stopped in the hallway cupboard for a couple of blankets. I returned to the living room, draped one over them and took the other one with me to the recliner.

★

The next morning, I awoke to the smell of bacon. I rubbed my eyes and checked the clock on the fireplace mantle. It was nearly ten. How had I slept so late? Usually, I got to bed about three in the morning, only to be woken by Scarlet around seven or eight—sometimes much earlier.

I scanned the living room. Where was she?

A low murmur of voices floated from the kitchen, and I left the recliner. Following the heavenly scent, I tiptoed past the dining room. Scarlet was kneeling on a stool in front of the stove next to Liam. He flipped a strip of bacon with tongs.

"Depends what you prefer. If you want it crispy, we

should wait another minute or two." Liam handed her the tongs, his hands hovering around Scarlet in case she lost her balance.

"Morning," I said.

"Mommy!" Scarlet scrambled off the stool. "We're making you breakfast."

"Yes, I see that." I stooped to be eye level with her. "And after we eat, we'll go to the park, as promised."

"Can Liam come?"

Knots wound in my stomach. "Uh..."

Liam grinned, obviously enjoying this awkward turn of events.

"I'm sure he has things to do, sweetie." *Maybe leave town or get a hotel if he's planning to work tonight.* I ruffled her hair and stood.

Scarlet shook her head. "Nuh-uh. He's on vacation."

I gave him a look that said he'd better not cross me. He merely shrugged, his grin widening. He needed to be a lot less sexy while he was in my house. Commanding myself to ignore him, I refocused on my little girl. "He's not staying."

"Why not?" Her bottom lip pushed out.

Oh, screw it. Liam was probably dying to get away from us. Yeah, sure, he was making breakfast with a toddler now, but that didn't mean he wouldn't get tired of her any minute. Most guys his age did. No way would he go to the park with us, but I'd let *him* be the bad guy and disappoint Scarlet. "Liam, would you care to go to the park with us?"

"I'd love to. Thank you." He revealed beautiful white

teeth as he plucked bacon out of the pan and laid it on a paper towel.

How the hell had that happened? And why would Liam want to hang out with a four-year-old kid? Okay, whatever. We'd have breakfast, then get ready and take Scarlet to the park. He'd take off soon after, and I seriously doubted he'd show up for work later. I'd never see him again. I resented the thud of disappointment beneath my ribs. I couldn't let myself go there. No way.

"While we finish making breakfast, why don't you go get dressed?" I told Scarlet.

"*I'm* making breakfast." She eyed my sweats and wrinkled her nose. "*You* go get dressed."

I followed her gaze to my paint-streaked orange sweats. Oh, they were disgusting. If only I'd flipped on the light last night when I'd plucked them from the drawer.

Liam cleared his throat, then directed his words to Scarlet. "I bet you can get dressed superfast. When you come back, we'll throw the eggs on."

"Okay." Scarlet skipped to her room.

Trying not to imagine what I must've looked like, I planted a hand on my hip. I didn't care how hot this guy was. He had no business manipulating us into an outing where Scarlet might think we were a family. I especially didn't want her getting attached to him.

"What the hell are you doing?"

"What do you mean?" His brows shot up, then he returned to the pan. "I'm pretty sure I'm fixing us something to eat."

I closed the distance and lowered my voice. "What's

with accepting my invite? You were supposed to say no."

"I was?"

Damn if Liam didn't look innocent. God, why hadn't I anticipated this? Since having Scarlet four years earlier, I'd dated only occasionally. None of the guys had been serious enough to stay overnight. Having a man in the house upon waking was a novelty to Scarlet. I'd let her enjoy it this time, but first chance I got, I'd get rid of Liam. I couldn't allow her to get hurt.

Scarlet scuttled past me, wearing jeans and a sparkly pink top.

"That's a pretty shirt." His expression softened as he smiled at her.

"Thanks." She climbed back onto the stool. "I like 'em scrambled."

I located a bowl and set it on the island behind Liam, then went to the fridge to get the eggs.

"Can I crack them?" she asked.

The mere thought of the resulting mess had me cringing. I was about to open my mouth and deny her request when Liam beat me to an answer.

"Sure, you can." Liam pulled an egg from the carton. "I'll do the first one." He tapped the egg on the side of the bowl, then pried the shell apart, letting the contents spill into the bowl. He handed another egg to Scarlet.

I wondered if Liam knew what he was getting into. But as Scarlet crushed the shell and egg white slopped onto the counter then dripped to the floor, Liam snagged a paper towel and quickly wiped it up.

"Good job." He handed Scarlet another egg and I twitched.

She beamed. Seeing how proud she was of herself, I kept my mouth shut, grimacing as more egg spilled onto the counter. Like a pro, Liam tore off more paper towels, wiped up the slime and handed her another egg.

Between the loss of perfectly good food and the mess — not to mention the waste of paper towels — I steeled myself to keep from shoving them aside and finishing breakfast myself.

Scarlet never helped me in the kitchen. Not because she hadn't asked five million times, but because I'd always been in too much of a hurry and didn't want to take the time to clean up. But after seeing how happy she was to help, I felt bad for denying her all those times. I'd have to make it a point to slow down and let her pitch in more. Doing it herself was the best way for her to learn.

While they finished making breakfast, I set the table. Scarlet chattered nonstop, and when she drifted to her doll collection, I was sure Liam would run screaming. But he didn't fly out the door; he told her about his car collection. He seemed too old to be collecting toy cars, but maybe he was referring to what he'd accumulated as a kid. In any case, Liam was humoring Scarlet, and my insides hummed.

Liam distributed the eggs onto three plates, then Scarlet brought them to the table and climbed up onto her booster seat.

He dropped two pieces of bacon on my plate. "More?"

"No, I'm good. Thanks." I eyed Liam as he divided the remaining eight pieces equally between him and Scarlet. I liked how the muscles of his arm bunched as he held the iron skillet.

He returned the pan to the stove and joined Scarlet and me at the table. "Dig in."

I chewed and swallowed some of the fluffy eggs, my mouth watering for more. "This is great."

"It's pretty much all I can do in the kitchen. I go out to eat a lot."

I forced my mouth shut and stifled the impulse to offer to take my turn at making breakfast tomorrow. He wouldn't be around. If he was, he wouldn't be staying at my house.

"Wanna see all my dolls?" Scarlet stared up at Liam with wide, innocent eyes.

Liam pointed at the eggs. "Are you done eating?"

"No." She shook her head.

Liam chuckled. "Maybe you should finish your breakfast first, huh? Then I need to talk to your mom a minute."

My stomach dipped. What did he want to talk to me about?

Scarlet stuffed her mouth full of eggs and the last piece of her bacon, then slid off the chair and disappeared.

"You're good with kids. Personal experience?" I tore a piece from a strip of bacon and popped it in my mouth.

"Yeah, when I'm in town, I spend a lot of time with my nephew. He's around the same age as Scarlet. She's four?"

"Mm-hm." I pushed the egg around on my plate,

giving in to my desire to know more about him. "No kids of your own then?"

"God, no." He laughed and speared a clump of eggs. "I'd never be stupid enough to get a girl knocked up. No kids for me. Nope."

He might have been one of the most gorgeous guys I'd ever laid eyes on, but apparently, his brain was wired to shut down when his mouth opened. I doubted a crowbar could pry his foot out.

Liam froze before opening for another forkful, his smile slowly fading. "That came out wrong. I meant that I'm not ready to start a family. I'm only twenty-four. Still have plenty of time."

"And I'm two years younger than you. I manage." I lifted one brow.

Liam stopped chewing. "You were eighteen when you had Scarlet?"

Yeah, now he was thinking. "Pregnant at seventeen," I chirped, tilting my head and expecting him to bolt any second.

"Did you graduate?" he asked.

"I was a year ahead. Graduated early, just before I gave birth."

"You were ahead because you were so smart?" He took another bite of eggs.

I swallowed another mouthful. "Yes. I was a total math nerd, among other things."

And that was all I wanted to say on the subject. Most people were too curious about the young single mom with no husband or family around to help. I didn't intend to let Liam go there. He didn't need to know the gory details. Judging by his phobia over having his own children, he wouldn't be riding in on his white horse to rescue me.

Not that I needed saving. I sure as hell didn't want his sympathy either. Time to change the subject. "So when you're home, you see a lot of your nephew. What do you do when you're out of town?"

"Miss him, I guess."

Warmth spread through me. I loved that he cared so much for his nephew. "I meant what do you do for work?"

"Oh, uh..." His eyes swept the room before he drew in a deep breath and met my gaze. "Listen, Em, I'm an awful liar. Terrible at it. Maybe we shouldn't talk about my other life."

My brows furrowed. "Is it illegal or something?"

He laughed. "No. I'm just trying to figure some things out, and that means getting away from it for a bit."

"But that life includes your nephew. Why would you leave town instead of spending time with him?"

He glanced down at the scraps of remaining food. "My sister wouldn't let me see him."

That got my interest. "Why?"

Liam scowled and nudged his plate away. "She thinks I'm a bad influence."

If his own sister thought so, that was proof my instinct was correct. "Are you?"

"I never thought so before." He pushed off the chair and carried his plate the few feet into the sink.

That wasn't a clear no, which made me think he wasn't sure. But I was. He'd admitted to having a one-night stand the other day and, by the way he'd handled Bobby, it was obvious he wasn't afraid to get into a brawl now and then. He also threw a lot of parties where there was enough alcohol involved to warrant a bartender. And now his sister wasn't allowing him to see the nephew he loved.

I stilled my stuttering heart, willing myself to purge all fantasies of touching that cute little muscle at his hip or any other part of him. No matter how sweet he was for helping me at the bar last night and fixing breakfast with my kid, in reality, Liam was not a good guy.

I pushed myself off the chair, glancing over my shoulder to make sure Scarlet was still gone and wouldn't hear me. "Any chance you'll be a bad influence on Scarlet at the park?"

"Absolutely not." He found a sponge and hit the counters. "Not if she doesn't know about my other life."

I rocked back on my heels. "What other life?"

His hand halted, along with the rest of his body, as if he were anchored to the floor. "Listen, Em, you don't want to get caught up in that crap."

Probably not, but I was more curious than ever. "Is your lifestyle that bad?"

"My sister thinks so." He rinsed the sponge under the faucet.

I groaned inwardly, wishing he'd cough up what I wanted to know.

"Liam!" Scarlet barreled past me. "Come meet my dolls now."

He squeezed the water out of the sponge and set

it on the sink. Facing me, his eyes looking haunted, he said in a hushed voice, "I might need rescuing in a few."

I giggled. "I'll finish getting ready and come get you soon."

True to my word, I scooped Scarlet into my arms eight minutes later and swiped her doll from the table, then ushered her out the door. Just before the driveway, I stopped. "Forgot I don't have a car. Stupid Bobby," I mumbled.

He gripped my hand and tugged. "We'll take mine."

I pulled back again and wiggled my tingling hand out of his grasp. "You don't have a car seat for Scarlet."

"Sit in the back with her. If we get a ticket, I'll pay for it." He jerked his head toward the car. "C'mon."

Having Scarlet without her booster didn't seem safe or responsible. But it was short drive, and I could hold her tight. Taking Scarlet's hand, we trailed after Liam.

When we stopped at the end of the curb, Scarlet gawked. "This is your car?" she asked. "It's pretty."

"I hope so. It cost enough." His eyes went wide. "I mean, real cars cost more than toys."

I made a mental note to Google the model. As I rounded the bumper, I checked the name on the trunk. "The Wagon Wheel isn't far. We should stop by and grab her car seat before the park."

"Not a problem." The engine purred to life. It had to be forty or fifty years old, yet it ran better than mine. Yeah, I'd definitely be researching this car.

When we swung by the bar, Liam jumped out to retrieve Scarlet's car seat, and then he buckled it in the backseat of his car. Though I felt useless, being pampered a little wasn't awful. I'd been doing everything all by myself for so long, having help was a new experience for me. I liked it.

I mentally cleared my head, vowing not to get used to this. Liam would be leaving soon, and I'd get back to my life. Without him. As I strapped myself in, melancholy stole into me. I didn't love being single, but I had higher priorities than chasing a guy who wasn't good for me. One day I'd meet an amazing guy who wasn't Liam. Until then, I had to be okay with him not being The One.

He rotated the key in the ignition, and the engine purred. Before putting the car into gear, he dug into his pocket for his cell. He squinted at the screen. "Who'd call me from the seven-seven-five area code?"

"Rocko maybe?" I answered, shaking off the gloom. "Does it start with two-six-seven?"

Liam tapped the screen and shot me a quick look. "Hello?" He paused, his brows drawing closer as if he'd gotten bad news. "Six thirty?"

Liam was going to say no, I was sure of it. Oh, man, I hoped Rocko had a backup plan. I so wasn't handling Saturday night alone.

"Yeah, sure. ... See you then." Liam dropped his phone into his lap.

My emotions ping-ponged between relief that I'd have competent help behind the bar and fear that after working so closely with him for eight hours I'd be even more attracted to him.

CHAPTER SEVEN
⋆ *Liam* ⋆

From where I sat on the park bench, I got a perfect view of Emma's backside while she pushed Scarlet on the swing. I'd thought the short skirt last night was distracting. These snug jeans were worse because the shape of her ass, every little luscious swell, commanded me to look.

This sweet, wholesome girl had turned me into a pervert.

While I'd been fixing breakfast with Scarlet, I'd made myself a promise to drive them to the park, take them home, then gather my things and say good-bye. But when Rocko had called to confirm me for six thirty, I'd taken one look at Emma and wanted to stay. And as I listened to Scarlet laughing while her swing soared high into the air, I didn't find an ounce of regret in me for that decision.

I doubted any nice girl who was struggling to raise a kid on her own would be casual about a fling. And I'd never push it with Emma. But if I wasn't going to try to sleep with her, what good was she to me? Why the hell was I at the park with her and her kid?

Emma lifted Scarlet off the swing and headed toward

me. She stopped just short of the concrete, with her feet in the sand, and swooped down for Scarlet's shoes.

Don't do it Liam. "Let's drive to the lake and get some lunch."

Her body stilled. "Tahoe?"

God, the look she gave me made me feel like I had lice or something. Could she act any less interested in me? "Yeah, I haven't been there in a while. I remember it being really pretty."

"Can I drive?" Scarlet asked, as her mother tied her shoelaces.

"If your mom says it's okay, sure. But you have to drive from your seat in the back. We'll do it together."

Scarlet grinned as she bounded toward me and crawled into my lap, showing tiny white teeth. The scent of watermelon wafted up my nose, and I arched away, not sure what to do with her. When she'd fallen asleep on me last night, it had been easy since the only thing left to do was close my eyes. Breakfast had been effortless too. Just supervise while she cracked an egg or two. But in my lap... was I supposed to hug her or something? My arms hung limply at my sides.

"Sweetie, Mommy can't go to the lake." Emma bent down to throw Scarlet on her hip. "I have things to do before going to work tonight."

Understanding dawned on Scarlet's round face, and she squirmed in her mom's arms until she could see me. "We'll be back before Mommy goes to work, right?"

Emma's mouth parted in stunned disbelief. Oops.

"You can't go without your mom," I said quickly,

and Scarlet's mouth turned down.

Emma expelled the breath from her lungs, then angled her head to give me the eye while answering Scarlet. "Fine. We can go to the lake, and I can do some of my work later. We'll have lunch and maybe walk around for a few minutes, then we drive back. The end."

"I love you, Mommy!" Scarlet flung her arms around Emma's neck, then wiggled out of Emma's hold and ran toward the monkey bars.

"What just happened?" I asked. "I thought she wanted to go to the lake."

"Short attention span." Emma laughed. "She'll be back in a minute and still want to go."

"You sure it's all right? I should've talked to you before mentioning it. Sorry." I loved the idea of hanging out with Emma a little longer before our shift began, but I didn't ever want any woman to feel forced to be around me.

Her mouth curved up. "It's okay. I'm having a nice time. It's been a while since I've goofed off all day."

"It's hardly a whole day though. You're working tonight," I reminded her, feeling guilty that I was taking a full month off. But before my first single had hit the Top 100, I'd done my fair share of grueling work—framing houses for the meanest son of a bitch ever to walk onto a construction site and another stint when I'd done reroofing during a heat wave. When I'd finally gotten home and fallen into bed, I'd never been so exhausted in all my life.

And I didn't have a toddler to take care of during

my free time. Emma did mom duty during the day, worked on her feet for eight hours, then woke with her kid in the morning and made breakfast. I could spend forty-eight hours straight in the recording studio, and I'd have it easier than she did.

"Where's her dad?" I asked.

Emma studied me for a moment, like she was trying to decide what she should tell me. "What do you do for work?" One side of her mouth curled up.

My brows strained closer together, then I sucked in air before shouting, "Scarlet, time to go!"

As soon as Scarlet landed at the end of the slide, I headed back to my car. I opened the door and flipped the seat forward. By the time I finished, Emma was there. I reached for Scarlet and tucked her in the seat.

"I can do that, you know." Emma tilted her head.

I finished securing Scarlet then straightened and brushed a tuft of hair out of Emma's eyes. "I know. But you shouldn't have to."

She flinched and took a step back. "I don't need you to take care of me. I do just fine by myself."

I sighed, got behind the wheel, and waited until she got in on the other side. "Yeah, you do. But it's not a crime to catch a break now and then."

Emma fastened her seatbelt. "Look, Liam—"

Here we go. I wasn't sure what I'd done wrong, but her tone told me I'd screwed up big time. Women! "Yeah?"

"Why are you here? With me? With us, I mean. I

thought you were just passing through."

I shrugged. "I like this town. I like *you*. For the first time in a long time, I'm not stressed out, and I'm not in a hurry." I fired up the engine and gazed into her eyes a long moment before finishing. "It's kind of cool."

I had no idea what she made of my answer because she readjusted herself in her seat so she had a view of the mountains. Other than the occasional reply to Scarlet, Emma didn't say another word until we arrived at Lake Tahoe.

★

"When's her nap time?" I asked Emma as tears streamed down Scarlet's cheeks. We'd had to step out of a shop because Scarlet had made a huge fuss about not getting a toy.

I'd almost offered to buy it just to shut her up, but the one time I'd done that with Xander, Faith had chewed me out. The next time I'd taken him somewhere, he'd thrown another tantrum and I'd realized my mistake. Let them have their way after pitching a fit, and they assume you'll break down again.

"Soon. I'm thinking she's hungry though."

Emma hadn't said much while we were perusing the tourist shops. Maybe Scarlet wasn't the only one who needed refueling. I pointed to a restaurant. "I'll buy you lunch."

"No, I'll get it. You already made me take your share of the tips, and then you sprang for gas to get here. It's not right for you to pay for everything." Her cheeks glowed red. "I'm not your girlfriend."

Right. She wasn't my girlfriend. Strangely, my

heart thrummed at the idea of her and I belonging to each other. I blew it off as hunger. Which would need to be rectified and paid for shortly. By the looks of her house, I had a hell of a lot more funds to play with than she did. Seemed silly for her to spend her own money when she might not be able to afford it and I'd never notice it was gone. "You gave me a place to sleep last night, and this morning I ate your food. Today's *my* treat." I opened the door for her.

"You gave me all your tips." She waved an index finger at me. "I owe you."

"We're keeping score?" I tossed her a mischievous grin. "Would've cost me a couple hundred for a decent hotel, minimally, and breakfast would've set me back at least fifteen bucks. The way I see it, I owe *you*."

"Your share of the tips was more than that. I'm the one who owes *you*." She rolled her eyes, then held up two fingers for the hostess. "Two adults and a booster seat, please."

I trailed behind Emma and Scarlet, trying to picture myself leaving tomorrow. I wasn't feeling it. I wanted to stay and hang out with Emma, get to know her. But what was the point if I didn't do relationships? Though Emma intrigued me, she impressed me as the type who went in with her whole heart. I didn't want to hurt her. And I sure as hell had no intention of playing daddy to Scarlet.

The hostess stopped in front of a booth, and I slid in on one side while Emma put Scarlet into a booster on the other side. Seated next to Scarlett, Emma met my gaze, and my heart skipped a beat. God, what was it about her? Yeah, she was super pretty, but it wasn't only that angelic face that had me practically mooning over her. It was the way she moved and how she smiled so freely. That she'd gotten pregnant at seventeen and didn't regret it, and the way her eyes lit up every time she looked at her daughter.

In another time and place, I wouldn't resist trying to hook up with her. Not that she seemed the least bit interested. In fact, she nearly flinched every time I got near her. That was probably for the best, because if I thought for even a second she'd go for anything short-term with me, I'd be all over her. The idea of getting my hands on her made me all sorts of... I pushed away the visions of getting naked with her between the sheets.

Not gonna happen.

I'd enjoy her company for a few days, just as friends, then I'd move on. But first, I needed a place to stay. "Any good hotels in Gardnerville?"

CHAPTER EIGHT

★ *Emma* ★

Was Liam serious? I tried to envision him sticking around and working at a small-town saloon during his vacation. Even if he made it through a week, no doubt he'd become a jerk at some point; with my luck in the love department, it was bound to happen. And then he'd leave. Rather than put myself through all that, I wanted to fast-forward our relationship to the part where he jumps ship.

"There's a decent enough hotel about five miles away, but it's not exactly five-star. I clamped my mouth shut, determined not to offer Liam the garage again. "Nearest nice hotel will have you driving forty minutes to get to work every day."

"Hell, no." His head swayed side to side. "I'll ask around tonight and see if anyone wants to rent me a room for a few days."

Like me. I didn't *need* a tenant, but the extra money would get me that much closer to replacing my car. *Don't do it, Emma. Don't do it!* "What's your budget?"

"Can I get you something to drink?" a woman asked.

I'd been so engrossed in my Liam dilemma, I didn't notice the server standing at our table. While we gave her our drink orders, I commanded myself to drop the subject. Liam wasn't going to stay under the same roof as me. Of course, technically, the converted garage had its own roof...

When the waitress rushed off, Liam returned his attention to me. "I have some money saved up. I guess most landlords would want a month's rent and a deposit. Real estate's got to be cheaper here than Hollywood. A thousand for a month, maybe? You think it'll be more than that?"

"To rent one room? I'm sure you could easily get something more than adequate for a lot less." *Don't offer him your converted garage. No, Emma.* "I'll check around too."

The server arrived with our drinks, then quietly slipped away.

I lifted the small glass to give Scarlet a sip. She'd quieted down since coming into the restaurant, but it wouldn't last unless I got some food in her. Not wanting to make Liam an offer I couldn't take back, I stalled while considering my options as I rummaged through my purse for my phone. I handed it to Scarlet to play with.

I'd been with Liam half the day, and not once had he flirted with me in any way or hinted he was interested in me, even a little bit. In fact, I was beginning to think the only reason he'd taken us to the lake was because he had nothing better to do. I probably reminded him of his sister, and being with Scarlet made him miss his nephew less. That's all it was. Which made him a perfectly safe tenant.

If Liam ended up being a tool and me renting him the garage ended up being a mistake, it wouldn't matter. Because if I was right about him and he wasn't a commitment kind of guy, he wouldn't stick around any longer than necessary. A week max. All my contemplating would be pointless if he didn't want to rent out the garage.

"You could stay right where you are. Your stuff is already there, and it's close to the bar."

"Great," he answered right away. "Why don't you keep all the tips for the next several days until Duke comes back, and we'll call it even?"

What kind of person gave away their earnings so easily? Was he loaded or something? Maybe he was some spoiled rich kid who'd never had to earn it himself. That theory certainly fit with the expensive car he drove and his ability to take a month-long road trip. Any of the above scenarios made me even less willing to take his charity.

"No way. Are you kidding?" I didn't wait for him to answer. "I'd charge anyone else a fraction of that." Before he had a chance to reply, the server returned.

After we put in our orders, I gave Liam a figure. He countered me with a higher figure. What the hell? Whatever. We could do that all day, and I probably wouldn't win. "You'd be overpaying, but I'll agree if that includes food. I cook from scratch every day."

"Deal." He grinned and held out his hand for me to

shake.

"Okay." I reached out my hand, and his warm fingers wrapped around mine. Chills snaked up my arm as our eyes met. My stomach bottomed out. Even if he wasn't into me at all, I couldn't deny my attraction to him. And now we'd be living together.

I was in so much trouble.

★

Scarlet slept the whole way home while I stared out the window. I knew Liam wasn't interested in me. There was no chance anything would happen between us, especially if he never made a move on me. But he was still hot. And seeing his sweeter side with Scarlet made me wish I was the kind of girl who would be satisfied with a fling.

As my house came into view, so did my car. I'd abandoned it at the bar last night and visited it this morning to get the car seat. How did it get home? The Shelby rolled to a stop, and I glanced in the back to make sure Scarlet was still asleep. After opening the window for her, I climbed out.

"Emma, let me handle this," Liam shouted as he clambered out of the car after me.

I was already stomping toward the front porch. "What the hell, Bobby? How did you get my car here? You don't have a key. Or did you make a copy last time you worked on it?"

"Oh, hell, Emma, I got scruples. I don't make copies of customer's keys. Besides, I don't need to do that when I can hot-wire the starter. Those older cars don't need keys with those fancy chips. Thought you'd need your car for work tonight." His eyes lit up but grew a cloudy shade of blue when he spotted Liam. "What's he doing here?"

I took a deep breath and planted myself in front of him, blocking him from going after Liam. "None of your business, and you need to leave."

He pushed past me, marched across the lawn, and shoved Liam. "Thought you had enough sense not to come back. If you think you can take me sober, feel free to give it your best shot."

"I don't want to fight you, man. Just walk away now, and you'll be free and clear." Liam held up his palms and moved to get around Bobby.

Bobby snorted, yanking Liam's arm. "You're trying to steal my girl, and I'm supposed to let you?"

"I'm not your girl! We went out *once*, and that was months ago. Let it go, Bobby. Leave."

"Take your hand off me." Liam glanced down at the fingers fastened onto his arm, then pinned Bobby with a cold stare. "I'm not going to say it again."

"Or you'll what? Try to take me down?" Bobby laughed. "Good luck with that."

"Bobby, no!" I yelled as he drew up a fist.

Liam moved faster than my eyes followed, and the next instant, Bobby was face down in the dirt, same as the night before.

"I can take you drunk, sober, in a train, or on a plane." Liam wrenched the arm back a little farther, and Bobby yelped. "Now that you've returned Emma's car, you have no reason to come back. If you bother me or

Emma again, I'll break your nose. Got it?"

As Bobby nodded, his cheek slid against the grass. Liam unlocked Bobby's arm, and Bobby righted himself to his feet, rubbing his shoulder as he booked it down the sidewalk.

I wasn't sure what to think. Liam had taken on a guy who had probably forty pounds on him and hadn't broken a sweat. "Where did you learn to fight like that?"

He straightened his shirt that had become askew during the scuffle. "That wasn't fighting. Not even close."

Whatever. I dashed to the car, but Scarlet was still asleep. I spun, expecting Liam to be several yards away. But he was right in front of me and very close. I backed up against the car to create distance. "You didn't answer my question. Where did you learn to do that?"

"Back home. Took a few lessons."

"Only a few?" Obviously some form of martial arts. "What belt did you get to?"

His eyes darted away uncomfortably. "Black. But it was a while ago."

I gave a quick dip of my chin toward his raw knuckle. "Is that how you hurt your hand, by getting into a fight?"

"No." Liam laughed once. "I got mad and hit a wall."

I blinked, not sure what to say to that.

He cleared his throat. "Well... as soon as we get Scarlet inside, I'm going for a quick run."

"A run for what?" I asked.

He held back a grin, his lip twitching. "Not an

errand. You know, jogging?"

"Oh, right." Heat crept up the back of my neck at how naïve I'd sounded.

Liam carefully unclasped the seatbelt, then lifted out the car seat. He carried Scarlet into the house, then lowered her to the floor without disturbing her.

"Thanks for bringing her in." I tucked a blanket around her, then glanced up at Liam. "See you in a bit, I guess."

He went out the back door — to change into sweats, I assumed. A few minutes later, I heard the door slam to the garage, and I peeked through the front curtain, careful to stand where he couldn't see me. He was out on the curb, stretching next to his car. And looking damn good doing it.

Warmth pooled in my belly as his lean, strong thighs elongated and the muscles in his arms flexed when he twisted from side to side.

Blowing out a shaky breath, I stepped away from the window and spent the next few minutes tidying up. I wasn't horribly anal about how I kept my house, but I wasn't crazy about clutter either. Mostly, I didn't want Liam to think I was a slob.

Wait... why should I care what Liam thought? I didn't even know how stable he was. Hadn't he, after all, admitted earlier to becoming so angry that he'd hit a wall? That said, Breanna had a point. At least he was honest. He could've lied about his knuckles and said he got hurt on a construction site or something.

Unfortunately, knowing the truth didn't make me

feel any safer with him. That kind of temper wasn't good for anyone. Yet I was drawn to him like a toddler to permanent markers. And he'd be my tenant for a while.

CHAPTER NINE
★ Liam ★

Why did I have to open my mouth and tell Emma how I'd hurt my hand? It's not like I got my kicks from hurting people. And I'd never hit a girl. I hit the wall because... well, because I could. Figured I'd get out some of the anger, and I knew I could afford to get the wall fixed.

Sadly, after the drywall had crumbled and my bloody hand throbbed, I hadn't felt any relief. Not something I planned to do again anytime soon. But Emma didn't know me, and she had no idea what I was capable of. She probably thought I was some kind of thug. Or psycho.

That was just as well though. As attracted as I was to her, I didn't need her to feel the same way about me. No way would I be able to keep my hands to myself. On the upside, any exercise I might get with her would be a hell of a lot more fun than running.

But if I went there with her, I'd probably walk away feeling guilty. I needed to put my efforts toward women who didn't want more than I was willing to give.

I booked it to the garage, stowed my few belongings in the closet, then changed into sweats and headed out front to warm up.

The exertion felt good. Liberating. Once I'd done my usual four miles, I went straight to my new digs so Emma wouldn't see me all gross and sweaty. While I cooled down, I poked around. There wasn't much to see—a small bathroom with a shower, a smaller kitchenette with a refrigerator that came up to my thighs, and an A/C unit in one of the windows. The past few months, I'd lived in a huge house by myself, and yet the size of this room didn't bother me.

While my laptop booted up, I checked my texts. Five from my sister asking where I was. I texted back with, "About four hundred miles away. Will check in with you next week." My manager Aidan had also texted, wondering what the hell I was up to. I copied the text to my sister and pasted it for him.

Next, I researched Gardnerville, hoping to find something interesting to do tomorrow with Emma and Scarlet. Yeah, right. No way would she go anywhere with me again after learning how I'd hurt my hand. She'd already been reluctant to take me to the park with them and then the lake. It never hurt to ask again, but I fully expected to get shot down.

"Liam?" Emma followed it up with a knock.

I sprung off the bed and opened the door, a grin waiting for her. "Hey."

She grimaced. "I was wondering if you knew how to fix a leaky pipe."

"Depends." I shrugged and stepped over the threshold. "I can take a look."

She moved out of my way and fell into step beside me. "I'd appreciate that."

"Why not call the landlord?" I asked. "Isn't it his job to send someone over?"

"It's almost five. No one'll want to come out this late. And if they did, it wouldn't be done before I have to leave for work." She groaned. "And I have a four-year-old who gets into everything. I just need it fixed."

I motioned for her to go into the main house ahead of me and she led the way to the kitchen.

"Liam!" Scarlet launched herself at me, her arms snaking around my leg.

I hesitated a moment before giving the top of her head an awkward pat. "Uh... did you have a good nap?" My eyes landed on Emma, hoping she'd rescue me.

Obliging, Emma maneuvered Scarlet away from me, opened the door below the sink, and pointed toward the inside. Water dripped from a pipe, the drops melding to the small puddle on the cabinet floor.

In theory, the lower pipe should connect to the one traveling up into the sink. Instead, there was a hairline gap between the two. Once I'd reunited the pipes, I snagged a paper towel to dry them and turned on the water. I stooped over again to check the pipe. It was dry.

I straightened and shut off the water. "Pipes came apart. I'm not a plumber, but even I know that's not going to hold forever. Hopefully, it'll stay long enough for the landlord to send someone here."

"It's not leaking anymore?" As if not believing me, she ducked and examined the pipe herself. "Wow. If you need a job, I can put in a good word for you with the landlord." She grinned as she stood again, bumping her backside against the counter.

"No, thanks." I tossed the wet paper towel in the trash, then circled back to her. "I already have a job."

"Which is?" She lifted one brow.

"Nice try." My mouth curved up. As I twisted around to lean against the sink next to her, our elbows brushed. She didn't move out of the way and pinpricks covered my skin where I'd touched her. The temptation to kiss her had my palms curling around the edge of the counter. Then I remembered Scarlet was just on the other side of Emma. "And anyway, I'm leaving in a few days. I can't stay and get another job."

She canted her head. "So you keep reminding me."

More like I had to keep reminding myself so I didn't get caught up in Emma and how much I wanted to spend time with her. What the hell was wrong with me? I was a nail-and-bail kind of guy. I slept with girls I barely knew and rarely spent the entire night with them. If I ever did, it wasn't because we were sleeping. So why did I find myself wanting to spend a whole day with this woman, even knowing she was untouchable?

I surveyed the orderly kitchen. "Need help with anything else?"

"Depends." She eyed Scarlet. "If you kept her distracted, dinner will be ready in a few minutes. If I have to entertain her, might be an hour before food's on the table."

"W-what would I do with her?" I asked. Making eggs with kid had been easy, but I figured that had been a fluke. Not everything with little people always went smoothly. Not even with Xander. The only reason I survived him was because I knew him so well that I anticipated problems before they got messy.

Emma disappeared, then returned and presented me with a box of paper and crayons. "This could keep her busy for hours."

How hard could it be hanging out with Scarlet while she scribbled and colored? Emma would be nearby, so if I ran into any snags, she'd be there to step in.

I relieved her of the box, and took them to the table where Scarlet drew pictures while her mom fixed dinner. Every now and then, Scarlet would ask a question and Emma would spin around and answer. She'd flash us both a smile, as if she wanted to include me in that happy moment. My heart almost jumped into my throat every time she did it. And this weird, fuzzy feeling came over me... like I belonged. Like I was important, and my being there meant something to both of them.

Had to be my imagination. For the moment, I was only a babysitter for Scarlet and a tenant for Emma. And, seriously, that's all it could ever be.

While rinsing my plate after dinner, I glanced over at Emma who was already hitting the counters. "I'll do that. Babysitter will be here soon. You don't have much time with Scarlet."

She eyed me a long moment, then shook her head and resumed running the sponge over the table. "For what you're paying on room and board, housework should be part of the deal."

I didn't want to argue with her about money again. "Need a ride to work?" When she didn't answer right away, I barreled on. "You'd save on gas money. And your car won't be around for Bobby to take apart." Not that Bobby couldn't find the car here if he wanted to mess with it.

With her back to me, her hands stilled on the sponge. Then she slowly swiveled around. "Why are you so nice to me?"

My gaze wavered as I wondered if I was walking into a trap. "Uh... why wouldn't I be? Would you rather I be a dick?"

She turned back to the counters and began wiping them furiously. "I'm sorry. It's just that you don't seem domestic, but you're offering to help me. From what I've seen so far, you're not the sensitive type either, yet you're playing with crayons to make me and a four-year-old happy. It doesn't make sense."

She had a point. But how could I explain it when even I didn't understand why I was there and doing those things? Besides, I wasn't big on sharing my feelings. I sure as hell wasn't going to start spilling my guts to a virtual stranger no matter how badly I wanted to drag her to the bedroom.

When I didn't say anything, she forged on. "Sometimes.... Sometimes I wonder what's in it for you."

Her lack of faith in me was astounding. Did she think I was trying to con her somehow? With what she already knew about me, I couldn't blame her. I didn't want her to think well of me anyway, because that might open the door to her liking me more than she should.

For now, I only needed to know one thing. "So you don't want a ride to the bar?"

Her face softened. "I wouldn't mind going with you if you're still okay with that. We should leave in fifteen minutes or so."

"I'll go change." I exited through the back door off the kitchen, restraining myself from banging the door shut. It shouldn't bother me that she was suspicious of my motives—I hadn't given her a reason to feel otherwise. And I wasn't going to.

I took a five-minute shower and put on some old ripped jeans and my favorite T-shirt. It was well-worn, with the band name so faint that the words were unreadable. After finding my car keys, I locked up and sprinted to the main house.

Scarlet sat watching TV and playing with her dolls, while Emma spoke with the babysitter. Emma looked stunning in a blue tank top and a black skirt that didn't quite reach halfway down her thigh. As my eyes devoured her shapely legs, I hoped I wouldn't have to beat up too many guys tonight for ogling her.

When she spotted me and beamed, my heart pounded. What the hell was that? Jesus, if one of my buddies had behaved this way, I would've ribbed him mercilessly. Shock at my body's reaction had me standing there staring at Emma. The last thing I needed was for this sickness, or whatever it was, to get any worse. But I couldn't seem to stop it.

When I didn't smile back, hers dulled. Whatever. It was for the best. Her sweet smiles and generosity were not helping my condition. She could stop that crap anytime.

I jiggled my keys at her. "I'll wait for you outside."

I stormed out the front door, hopped down the steps, and went to the passenger side to unlock it. When I circled around, Emma was approaching, so I went ahead and opened the door all the way for her. She gave me a puzzled look, then scooted in and pulled her skirt down as she wiggled in the seat. I paused to admire her legs but closed the door as she glanced up at me. I'd almost gotten caught perving on her again.

Emma was quiet until a couple of blocks before we got to the bar. "I'm sorry about earlier."

Though I'd been irritated, I also knew her reasons were valid for assuming I was an ass. "Forget it," I said, braking for a red light.

"It *is* kinda strange though." She twirled her long blond hair around her finger. "Here's this hot guy who is doing nice things for me, but..."

I threw her a quick glance. "But what?"

"You don't flirt with me or make lewd comments the way other guys do. You don't try anything with me. You're staying in my garage, eating dinner with us, and hanging out with my kid. But you're obviously not interested in me, which makes me wonder why you're still here when you made it very clear from the beginning that you were just passing through."

Not interested? Was she crazy? My gaze fell to her skirt again before I forced it back to the road. I was a horrible liar, and if I jumped in on this topic, I'd end up telling her that all I wanted to do was forget about everything else and spend a week with her in bed.

Moments later, I rolled into the parking lot and couldn't get out of the car fast enough. As I raised the key fob to lock up, I noticed she wasn't out of the car yet.

What was with women and how slow they were to get out of cars?

I went to her side to see what was holding her up. Right then, she emerged but avoided making eye contact with me. Great, I'd made her feel bad. Now I *really* felt like an ass. I'd wanted her to keep a distance so I wouldn't hurt her, but she'd gotten hurt anyway. I didn't want her going into work upset.

"Emma." I slung an elbow on the top of the open door, trapping her in that small space. "I'm the one who should be sorry."

She lifted her chin. "Sorry for what? For not being attracted to me? I wasn't asking you to be." Her words tumbled from her lips. "I just think it's strange you're here."

God, my nose tickled from the smell of fresh soap and whatever else was coming off her hair and the hollow at her throat. Floral something. The scent gave me an urge to run my hand up her thigh. Instead, I ran it through my hair. "You've got it all wrong. Trust me, under different circumstances, we'd be in bed right now and way too busy to go to work."

Well, so much for keeping my mouth shut. Why couldn't I be a gentleman around her without blurting out all my thoughts and crimes?

"In bed?" She swallowed, her cheeks flushing.

That word from her mouth brought all kinds of sinful images to mind, and they all involved her. I inched toward her, the warmth radiating off her and seeping into my pores. She backed up against the inside of the door, and I pressed closer. "The only reason I haven't tried to sleep with you is because I thought I was doing you a favor."

Emma licked her lips while eyeing me cautiously. "So... you're holding yourself back to spare me?"

"Pretty much." Damn, I wanted to kiss her. Just once to see if she tasted as good as she looked. And who knew? Emma might surprise me. Maybe under that good-girl façade was a wild woman waiting to cut loose. "But right now, I can't think of a damn reason to hold back."

I zeroed in on her full pink mouth and that plump lip that begged to be sucked. Her gaze drifted to my mouth, and her lids drooped. Slowly, I moved my arm off the door and leaned in.

CHAPTER TEN
★ *Emma* ★

As Liam slid his palm around the nape of my neck and slowly inched toward me, I knew I should push him away. Kissing him was a bad idea. But since seconds ago when he'd admitted to wanting me, all I could think about was feeling him against me. Maybe I needed to get the kiss out of the way so my brain would start working properly again.

He paused with his mouth hovering over mine, as if asking for my blessing.

Oh, to hell with it. I dropped my purse on the seat, raised my chin, and slipped my fingers though the belt loops of his jeans. He moved in closer, and I inhaled sharply before his lips brushed my own. He moved his mouth over mine, lingering, teasing, then grazed my bottom lip with his teeth just before he withdrew. Shivers danced over my arms, and my stomach dipped.

I barely caught my breath before his mouth came crashing down on mine again. I opened for him, and our tongues tangled, causing tingles to spread out from my belly. He took the kiss deeper. As dizziness swept through me, a small moan escaped my lips, and I gripped his arms to keep my balance.

Abruptly, Liam muttered a soft curse, stepped away, and ran his hands over his head. "I promised myself I wouldn't molest you. What the hell is wrong with me?" He dropped his arms and stepped back.

Nothing was wrong with him. Absolutely nothing.

A car door closed with a soft thump, and I remembered where I was. Crap, I hoped no one had seen us kissing. Horribly inappropriate in the workplace. "We'd better get inside, or we're gonna be late." I slipped between Liam and the door and forged ahead on wobbly knees. Oh, man, that boy could kiss.

Before I got to the double doors, Liam was there opening one side for me. I glanced at him uncertainly before brushing past him. Inside, Liam removed his jacket and exposed his sinewy arms. My belly danced again.

If my body reacted this way every time I caught sight of him, it was going to be a very long night.

★

As we closed up the bar at the end of our shift, I regretted driving in with Liam. The entire night had been awkward except for the three minutes I'd spent on stage doing my obligatory karaoke song and a short time later when Liam had done his—he'd butchered one of my favorite songs by Linkin Park. The night before, I'd thought he could carry a tune. I was dead wrong.

As I dried and put away the shiny glasses, I shuddered, remembering how Liam had repeatedly tripped over the words of the song. The only reason I wasn't hideously embarrassed for him was because he looked like he was barely suppressing his laughter. If it didn't bother him, why should it bother me? Whether Liam could sing or not, he was sexy as hell.

The ride back home was spent in silence. It had been a crazy-busy night, and I didn't have the energy to agonize over Liam or what that kiss had meant to him. I knew I'd be fooling myself to think the one kiss would lead anywhere. Well, obviously, it could easily lead to the bedroom, but I wasn't going to allow that. Not when I knew — and he'd openly said — that he wouldn't be sticking around. Among other confessions.

Besides, even if he changed his mind and stuck around, he'd never be capable of being a father to Scarlet, especially when he had no idea what to do with her. He'd figure it out if he put in the time, but he'd have to *want* to try. I knew he wouldn't. If his own sister worried he was a bad influence over his nephew, he certainly wouldn't be any better for a four-year-old girl.

I would not fall for this guy, no matter how delicious he was to kiss. No way. And wasn't that kiss supposed to help me to stop thinking about him, get him out of my system? Epic fail. I sighed and dropped my head against the back of my seat.

The car stopped in my driveway, and Liam climbed out. By the time I gathered my purse and fished out my house key, Liam was opening my car door. I stood, but he didn't back up and make room for me to pass him. We'd come full circle to where we'd begun the evening — with me trapped between him and his car door.

And, damn, I wanted him to kiss me. No matter how hard it might be to keep my distance, that was exactly what I needed to do. I mean, he would dump me eventually anyway, right? Why put it off? "Uh, Liam... as nice as that kiss was..." I averted my gaze.

He tucked a wayward lock of my hair behind my ear, and the skin at my temple warmed. "A moment of weakness. Won't happen again." But his gaze dropped to my lips, and he was still standing in my way.

The memory of his mouth over mine had me holding my breath. I wanted to grab a fistful of his T-shirt and yank him closer.

My breath whooshed out in relief when he stepped aside so I could pass. Disappointment washed over me at how much I'd wanted to kiss him again. I needed to get over it. He was just a guy. A fight-starting, promiscuous troublemaker.

Ignoring the rush of blood roaring through my extremities, I made a run for the front door and unlocked it. "Good night," I threw over my shoulder. As I darted inside, I snuck a peek at him through the living room window as he crossed the lawn toward the driveway and disappeared into the garage.

Yep, he had some unsavory qualities. Too bad Liam was also gorgeous, sexy and a phenomenal kisser. I couldn't help wondering what else he was good at.

★

The next morning, I woke to my mattress quaking

under the weight of Scarlet's jumping. Scarlet always woke me early. I usually made up for my lack of sleep by napping when she napped, or else getting through the night at the bar would be grueling. But with Liam there yesterday and our impulsive outing, she'd napped in the car and I hadn't.

As I opened my eyes to see Scarlet, I rubbed my lids. Tired or not, even a bad day spent with Scarlet was a pretty damn good day. In fact, I felt surprisingly well rested. "Good morning, cutie pie."

"Hi, Mommy." She smiled down at me. "Where is Liam taking us today?"

That woke me up. I rolled over and pushed up on my elbow. "Nowhere. He has his own life, sweetie. He can't hang out with us all the time."

Her tiny brows scrunched toward the middle of her forehead. "Don't you like him?"

That was an understatement. But my goal was *not* to like him, which meant I couldn't spend any more time with him than necessary. "He's okay."

"Well..." She cocked her head. "If he's not your boyfriend, why does he live here?"

Boyfriend. That word in connection with Liam made my knees turn to jelly. "He's renting the room, sweetie, like Karen used to."

She tugged on my covers. "I'm hungry."

"Of course you are." Snickering, I climbed off the bed and made a quick stop at the dresser mirror to check myself. The scent of the coffee inundated me, trumping my desire to fix my bed hair. As I headed toward the kitchen, the patter of little feet echoed on the hardwood floor behind me. Still groggy, I went straight for the coffee pot when I noticed Liam sitting at the dining room table. He wore a snug tank that flaunted more than his muscular shoulders and arms. I struggled to keep my gaze on his.

I figured he'd made the coffee, but I had expected him to return to his room, not still be in my house. My hand automatically reached for my tousled hair. "Hi. You're up early."

"It's almost ten." He took a sip from a mug.

I glanced at the clock on the microwave and frowned. That explained why I wasn't suffering from sleep deprivation. "Scarlet should've woken me hours ago." After scanning the immediate vicinity, I realized she'd run off again. My, she was busy.

He lifted one shoulder. "I came in to make coffee around eight, and she showed up a few minutes later. Figured I'd keep her occupied with breakfast while you slept in."

While I slept in? And she'd already eaten, which meant I could relax and eat in my own time without battling to get her fed first? That was the nicest thing anyone had done for me in so long. But why did it have to be Liam? Why couldn't it have been Breanna or one of my other friends doing something sweet for me? Someone I wasn't dying to kiss again.

"Don't sleep much, do you?" I asked, finding a mug in the cupboard.

"I go through phases." He eyed me over the rim of his own mug. "In a couple of months when it gets colder, I'll want to lie in bed all day."

I could totally visualize myself there with him. In bed. All day. I shook off the thought and reached for the coffee pot. *Stay focused, Emma.*

"Mommy!" Scarlet burst into the kitchen.

"Yeah, baby?" I replaced the pot and ran my hand over her baby-soft curls.

"When I grow up, I'm going to have a million puppies," she announced. I bit my lip. "Bye." She bolted out of the kitchen.

"She moves on quickly." Liam stared after her.

"Yeah, she does." I glanced into the living room to find it wasn't a total disaster. "What have you guys been doing for two hours?"

"I helped her get a bowl of cereal. After a few bites, she started asking questions about dogs and how they got tamed. So we looked up the history of canine domestication on the Internet." He hitched a thumb toward the laptop sitting in the living room on the coffee table. "She wants a puppy."

I rolled my eyes. "Only because she's not the one who has to pay for it and take care of it."

"Pets are good for kids. I remember when I was five and my mom surprised us with a puppy." His eyes had a faraway look, and one side of his mouth curved up. "My sister and I could play with that dog all damn day. Animals change you somehow."

Easy for Liam—with the fancy car and the month-long vacation—to encourage my daughter to get some damn puppy when he wasn't the one who'd be stuck with it. I liked animals. I did. Though I wouldn't mind having a dog one day, I had more appreciation for them when I was younger. Now, as a single mom, all the responsibilities fell on me. A pet would be another mouth for me to feed when I was already overloaded.

I folded my arms over my chest. "I'm not getting a dog."

He nodded, then set his mug on the table. "What if I paid for it? You have a good-sized backyard."

"No," I snapped. Why wouldn't he mind his own business and drop the puppy subject? I barely had enough time to spend with Scarlet as it was. "Did you mention to my daughter that you'd bankroll a puppy?"

He spun and faced me. "No. I wouldn't do that before talking to you."

"Well, please don't." He needed to stop right now.

He raised a palm. "Whoa. I offered to spring for a puppy that your daughter is dying to get. Why is that so bad?"

Why indeed? I took a moment to wonder if I wasn't overreacting because he was being so generous. When we were away from the bar, it was easy to forget all the reasons I shouldn't be with him. The sweeter he was to Scarlet and me, the less important all those reasons became and the harder I might fall for him.

God, why wouldn't he leave already? Even as the desire to be rid of him hit me, another emotion took its place—hope that he would stay.

I'd be a fool to think I'd be the one to change a guy like him. I couldn't stop my first boyfriend from cheating on me or change Kyle before he'd OD'd and left Scarlet without a father. I couldn't make Bobby less jealous and possessive or fix any other totally wrong guy I'd ever dated. If my taste in men didn't improve, I'd be single the rest of my life.

Liam would never be an option for me in that way because I would never be his type. He needed someone racier, who would sleep with him on the first date or challenge him in ways I never would. No point in me mentally going there.

I lightened my tone. "Scarlet's too young to bathe the dog and feed it. It would only be more work for me." Suddenly self-conscious over my raggedy T-shirt and baggy sweats, I shrunk away. "I have to get dressed."

"While you do that, I'm going for a run."

"Okay. See ya." A part of me wanted to shadow him. Why did I love the idea of him straining his muscles and getting sweaty? I needed to get that image out of my head.

As soon as I heard the back door shut, I raced into my room. Okay, so he'd said that the only reason he hadn't tried to sleep with me was because he was trying to do me a favor. But what did that even mean? I knew why *I* thought sleeping with him was a bad idea, but what was *his* reasoning? Probably because he knew he was bad news.

When I should've been prettying up, I got comfortable on my bed and booted up my laptop. Time to research this guy and his car. I typed "Shelby classic" in the search engine. After a couple of minutes, my eyes were bulging. Some of those cars sold for nearly two hundred grand. Most of the images looked like Liam's car, but I couldn't tell if his was the big-ticket item. My gut told me it was. The way he didn't seem to care about money, the guy had to be loaded. Trust fund?

Back in the search window, I entered "Liam Blackwell." I scanned the first few results, then closed the laptop in disgust. No Twitter account, no Facebook page, no Instagram, no Tumblr. It was as if he didn't exist. I needed more info on him, but I didn't have a prayer of squeezing the information from him.

I changed into a pair of jeans and a T-shirt, then washed up. As I tiptoed into the kitchen, Liam slipped in from the back, über-short hair glistening from a shower and his T-shirt hugging his wide shoulders.

"Mommy, look what I drew." From her seat at the kitchen table, Scarlet handed me a piece of paper. I saw her likeness in the small orange figure and me in the medium sized person. But who was the guy? I clamped my mouth shut, not wanting to know if it was Liam. God, what was with him and women? He'd cast a spell on the babysitter, then me, and now my daughter.

CHAPTER ELEVEN
★ Liam ★

Emma's mouth softened as she admired the picture Scarlet had drawn. It was probably too much to hope that the dark-haired stick figure was meant to be her real father or an uncle or something. I was fairly certain it was supposed to be me — his hair was clipped close to his scalp, like mine.

Just the thought of full-time parenting had my blood running cold. I loved being a part-time uncle, taking Xander when I chose, then giving him back when I felt like it. I enjoyed getting him all sugared up, knowing I'd be dropping him off soon and wouldn't be dealing with the consequences. Spoiling kids and raising them were two drastically different things.

But if I had to, I'd take care of Xander. Thankfully, that would never be an issue because my mother would snag her grandson before I ever had a chance at custody. That was just as well. I wasn't ready for fatherhood, especially to a little girl. I wouldn't even know where to begin. Little girls generally didn't want to learn martial arts or have much to do with sports. What else was there? And I could never be her real dad. God forbid I should end up like my own stepfather, Carl, who'd been saddled with two kids he'd never wanted.

"What a pretty picture. Thank you, sweetie." Emma plucked a magnet from a drawer and used it to stick the paper on the refrigerator. "Mommy has to work tonight, and I have errands to run first. Let's get you fed and dressed, so you can go with me."

"Mommy, no." Scarlet screwed up her nose, shaking her head dramatically. "Can't I stay with Liam?"

Emma fished out a pan from a cupboard and turned on the stove. "I'm sure Liam has things he needs to do, sweetie."

Scarlet blasted me with her gorgeous, blue eyes. "You can't stay with me?"

Damn, she was cute, dimples and all. And the way she looked up at me, pleading with those enormous eyes, I would've done anything she commanded — even have a tea party with her dolls.

"Like your mom said, I have things to do." Yeah, stare at the walls in my room.

I didn't want to play daddy with Scarlet or anyone else, but something about this little girl drew me in. She seemed to want me around too. What was the harm in that? "I should be done by the time you two get back though."

"We can bake cookies!" She squealed and dashed to her room.

"I can't bake." I pivoted toward Emma with what must have been sheer panic in my eyes. I'd been an idiot to think I could be anywhere near a four-year-old girl and not get burned.

"Don't worry," Emma said, reaching for eggs. I located some bacon and held it up for her approval. When she nodded, I looked for the pan.

"It's a play set. All plastic with nothing dangerous to hurt a kid. And she already knows how to use it." She cracked eggs into a bowl.

That didn't seem so bad. And I might even get to eat the cookies. "I don't have anything to do today," I whispered so Scarlet wouldn't hear, "but if you don't want me to babysit so you can run errands, I'll back you up. Just tell me what you want."

Emma emptied her lungs, her shoulders slumping. "It's not that I don't want you to. But I can't impose on you that way. She's not your responsibility. Besides..." She licked her lips. "I've known you less than forty-eight hours."

I held up a hand. Although being with Scarlet for a few minutes no longer seemed thoroughly terrifying, I couldn't blame Emma for not feeling one hundred percent comfortable with me as a babysitter. "I get it. No worries."

When we'd finished eating and Emma began clearing the table, I nudged her out of the kitchen. "I'll finish up. You go."

"That's not part of the deal." Emma glanced at the clock on the microwave. "Damn it, I slept too long, and now I'm behind on everything." She moaned and met my gaze. "Yes, thank you."

While I scrubbed the pan and wiped the counters, I listened to Emma beg Scarlet to decide what to wear. To make sure Emma didn't need anything else, I hovered around the dining room table.

Emma strode back into the living room, her mouth tight. "Anything in particular you want from the grocery store?"

She looked stressed enough without worrying about feeding me. "I'll eat almost anything."

"Favorite snacks?" She found her purse and checked for keys.

"Whatever you normally buy." I slapped on an easy smile in an effort to get her to relax. "Except get a lot more of it." In my peripheral vision, I glimpsed Scarlet who was scowling at her clothes, her mouth turned down. I guessed Emma had won the battle. "That's a pretty dress."

Scarlet quit pouting and grinned up at me. I smiled back, warmth filling my chest.

"Okay, sweetie, let's go." Emma extended a hand for Scarlet to cling to, and they headed out.

I was about to return to the garage to get showered but ended up at the living room window. By the time I peered through the curtain, Scarlet was in the backseat and Emma was climbing into the driver's side.

Only seconds had passed before the driver's-side door opened again, and she went around to the backseat. Scarlet scrambled out, and Emma threw her on her hip, then stormed toward the house, reaching for her cell with her free arm. I opened the front door.

"Bobby, what did you do to my car?" she barked into her phone wedged between her cheek and shoulder as she barreled over the threshold like I didn't exist. She let Scarlet slide to the floor. "It won't start. What did you do?" A moment later, she smacked the phone off, shoved it into her pocket, and paced.

"You think he messed with your car again?" I asked doubtfully, not sure Bobby was stupid enough to come back. And even if he'd returned, wouldn't he have made his presence known? Bullies generally wanted the attention.

"I don't know." She dropped her purse onto the sofa and stared at it. "The car's old, so who knows?"

Back when I was a struggling musician, I didn't have enough money to pay someone to work on my car. I'd quickly figured out how to fix most things. I could probably take a look at her car and tell her what was wrong with it, maybe repair it myself. But driving her around and spending the day with her seemed a much better idea.

"It's Sunday. Auto shops won't be open." I waved my keys in front of her. "I'll drive you."

She rubbed her fingertips into her temples. "You've already done enough."

I made an exaggerated show of looking around. "See any hotels around? 'Cause I'd be homeless if not for you. Let's go." I strode to the front door and glanced over my shoulder with my hand on the knob. "C'mon. It'll be fun."

At my car, I opened the back door, then went to Emma's Honda to retrieve the car seat. Emma and Scarlet appeared as I was strapping it in. I stepped aside, and Emma lifted Scarlet up into the seat.

"We left Matilda all alone," Scarlet said as Emma was buckling her in.

"I can get her." I held out my hand for the house key, and Emma dropped it onto my palm. "She's the one with black hair?"

"Yeah, I think she ended up in my room on the dresser." Emma scrunched up her nose. "Go on in."

I jogged into the house, slowing as I neared Emma's bedroom door. When I opened it, the scent of flowers rushed me, and the memory of Emma's flushed face after we'd kissed swam before me.

Stay on point. I could not allow myself to think about that kiss *ever* again. It would only lead me to violating Emma further, and she'd end up despising me if I broke her heart.

I'd told Emma the kiss had been a moment of weakness and it wouldn't happen again. I needed to mean that — unless she insisted otherwise. I didn't see that happening though. Whatever went on between us, when I left Gardnerville, I wanted her to remember me as something other than a complete jackass.

Spotting Matilda, I sped toward the dresser and reached out to snag her when a small rectangular piece of paper caught my eye. I set the doll down and picked up the wrinkled, coffee stained check. It was made out to Emma Taylor in the amount of fifty thousand dollars, dated over five years ago.

What the hell? Why would Paul and Melissa Hauser, whoever they were, give Emma that much money? And why hadn't Emma cashed it? That would go a long way to handling her car situation or helping her buy a house.

I placed the check on the dresser, snatched the doll, and hurried back to reunite her with Scarlet. Once behind the driver's side, I turned toward Emma. "Matilda was right where you said." I paused a moment. "Sitting right next to a check for fifty grand. You can't miss it."

Emma rolled her eyes and scooted away from me.

"I guess you never needed that in the past five years, huh?"

"It's a long story."

I tossed a grin her way. "I have all day."

She glanced over her shoulder to Scarlet who was preoccupied with the scenery, then back to me and whispered, "Grandparents on her dad's side."

"Oh?" I pulled out into the street.

"Hang a right onto the 395."

I obeyed, trying to think of any other reason they'd give Emma that check and why she wouldn't cash it. "They tried to buy you off?"

"Yep. Before I got pregnant. When he refused to give me up, they disowned him. He was over eighteen by then and got access to his trust fund. Within weeks, he'd blown nearly all of it and OD'd on heroin."

"He was an addict, but *you're* the one who wasn't good enough? What a joke." I hung a right onto the main street and snuck a glance her way. "Awfully young to be on heroin."

She lifted one shoulder, her mouth set in a grim line. "Drugs don't discriminate, and dealers sell to anyone who can pay."

"That's too bad. He obviously had some good qualities, or you wouldn't have loved him."

Emma's gaze snapped to me, and her eyes watered. "Yeah, he had his qualities." She inched away from me again. "But with him came a lot of negative emotions and stress. I can't afford to have that kind of drama in my life again."

Especially not now that she had a daughter to raise. All by herself. "What about your parents or siblings? Are they around?" I asked.

"I'm an only child, and they had me late in life. My dad had some health scares and can't work anymore. He's almost seventy now. I didn't want them to feel obligated to help me."

"They don't know about her?" I aimed a thumb at the backseat.

"No." She glanced away for a moment before sucking in a deep breath. "They disapproved of my choice in boyfriends. Grounded me, took away my cell phone, my laptop and anything else they could think of to get me to stop seeing him. Eventually, I just took off."

I rubbed my chin, the muscles between my brows pulling. "You haven't seen them since?"

"No." She drew up a knuckle and swiped under her eye. "I send them a card for Christmas, their anniversary, Mother's Day, Father's Day and birthdays, so they know I'm alive. But I never give them a return address or phone number." Her hands fidgeted in her lap. "They live in Oxnard, a couple of hours from LA. Easy to keep secrets when they're hundreds of miles away."

Didn't matter how pissed off I was at Faith for disapproving of my lifestyle, I'd never abandon her and Xander. I might be taking a break now, but my sister was going to find me on her doorstep soon enough. "But why not tell them? You should be proud of what you've accomplished."

"It's been so long now." Her eyes pooled, her voice just above a whisper. "I guess I'm afraid they won't forgive me."

"Forgive you for getting knocked up?" I asked, casting a quick glance her way.

She chewed on her lip. "Yeah. And for being so rebellious."

"You don't strike me as the rebellious type."

"Normally, I'm not," she said. "But I would've done anything for Kyle. And my parents pushed too hard, which only drove me further away. So, yes, I rebelled."

For a moment, I wondered how life would be if I had that kind of love from a girl like Emma. One thing I knew for sure: if Kyle spent all his money on drugs, he hadn't earned that love. If I took a chance on her and told her who I really was, could she ever love *me* that way?

Oh, man, I needed to get out of my own head. Never going to happen.

"You still love Kyle?" I asked.

"No. My mourning ended as soon as I realized he'd nearly drained our accounts to support his drug problem. I was pretty angry with him for a long time. You know, with a baby on the way and no family to fall back on. I was screwed."

I wondered how her parents must feel to have lost touch with their only child. If Xander disappeared, I'd be beside myself. "So, your parents... If Scarlet wound up in that same situation, would you forgive her?"

At a red light, I braked and snuck a peek at Emma. Her eyes were filled with tears, her chin trembling. "I'm sorry," I said. "Didn't mean to upset you."

"It's okay. I never looked at it that way." She gave a watery laugh. "I guess I'm a terrible daughter."

"Not necessarily. Besides, one visit might change everything."

Her head swung side to side. "Even if I were brave enough to see them, I can't afford it. Unless I want to be in a car with a four-year-old for six or seven hours, there's the airplane fare for two and missed wages from time off work. Maybe I could figure out the money stuff, but it's not just Rocko who'd have to do without me, but my bookkeeping clients as well."

I'd never gone more than a few weeks without seeing my mom or sister. San Diego was an easy commute from Los Angeles, so we visited each other often. If my bio dad weren't a total deadbeat and I had any kind of prayer of locating him, I probably would've wanted to see him as well. Hell, I didn't even go that long without seeing my ex-military stepfather who'd always spent more time shouting than listening.

Rather than rely on family, Emma had figured out a way to do everything on her own — as a single mom. Without any kind of safety net and without cashing that check. At that moment, I didn't think there was anyone in the world I respected and admired more than her.

"Where are we going, by the way?" I asked, trying to squash the urgent need to take care of Emma, protect her. And not just for the next week — though she obviously didn't need my help. Emma was a survivor.

"We should pick up some groceries. There's a market another block up. Scarlet will be in school tomorrow, and I have part-time work Monday through Friday. If I don't get it done today..."

"Gotcha covered." I stopped for a red light and jerked my head to the right. "Turn in there?"

"Yeah, that's it." She glanced into the backseat, her eyes lighting up at Scarlet. "No junk food," she said firmly but gently. "The rules don't change because Liam is here. You throw a fit, and you won't get what you want. Won't get any TV later either. Okay, sweetie?"

A half hour later, I was loading groceries into the trunk of my car. "Any other errands?"

"I have to pick up stuff from the office for a couple of bookkeeping clients."

"They're open on Sunday?"

"No. I have a key." She gnawed on her lip. "You shouldn't have to drive me around."

"We're already out and, like I said, I have nothing to do today. May as well make another stop."

Emma slumped against the seat. "Okay. I appreciate your help. We can go straight home after this though, I swear."

"Not a problem." Almost out of the parking lot, I glanced over at her. "Right or left?"

"Make a right." Her voice sounded strained, as though she hated being forced to depend on people. As soon as we got home, I'd take a look at her car. In the meantime... "So why keep the check on your dresser? Isn't it a constant temptation to cash it?"

"I never want to forget what kind of people they are. In case they ever show up and try to weasel their way into Scarlet's life, I want that check sitting right there to remind me why they gave it to me in the first place. And anytime I feel like I'm drowning, I can look at it and know that I survived before without selling my soul. I'll survive again."

I opened my mouth to speak, but she interrupted me. "Pull over at that gray building. It'll only take me a minute to run in."

Emma was out of the car as soon as I parked. Scarlet and I talked about which kind of dog she would get one day—her first of the million—and what she would name it. Apparently, only a lab would do, but she wasn't picky about color.

About three minutes later, Emma returned, carrying a stack of folders. I started the car. "Home?"

"Yeah."

"You know," I began, "If the Hausers have tons of money, what's the harm in taking it? Considering they're her grandparents, it's not inappropriate for them to help out. And it would make things a lot easier for you. Any normal person can barely reach adulthood without selling their soul in one way or another. Weddings are a good example of that."

Her mouth dropped open, and I wondered what I'd said wrong.

"You don't believe in the institution of marriage?"

Her brows rose dangerously high on her forehead.

"I agree with the *idea* of it. But in reality it rarely works out. People get divorced now more than ever." I shrugged and changed lanes, noting that I could barely hear myself over Scarlet's singing.

Emma handed Scarlet her cell phone, and the backseat got super quiet. "Maybe if people had more conviction in their commitment, they'd try a little harder to make it work and not give up so easily," Emma said.

Conviction wasn't any guarantee that a relationship would work. My sister Faith was proof of that. My mom too. Hell, I'd been in love once. She'd minced my heart into tiny pieces and chucked them down the garbage disposal. Like I'd ever fall into that trap again.

"You can't predict the future. Marriage is more like blind faith, putting your trust into something you can't control. Throw in a little bad judgment, a sprinkling of bad karma, and most of the time it just ends up being false hope."

Emma was quiet for so long, I glanced over to find her staring at me. "What?"

"Wow, someone really hurt you. It must have been bad."

I laughed once to cover up the sick feeling in my gut. Tamara had been the head cheerleader, and I'd fallen for her in a big way. She was all I thought about back then, marrying her and building a life with her. After dating her through most of senior year, I'd caught her cheating on me. For an entire week, I'd been too ruined to go to school. I had no plans to let any woman have that much control over my emotions ever again.

Though I contemplated the road ahead, I felt Emma's gaze on me. Unless I planned to sprout a pair of boobs and start talking about my feelings, I needed to wrap up the topic of my love life and steer her off it. "I've had a few relationships that didn't work out, and some of them were messy. But that's usually the way of it, right? If it wasn't bad, it wouldn't end." I slowed for a red light. "So... bookkeeping, huh? Are you a CPA?"

"No, not yet. I've got all the required semester hours, but I need to take the state test."

I cast her a quick glance before moving through the intersection. "When we get back, I'll have a look at your car. It might be too complicated for me to fix, but it wouldn't hurt to look."

"I can't ask that of you. I—"

"You're not asking. I'm offering." What was with Emma? She needed help, and I didn't have much else going on. She should accept it already. "You'll need a car at some point, and you don't have many choices. Spend money on a mechanic who might rip you off, buy a new car, or walk with Scarlet everywhere."

She blew out a breath. "When you put it that way..."

CHAPTER TWELVE
★ *Liam* ★

After Emma and I lugged the groceries inside, I entertained Scarlet while she put them away. Scarlet was growing on me, and the more time I spent with her, the easier I found her to talk to. Same as Xander, she wanted to be heard and have someone to laugh with. Kind of like adults, except smaller.

As we baked cookies in Scarlet's little pink oven, I snuck peeks at Emma from the kitchen table while she made grilled cheese sandwiches and heated up soup. She was fascinating, that confident posture and those efficient moves. She didn't waste time, and I couldn't figure out why that was so incredibly attractive to me.

"What nights do you have off?" Maybe she'd agree to go out with me to a movie or something.

"Same as you. We work Thursday through Sunday. Stephen does the other nights."

After tonight, I'd have three days off in a row. What the hell was I going to do with myself all that time?

"But if Duke returns to work on Friday, you're off

the hook."

With her back to me, I couldn't read her expression and had no idea if she loved or hated that scenario. My best guess was indifference. Did she expect me to leave since I'd been threatening to take off since the moment I'd met her?

I stiffened. This was a much bigger problem than merely amusing myself for three days. If Rocko no longer needed me, I had no real reason to stay. My room was paid up through the whole month though. Technically, I could use it that entire time. And do what, hover around Emma?

God, what was wrong with me? I drove her around, offered to fix her car, and clung to her like a groupie. Even spending the whole day with her wasn't enough.

Probably just Forbidden Fruit Syndrome. It would pass. It always did; I just had to wait it out. In the meantime, I'd make good use of my time with her. Without touching her.

Now that I knew Emma's views on marriage, I knew I'd never get a chance to nail-and-bail with her. Even if she wanted a short-term relationship, she'd never choose me. Maybe if I hadn't blurted out that bit about the one-night stand and slipped to her that my sister had accused me of being a bad influence. Plus I'd almost gotten in three fights in less than twenty-four hours. She had to think I was a bit of a douche. Hell, right then, even I thought I was a douche.

"Scarlet, are you ready?" Emma asked, patting the booster seat.

I scooped Scarlet up and set her on the seat, then

dragged the chair closer to the table. As soon as I returned to my own chair, Emma was standing next to me.

"Hungry?" She set a bowl of soup in front of me.

"I am now." I grinned up at her.

She smiled, and my insides trembled. *What the hell?* Oh, yeah, I was definitely inflicted with some hideous disease. Some ailment that made me delusional. I only *thought* I was happy. I only *imagined* Emma was someone I wanted to fall in love with, someone who would still intrigue me after years with her in a small town.

I needed to stop thinking about any of that. If I were to give in to my desires, we'd end up hurting each other. Whatever I felt for her, and vice versa, wouldn't last. It never did. I had to remember that.

She slid a plate in front of me. The grilled cheese sandwich looked great and my mouth wet itself. "How did you manage to work, take care of Scarlet, and go to school?" I asked as soon as she sat down with her own bowl of soup.

"I have a friend with a daughter around Scarlet's age. We used to take turns having them both, so we each got breaks. Still do now and then. And I was able to do some of the courses online, which I did while she slept."

I'd witnessed my sister struggle as a single mom, but she had help from family. And even then, she had a rough go of it. It couldn't have been any easier for Emma. "How did you pay for school?"

Emma bit off a piece from her grilled cheese sandwich, chewed, and swallowed before answering. "I had a scholarship that covered part of it. Student loans handled the rest."

She probably had a mountain of those unpaid loans. It

seemed wrong that I made a ridiculous amount of money and wouldn't notice those small chunks missing. I shoveled more soup into my mouth to prevent myself from offering to take care of them. Emma would never go for that.

"Did you go to college?" she asked, then took another bite.

"No." I shook my head without volunteering anything else that would lead to more questions about my life. I felt her gaze on me and steeled myself not to say any more. As soon as I finished eating, I put my plate away. "If you tell me where the key is, I'll have a look at your car."

Two hours later, I'd ascertained the car's problem stemmed from a bad alternator and an ancient battery. Before I decided on a plan of action, I strolled back inside the house for a few minutes to scope out the situation.

Scarlet was napping on the couch while Emma scowled at a ledger and her fingers danced over the keys of an adding machine. She didn't even glance up at me. If I went to the auto parts store, she probably wouldn't notice I was missing.

I thought about filling her in, but she'd never let me pay for any parts. Then I'd have to watch her struggle with moral dilemmas as she figured out how to come up with the money. No, thanks. I'd just take care of it. Up the road, maybe I'd clue her in after it was too late for her to do anything about it. Or maybe not.

Another two hours later, I rotated the key and her car purred to life. Done. But while I'd been under the hood, I'd noticed bad spark plugs, a cracked timing belt and dirty oil. Worse, the car needed new tires, and the brakes would be down to rotors in a few weeks. I could handle the minor stuff, but Emma was going to have to shell out some serious dough soon or buy a new car.

I'd worry about that another time. For now, I had to wash up and get ready for my shift at the bar.

Back inside, Scarlet was zoned out in front of the TV and Emma sat exactly where I'd left her at the dining room table, surrounded by a pile of paperwork. "Coming up for air anytime soon?"

Emma looked up from the stack of papers and smiled at me. "I figured out where the money's going. His business partner, who also does his books, is embezzling."

"I thought *you* did his books."

"Not yet, and his partner has no idea he gave me this stuff." She waved at the documents in front of her. "He had a feeling something was off and wanted a forensic accountant. He's lucky he took a chance on me. I'm good at finding out why numbers aren't adding up, tracking them and verifying expenditures, tracing them back, researching."

Sounded impressive. "Is that a thing, a real profession?"

She shrugged. "Yes, although usually the super-experienced CPAs do it. I'm already good at it."

"I don't think he'll allow his partner anywhere near the money once he learns about the embezzling. I'm guessing he'll probably want the guy to rot in prison while you handle it from now on."

"If he's smart." Emma checked the time on the microwave, and her eyes widened. "Oh, wow, I didn't realize how late it was." Her eyes shot to mine as her shoulders slumped. "Damn, I should've asked you earlier if you're okay with driving me to work again. Tomorrow's Monday, so I can take my car in, but tonight—"

"Absolutely." I thought about volunteering the news about her car. But if Emma knew it was running again, she wouldn't need me. "I have to shower, but that should only take a few minutes. When I come back, need help with dinner?"

She beamed. But I wasn't stupid enough to think her smile was meant for only me. She was still basking in her bookkeeping triumph. Which is probably why she hadn't asked about her car. Either that or she assumed I hadn't been able to fix it. More likely, she'd been so engrossed in work that she hadn't realized I'd been working on it.

"That would be great. I have a few things to do before I start dinner anyway. Meet you back here in a few?"

"See you then." I slipped out the back and went to my room.

By the time I changed and made it back to the main house, Emma had already started cooking. Stirring the red sauce, she glanced over her shoulder. "You're just in time. Water's boiling. Would you mind getting the noodles and putting them in the pot?" She used her free hand to point to a cupboard above her to the right.

"Let me wash my hands." As I gave them a quick scrub, I snuck peeks at her. She was wearing the same dress she'd had on all day, but somehow she looked sexier in it now. I loved the way it hugged her amazing curves. "Where's Scarlet?"

"Playing in her room. I'm sure she'll show up any

second."

I opened the cupboard, grabbed some linguini, and held it out for her approval. After a quick inclination of her head, I opened the bag and poured in half the noodles. When I swiveled to see if Emma wanted more, my mouth ended up only inches from hers. Cooking had never been this nice. "More?"

"No, that's good." She gave me that sweet smile, and most of the blood in my body rushed south.

I forced myself to pull back and covered the pot with a lid. "What else do you need?"

"Garlic bread." Emma picked a butter knife from a drawer and nabbed a small bowl from beside the stove. "I make this up ahead of time so it's always on hand." She lowered the flame on the sauce, and handed me the knife.

The butter smelled strongly of garlic and had flecks of what was probably oregano or basil. There were only three of us, so it didn't take long for me to slather several pieces of bread with her concoction. As I finished with the last piece, her arm brushed mine, and I willed myself to resist the overpowering desire to toss all the food on the floor and throw her on the counter. "This smells great."

"Did you try it?" When I gave her a blank look, she dipped her finger into the bowl and held it out for me.

Lick it off her finger? Her smile waned as if realizing where that could lead and she withdrew her hand. I captured her wrist and slowly raised her hand to my mouth. With my gaze locked on hers, I moved my lips over her finger and licked off the garlic butter. She shivered and her lids drooped.

I was quickly learning that *wanting* to resist her and actually doing it were two very different things. I was about to grip her hips and shove her against the counter when I heard a faint rustle.

"Mommy?"

In my entire life, I'd never been so desperately frustrated. Judging by Emma's reaction to having her finger licked, I probably could've lured her into something more if not for Scarlet's appearance.

I offered a smile to the little girl and backed away from Emma.

Since I'd become famous, I hadn't been the most honorable guy where women were concerned. But I hadn't been a total prick either—before I ever took a girl to my hotel, she always knew where she stood.

With what I knew about Emma, if I pursued her, she'd only hate me later when I left. I'd probably hate myself too. As much as I wanted what had been about to happen—or what I thought Emma had been about to roll with—putting the brakes on it had been the right thing. Thankfully, Scarlet succeeded where I'd failed.

"Hey, sweetie. Dinner's almost ready." As if nothing had almost happened, Emma brushed past me and fished for plates in the cupboard to set the table.

As soon as we'd eaten, Emma sprang from her chair, set the dishes on the counter, and slipped into her room to get ready. Lily arrived to babysit, and moments later, Emma emerged wearing jeans and a midriff-baring halter top, then we climbed into my car.

Although I wanted to talk about how much I enjoyed sucking on her finger — as well as other parts of her I wouldn't mind sucking on — I figured pretending it never happened was the best bet. Because if she hinted she might be open to a fling with me, I'd go for it without questioning her. I'd already proved how little control I had when it came to Emma.

★

Ladies' night ended up being as crazy as Friday and Saturday. We had fewer customers, but they weren't nearly as well behaved. Three hours in, I'd already cut off two women and three men and caught a couple getting freaky in the storage closet over a case of Corona. The only bright spot of the evening was that Rocko wanted my help keeping the peace, so he didn't make me do karaoke.

And right now, as I washed dirty glasses, a guy was standing by his stool to see over the bar to check out Emma's ass. He wasn't even trying to be discreet as he snickered with another guy sitting nearby.

A moment later, he tossed off a crude, sexual remark about Emma, and I'd had enough. Resisting the use of my fists, I stood in front of him, blocking his view.

He shot me an irritated look and motioned with his hand. "Get the hell out of my way."

Determined to handle the degenerate calmly, I glanced over at Emma to make sure I was positioned to cover her. "Did you miss class the day they were teaching manners? It's rude to stare."

He sneered. "I was too busy screwing your mother."

I reached over the bar, got an iron hold on his shirt, and yanked until his chest was flat against the bar. Then I dropped him. He slid off the bar top and scrambled on the other side to keep from falling on his ass.

"You need to show respect to *all* women, and not just Emma or my mother." When I turned, Emma was staring at me from the other end of the bar. "What?"

She made her way over to me and asked in a hushed voice, "Was that necessary? Del's not the kind of guy who lets something like that go. He'll come after you."

Though my entire body tensed at her warning, a part of me welcomed a good fight and the opportunity to teach him the lesson he missed out on while he was screwing my mother. I glanced over at him on the other side of the bar to see violence brewing behind his eyes while he sized me up. "Good."

"It's your funeral," Emma mumbled.

Breanna slid the tray onto the counter. "Four Long Island ice teas."

"Coming right up." I veered in the other direction, got out four glasses and began pouring in the booze. Feeling her eyes on me, I contemplated ignoring her. That lasted less than a second before I gave in. "Was there something you wanted to say?"

Breanna narrowed her eyes. "Shacking up with Emma, huh?"

I gave a quick laugh. "She's renting me a room. We're not even under the same roof."

Her brows knit. "You do realize if you hurt her, I'll use shards of glass to slice off your balls?"

I blinked before filling the glasses. "We're not involved," I said, keeping my voice level.

"Maybe not right now." She raised one eyebrow. "But I see the way she looks at you. And that jealous act just now said it all. "

My head whipped around, and I scowled. Why wouldn't Breanna shut up? If Emma was falling for me, I didn't need to know. That kind of information only made it harder to stay away from her.

"Emma is safe from me." I set two of the four drinks on the tray in front of her.

"We both know that's not true." She gave me look that had me on alert.

I loaded up the other two drinks. "The last thing I want to do is hurt Emma or Scarlet."

"Then don't. Or you'll regret it." She picked up the loaded tray then shot me a sly smile. "Thanks, sugar. You're a *saint.*"

A chill shot down my spine. Using my stage nickname didn't feel like an accident. She had to know about me. If she told Emma, I'd be out on my ass faster than Scarlet could change her mind. No way would Emma want me in Scarlet's life. I wasn't a positive influence on the young, as Faith had pointed out.

For the next five very long minutes, my gaze kept flicking to Breanna as I waited for her to come back. When she set her tray on the bar top again, a smug smile waited for me.

"How did you know?"

"Under normal circumstances, I probably wouldn't

have figured it out. You look totally different."

"Would you lower your voice?" I leaned over the bar so neither of us would have to shout. "What gave me away?"

"Nothing you did here. I had the TV on while I was working at home. You know, for the noise. A segment came on VH1 about Full Throttle. You've heard of them, right?" Breanna looked awfully amused.

I rolled my eyes. "Get to the point."

"Well, their hot lead singer? I was watching him but then the kettle whistled, so I went into the kitchen to make my tea." Her mouth curled up. "You were telling the interviewer about your latest arrest and what a raw deal you'd gotten, and I couldn't figure out why that voice was so familiar. I ran back to the TV, and it hit me."

"And what do you plan to do with this information?" My fingers white-knuckled the edge of the bar top. I loathed that she had something to hold over me.

She glanced around again to make sure there were no eavesdroppers, then tilted her head. "That depends on you."

Air whooshed from my lungs in exasperation. I'd do just about anything if Breanna would swear not to blow my cover. Emma would inevitably find out one day, but until then, I had her. I wanted her in my life as long as she was willing to be there. For the next week or so anyway. "What are your demands? Money?"

"I don't know." All traces of snark vanished and her shoulders fell. "Until I figure it out, don't you dare do anything to make her cry. Don't you dare." She gave me a last hard look before spinning around and leaving with her full tray.

CHAPTER THIRTEEN

★ *Emma* ★

What was up with Liam tonight? I didn't want to think about how Del might retaliate against him. And seeing Liam's heated exchange with Breanna, I wanted to hear what they were saying. Anything would be better than my imagination.

I'd been with Liam pretty much every moment since he'd first arrived, and I hadn't seen him do anything with Breanna other than deliver her drink orders. If he and Breanna barely knew each other, what was so serious? Maybe after we did last call and the bar cleared out, I'd pick his brain.

But as we worked, Liam rarely glanced my way. Anytime I spoke to him, his tone didn't invite more conversation. He barely spoke two words, much less explained why he was in such a mood.

Hours later, the rest of the staff had wrapped up their duties and left Liam and me to lock up. I thought of Del, and my shoulder muscles bunched. He was friends with Bobby. Liam seemed to do fine one-on-one, but how would he fare against two?

"Taking out the trash," Liam called out as he slipped through the back door.

When I heard a loud thunk, followed by shouting, I dropped the bar rag and bolted toward the back. By the time I threw open the door, Bobby and Fritz each had one of Liam's arms and Del had just landed a punch on Liam's jaw.

They didn't notice me as Del's fist flew at the other side of Liam's face. He aimed the next blow to Liam's ribs. And then another. I reached into my pocket and dialed 9-1-1, and when the operator answered, I rushed to fill her in. "Yeah, I'm at the Wagon Wheel. Bobby McConnell, Fritz Mantle and Del Johnson are beating the crap out of someone in the parking lot. Please hurry."

Del stopped his assault on Liam and slowly turned around. "You're calling the police?"

I lifted my chin. "Are you going to beat *me* up next?"

Del glared, but he didn't make another move toward Liam. "We'll finish this another time."

Bobby and Fritz released Liam, who stumbled to the asphalt. As I wrapped up my call to 9-1-1, they drove away in their cars, and I kneeled beside Liam.

He grinned, showing bloody teeth. "Aw, you saved me, darlin'."

I stood again and looked down at him. "This isn't a joke. They could've killed you."

Only a little unsteady, he dusted himself off. "I had everything under control. I was just waiting for the right moment." He chuckled as he scooped up the abandoned trash bag.

Hugging my sides against the chill, I scowled at him. "Why is getting beat up so amusing to you?"

Liam ambled to the giant garbage bin and tossed the bag, then turned around and headed toward me. "Because it took three of them to take me down, and the only reason they succeeded was because one of them clocked me as soon as I walked out the door. If you'd given me a minute or two more, they wouldn't have walked away." He smiled again. "And because when I see them again, that's when the real fun begins."

"You're planning on going after them?" I couldn't believe my ears. Liam's jaw was already swelling, and by the way he kept touching his side, I wondered if Del had bruised a rib. If I'd been later and not called the police, who knows what would've happened to Liam? And now he wanted to take on the three of them *again*?

Red and blue lights swirled in the night sky, gravel crunching under the patrol car. It slowed to a stop, and two officers climbed out. One of them was Dave, who regularly came in for coffee. "Someone called in an assault in progress?" he asked, scanning the lot.

While Liam practically ignored us, I filled Dave in on the after-hours excitement. I wanted Liam to press charges, but he refused. Dave and the other cop eyed him suspiciously, but in the end, they shrugged and walked away.

As soon as the cops left and we were back inside the bar, I invaded Rocko's office and emerged with a first aid kit. I snapped my fingers and pointed to a chair at one of the nearby tables. "Sit."

Liam obeyed, his eyes following me as I ducked past him to get behind the bar for some ice. I wrapped some chunks in a clean bar rag and returned to him. I gingerly touched his jaw, my fingers applying a gentle pressure until he turned his head and I could assess the damage on the other side. The cut probably didn't need stitches, but he'd be bruised tomorrow.

I pressed the ice against his jaw. "Hold this." My hands moved to his ribs and I laid my palm against them. "Does that hurt?"

He shook his head. "Not much. I've had worse."

I plucked some gauze from the kit and doused it in hydrogen peroxide so I could work the side that wasn't being iced. "What did Del say earlier that made you drag him over the bar?"

Liam winced when I ran the gauze over his skin. He hesitated so long, I wondered if he'd heard me. "Nothing," he finally mumbled.

"Yeah, it always pisses me off when someone does nothing." With one side all cleaned up, I soaked a fresh piece of gauze and moved to his other side. "I'm impressed you showed such restraint after that kind of an offense."

He grinned.

"Are you going to tell me what he did, or are you going to make me beat it out of you?" I found a cotton swab from the kit to work on the thin dirt-filled gap. A moment later, I felt the pressure of his hands on my hips and heat seared my middle and traveled to my toes.

"One of them hit me in the mouth." His voice had gone husky. "You should get a closer look."

The memory of our previous kiss ravaged me, and my stomach flipped. I only had to swing one leg over to straddle him, then bend down, and his full, soft lips would be mine. But where would we go from there? The more I kissed him, the greater our chance of ending up in bed. And when he eventually bailed, I'd feel worse for having slept with him.

I met his gaze, brushed a thumb across his mouth, and allowed myself a brief moment to fantasize about giving into my desires. "It's perfect." Then I backed up until his hands fell to his sides. "You'd never met Del before. What could he possibly have done?"

"I don't like you working here," he muttered.

What the hell? Did Liam think he had a right to tell me what to do, how to live my life? "Remember when we talked about selling our souls? Well, this bar is mine. Do I hate being at the mercy of drunk guys? Yeah, I do. But most of the guys here are pretty nice. Some aren't, but I deal. I have a kid to support, you know." I filled my lungs with a calming breath before continuing. "So what did Del do?"

He refocused on me, and his voice grew gravelly. "I didn't like the way he was looking at you."

My breath hitched, and I swallowed nervously. Lord, that bad-boy thing was working for me. "I spend eight-hour days at a bar, Liam. They're usually filled with guys who are drinking. They're gonna look. What are you going to do? Beat them *all* up?"

"Maybe." One side of his mouth curved up in that sexy way that made my insides tremble.

"Yeah, but why bother? You've made it pretty clear you're leaving when Duke comes back."

"What if I wanted to stay? For you."

For a split second, my heart soared. Then I reminded myself the kind of guy I was dealing with. It didn't matter what Liam *thought* he was feeling now; I couldn't see him making a lifelong commitment to Scarlet and me.

"After knowing me for only forty-eight hours, you'd move here and build a life with us? C'mon. You can't even tell me what you do for a living." I snatched another square of gauze and moved to the scratch on his chin. He didn't reply, which spoke volumes.

I threw away the used gauze and tossed the supplies back into the first aid kit. "Do me a favor, Liam. Don't kiss me again. Don't hint at it, and don't flirt with me. Unless you think you can deliver the goods, don't make promises you can't keep." Though breathing had become difficult and my throat had thickened, I gave him a hard look before spinning around and returning to cleanup duty. The sooner we got home, the sooner he'd disappear into the garage.

CHAPTER FOURTEEN

★ *Liam* ★

I rolled over and forced my eyes open, trying to figure out where the hell the pounding was coming from.

"Liam, breakfast is ready if you're up."

I shot out of bed and zoomed to the front door. The guest house was so small, I didn't have far to go. I flung the door open. "I'd love some. Thanks."

Emma's gaze trained on the waist of my boxers, then swept the length of my body. By the time she made it to my chin, a crooked smile awaited her. At least I wasn't the only one soaking up the view and unable to sample it. After the smackdown she'd given me last night, she deserved to suffer. Not that the verbal abuse she'd handed down hadn't been justified. But now that she'd laid down the law, I had no choice but to back off. Didn't like that. Not one bit.

"Put on a shirt before you come up, okay?" Her eyes pinched before she hiked up the driveway.

As tempted as I was to wear a tank—I so enjoyed her ogling me—I'd promised Emma not to flirt or hint at kissing or anything similar. She made her point well last night. Unless I planned to stick around to see if it might work between us, I had no business messing with her. No matter how much I wanted to run my hands up her thigh and feel her moving beneath me, it could never happen.

I'd always prided myself in following the girls' rules and fulfilling their demands. Unfortunately, this time the demand wasn't in my favor, and for the next few days or weeks, we would be strictly friends and I'd be forced to be the ideal tenant.

Except... it was Monday, and neither of us had to go to work tonight. What the hell would I do with myself all day, and how would I make an excuse to spend time with Emma?

But before I schemed of ways to worm myself into her day, I had something I needed to do. First, I had to park the Shelby somewhere secure in case the three idiots decided that jumping me last night wasn't enough. I'd rather they damage a thirty-thousand-dollar car than the Shelby, which was worth six times that.

After washing up, I threw on jeans and a T-shirt, then jogged to the main house. Emma was serving up an omelet.

"Liam!" Scarlet struggled to stand up in her booster seat, but the edge of the table prevented it. I closed the door behind me and flicked a finger under her chin, before dropping into a chair. Man, those dimples were growing on me. "Good morning, buddy."

"What are we doing today?" Scarlet asked.

"I'm doing laundry and chores," Emma answered before I had a chance to open my mouth. She sat down with us at the table and reached for her fork. "And you, young lady, are going to school. After that, you can have Cami over to play if you like."

"Yes, please." Scarlet speared a piece of egg.

"I was wondering..." I peeked at Emma between bites. "You'll need a new car soon. Any idea what kind you'll get?"

She lifted a shoulder. "I don't have many choices. It needs to be good on gas with low mileage. Something safe. I doubt I'll go for anything too fancy. Why?"

I wouldn't be able to drive a new car and the Shelby back to LA at the same time. I'd have to leave one here. Emma could use it. Didn't matter how fancy the new car was if it didn't cost her a dime. "What if you *did* have choices? What's your dream car?"

Emma looked pensive for a moment. "I'm not as comfortable in big cars. Makes me feel like I'm driving a tank. A smaller SUV would be easier to load kids into because I wouldn't have to stoop over so much. That's a ways off though."

"Color?"

Emma slanted her head, lips pursed as she thought about it. "Uh... White or silver hides the dirt better so I wouldn't be a slave to washing my car every week."

Wow, she was easy. Low standards or not, I had a much better idea what to buy. "How about dropping me off at the dealership later today?"

Her brows furrowed. "You already have a car."

My mouth pulled at the corners. "I'm well aware of that. I'd love to park the Shelby where those clowns can't key it or anything."

Emma's gaze bored into me. Probably trying to figure out how I so easily and casually could buy another car. "You're welcome to park it down the driveway behind the gate," she offered.

"Thanks." I shoved a forkful of omelet into my mouth, chewed, and swallowed. "Where's the closest dealership?"

"I can't drive you there. My car's not running. In fact, I should've asked last night if I could borrow yours to take Scarlet to school this morning."

"Your car's fine. Fixed it yesterday."

"You..." Her eyes reduced to slits. "Then why did I need a ride to work yesterday?"

"Because we were both going there anyway." My mouth turned up, my cheek bunching. "And now you get to chauffer me around. After my workout."

★

Several hours later, I parked in front of her house driving a brand new steel gray Mercedes-Benz GLK350. Yeah, she'd think it was too much and would never in a million years accept it as her own. I didn't plan on giving her a choice.

I strolled through the front door and dropped the car key on the dining room table. Scarlet obviously had a friend over because giggling reached me from her room. I poked my head into her doorway to say hello, but she only gave me a quick wave and went back to playing with dolls. Since I barely knew what to do with one little girl, much less two, being nearly invisible was a relief. By the time I made it back to the dining room, Emma was examining the car key.

"A Mercedes?" She strode with purpose to the living room window. After a quick peek, she shot me an accusative look. "Brand new?"

I shrugged. "Used ones tend to have more problems, and I don't want to deal with that."

"You do realize that you just dropped a big chunk of change on a new car to save you money from damage those guys may or may not cause to your other car? Anything they might do would probably cost less to fix than buying a brand new luxury car."

"Yeah, but now we have another car to drive in case yours breaks down."

Her eyebrows flew up, and she had a dangerous look in her eyes. "We?"

Oops, bad choice of words. I wasn't sure how to get out of that, since I really *had* intended to share the car with her. "Uh, is there anything to eat?"

She slammed a hand to her hip and scowled. "What are you up to?"

I blew out a breath. "I don't want to drive the Shelby while I'm here. So I got a new car, something that would work for you too in case you needed something to drive. No big deal."

She inclined her head, studying me. "Can I see the paperwork on the sale?"

What could it hurt? I rolled my eyes and dug into my back pocket, then thrust a folded envelope at Emma. She sent me a suspicious glance as she opened it and straightened the long sheets of paper.

"These are legal documents, Liam," she murmured.

"They need to lie flat in a folder, not crinkled up in your pocket. You clearly have no respect for your bookkeeper." She scrutinized the sheet a moment before inhaling sharply, then slowly her eyes met mine. "You just dropped over fifty grand. Cash. On a car you don't need."

I glanced up at the ceiling and chewed the inside of my lip. I had no idea what to say to that. "So... is there anything to eat?"

She stared at me a long moment, and I twitched under her gaze. Finally, she rose from her chair and opened the fridge. "Leftover lasagna from Friday. Or I could make you a sandwich."

"Lasagna sounds great." I sat at the table and eyed her on the sly as she put a generous portion into the toaster oven.

"What are your plans for tonight?" Then she began spreading the garlic butter mixture on a slice of french bread.

"I don't know. Thought I'd go out, maybe stop by the Wagon Wheel. See what's going on."

She set down the butter knife, flipped around, and folded her arms over her chest. "You wouldn't, by any chance, be looking for three guys in particular, would you?"

"Uh..." I tapped the table. "That lasagna ready yet?"

Emma blew out a breath, then slid the lasagna plate out of the toaster oven, replacing it with the garlic bread. "Will you please not make me visit you in the hospital?"

I grinned. "You'd visit me in the hospital, babe?"

"No. I don't go out of my way for reckless idiots." She stomped to the silverware drawer and got out a fork. On her way toward me, she grabbed the plate and set it in front of me. Then she went back for the garlic bread.

I dug in, closing my eyes as the flavors burst in my mouth. "Mm, you made this?"

"From scratch."

"Wow." I wolfed down another bite. "This is fantastic."

"I was going to make steak and baked potatoes for dinner tonight. Will you be around? I'm hoping you can squeeze me in around, you know, bar fights and blowing all your money."

I grinned before shoveling another forkful. Emma rolled her eyes, and I committed her ass to memory as she strolled away. She was a terrific cook, great with money, and she was beautiful — the perfect wife. But I couldn't think about that. Sure, providing financially for her and Scarlet would be no problem, but me being a stable father wasn't going to happen, and I'd bring too much drama into their lives. And if I ended up anything like the guy who'd raised me, I'd make a terrible stepfather.

A pang of jealousy hit me at the thought of her being the perfect wife for *someone else.*

★

After dinner, Emma shooed me out of the kitchen, leaving me standing there with nothing to do and no excuse to stick around. It was probably for the best since being near Emma would tempt me into flirting, and she'd already warned me against that. I was about to head out back when something tapped my hip.

"Read." Scarlet nudged me with the book again, staring up at me.

"Read to you?" I asked, taking the offered book.

Her head bobbed up and down. "Read it good."

I mashed my lips together to keep from laughing. "I'll do my best." How hard could it be? It sure beat playing with dolls, and it meant that I didn't have to leave right away. I followed Scarlet to the sofa, taking one end and leaning against the arm so we faced each other.

Scarlet listened quietly as I read the first page, then the second. Not my thing, since I wasn't into talking bears and skunks, but the illustrations were cute.

"No, not like that."

I peered over the book at her. "Not like what?"

"Mommy always changes their voices."

As ordered, I read the chipmunk's dialogue — I was nearly positive it was a girl — and raised the pitch of my voice.

Scarlet's cheeks dimpled as she snorted.

Pretending to be offended, I put the book down. "You're laughing at me?"

She giggled. "You sound funny."

The scent of grape hit my nose as I reached for her. "*You're* about to sound funnier." She squealed when I tickled under her arms. Her laughter rang through the air, and I wanted to hear more.

A shadow fell over us and I looked up to see Emma biting her lip. "Sweetie, it's almost bed time. Why don't you go find your pajamas, and we'll get you in the bathtub?"

Scarlet scrambled off the sofa and dashed into her room.

Emma gave me an apologetic look. "Sorry. Didn't

want to break up the fun, but she needs to wind down or she'll never fall asleep."

"No problem." I abandoned the couch. "I was only tickling her to get out of reading. I'm not that great with kids."

"You seemed to be doing okay." She backed up, reminding me she intended to keep her distance. And I needed to let her. "What about your nephew?" she asked.

"That's different. I practically helped raise him. But a kid I barely know, I'm not as comfortable."

"Getting good at anything just takes time and the desire to try." She collected the book and toys into her arms.

"I won't be here long enough to get good at that." I lifted a shoulder, leaving the lack of desire on my part unsaid.

Her mouth thinned to a straight line, her eyes hardening. "Right."

Hell, now I looked like an ass. But my gut was strongly suggesting that I not give Emma the impression that I'd ever be cool with being any kind of parental figure to Scarlet. The less time I spent with the kid, the better.

I checked the pocket of my jeans for my car key. "I should get going."

She cast me a suspicious glance. "As in going out, possibly to the Wagon Wheel?"

My gaze flitted toward the door. "Maybe."

Emma angled her chin down, a brow rising. "Don't be showing up on my doorstep, expecting me to tend to your wounds. Go to the hospital or go straight to your room all bloody."

"Roger that." I winked and slipped out the front. Just as I closed the door, something banged against it. Emma throwing a little pillow at me, I assumed.

Once I got to the Wagon Wheel, I parked the Mercedes at the end of the lot and scoped out the place. It was busy but not as packed as it had been the past three nights. I hit the clicker on my new car and strode toward the bar entrance.

As soon as I made it through the door, Breanna skidded to a stop in front of me, carrying an empty tray. "What are you doing here on your day off?" She focused on my bruised jaw. "And what the hell happened to you? Somebody jump you?"

"As a matter of fact, yes. Del, Fritz, and Bobby. Seen them tonight?"

Her eyes landed on a table near the stage. And there they were.

"Excuse me." I slipped past her but was delayed when she caught my shoulder. I flipped around. "Yeah?"

"Don't start anything, okay?" She glanced behind me. "Three of them and only one of you. Even if you could take them, they're not worth it. And besides, you don't want to risk messing up that pretty face any worse, do you?"

"Aren't you sweet?" Chuckling, I ditched her and took several long strides to the table, then passed it. After a quick leap up onto the stage, I nabbed the microphone and turned it on.

"Good evening, everyone. Bobby, Fritz, Del." I grinned down at them. "How about these bruises, huh?"

I pointed to my face. "Courtesy of these buffoons when they jumped me last night as I was taking out the trash." I shook my head. "I did *not* see that coming. And now I'm awfully curious to see if the three of you can take me in a fair fight when I'm expecting you. If you all would care to step outside with me right now, we'll have an opportunity to find out."

I rolled my eyes while the three idiots discussed it amongst themselves.

"We'll be happy to meet you outside when we're done eating," Del said, smirking and mumbling something to Fritz.

Seemed to me they listened to Del. I'd take him out first.

After replacing the microphone, I jumped off stage then barreled toward him. I yanked him up by his shirt and his chair toppled over. "Fritz, Bobby, follow us."

Once I'd gotten Del in a headlock—and not without some ferocious struggling on his part—I dragged him outside and tossed him to the ground. He slid a couple of feet across the gravel.

Fritz and Bobby appeared, along with half the people in the bar. "Bobby, Fritz, so glad you could join us." I stormed toward Bobby, who tried to run before I got a grip on his collar, and rammed my fist into his nose.

He shrieked so high-pitched I almost confused him with a girl. "You broke it!"

Del lunged toward me, and I clamped onto Bobby, shoving him in front of me as a shield. Hearing footfalls, I cast a quick glance around the parking lot. Del followed my gaze, eyeing Fritz running toward a car. Del took a few steps back. Yeah, he wasn't so tough when half his backup was fleeing and the other half was bleeding all over himself.

"Bobby was warned, and he didn't listen. Trust me, Del. If you do whatever it is you might be thinking, I'll send you to the hospital. That's a promise." I nudged Bobby aside and motioned Del to bring it on. "*Please* give me an excuse to hurt you."

A long moment passed before Del held up his palms. "We're even."

"Not until you look like this." I pointed to my swollen jaw. "But as long as you treat Emma and any other woman here with respect, I'll leave you alone. You don't, and I'll hunt you down. Your choice."

Fritz focused on something behind me, and I turned. Uh-oh. A cop.

"Dave, you saw how he attacked Bobby," Del said. "You're gonna arrest him, right?"

Dave stepped forward, his palm resting on the butt of his gun. "Depends. If you press charges, he might want to do the same to you for jumping him last night." He paused for a moment and stretched taller. "Seems to me everything's all settled now. Assuming you don't make any trouble around here with the ladies, as Liam said, we won't have a problem."

"But he attacked me," Bobby growled, holding his nose with his bloody hand.

Dave gave a sage nod as he regarded Bobby. "Isn't that what you did last night? When it was three against one?"

Bobby glowered at Dave, then shifted to me before

whirling around and storming to his car.

Rocko waved toward the entrance, shouting, "A round on the house for everyone!"

The crowd, including Del, rushed back into the bar, presumably for the freebie, leaving me alone with the cop and Breanna.

Dave considered me a moment, then spoke in a low voice. "You're getting away with it this time, but don't press your luck. Leave it alone."

"Good night." I saluted the cop, then headed back to my car.

"Wait," Breanna called out.

I stopped and pivoted on my heel. "Lecture time?"

"No." Her hazel eyes fixed on me. "In fact, I think that was nicely done. You could've turned it into a brawl, broke some furniture. You took it outside though and didn't do anywhere near the damage to them that they did to you. Except Bobby, but I know he had that coming."

True. I was betting Emma still wouldn't approve of how I'd handled it. But if I hadn't done something, those clowns would've thought nothing of pawing women. For all I knew, they'd do it again. But this time, they might think it through first.

"So what's up?" I glanced over at Bobby who was driving away in his truck, probably going to the hospital to have his nose looked at. "You have a list of demands? Is that why I'm not already in my car?"

Her shoulders pulled back, and her eyes flared. "I have one request."

My muscles coiled. "Let's hear it."

"Be upfront with Emma at all times. Except, of course, about your real life. On everything else, you'll tell her the absolute truth."

I was already violating that demand, since I hadn't told Emma I'd bought the car for *her*. But that probably wasn't Breanna's main concern. "You don't want me leading her on."

"Bingo."

I held up my right palm. "I swear that Emma will always be aware of my true intentions toward her."

"Good." Breanna seemed satisfied, but by her smug look, she was about to throw me a curve ball. "Because when you leave, if Emma feels violated or upset in anyway, I'll go to the media. I'll tell them how you rented a room from her and..." Her eyes darkened. "I'll tell them about her fatherless child and how you had a gig in Reno around the time Scarlet was conceived."

My insides turned to ice. "But it's not true."

"Yes, it is."

"I'm not Scarlet's father. I didn't even know Emma back then."

Breanna sighed. "That's not the point, *Saint Nick*. All I need to tell them is that you were in town around that time, which you were. They'll put the rest together themselves."

CHAPTER FIFTEEN

★ *Liam* ★

I was being blackmailed. What the hell was Breanna up to? "But why would you do that to Emma?"

Breanna raised her chin and straightened her shoulders. "Because she's my friend. If riding on your fame gets her a better job than bartending at the Wagon Wheel and getting perved on by guys like Bobby and Del, then so be it."

I wanted Emma out of there too, but I didn't want to risk my sister's wrath and my time with Xander. And if Faith thought I'd been careless or abandoned my own child, I'd have a harder time getting back into favor with her. "Well, it's a nonissue, because Emma knows where we stand. I respect her too much to do otherwise."

"Then we understand each other." At that, Breanna turned on her heel and went back into the bar without so much as a glance back.

By the time I leaped the front steps of Emma's house, it was quiet inside. Scarlet was probably fast asleep. Through the living room window, I could see Emma sitting at the kitchen table engrossed in ledgers.

I cursed my stomach for doing a summersault at

the sight of her. Since I didn't live in the main house, I tapped the door before opening it.

Emma rushed to me, examining my body for injuries. "You changed your mind about taking on three guys?"

I scoffed. "Hell, no. They just didn't get a chance to hit me."

"And you're not in jail." Her mouth tipped up at the corners. "I'm feeling a mixture of horror, relief, and admiration."

I laughed and tucked a lock of hair behind her ear. She didn't brush my hand away, and my insides warmed. But as tempting as it was to let my hand slide around the nape of her neck and yank her against me, I'd promised not to flirt unless I meant it. Hell, I'd promised Breanna I wouldn't make Emma cry. Breaking my word would land me in a world of hell. I *had* to behave.

"Did any of them have to go to the hospital?" she asked.

My gaze fell to my toes. "Only Bobby. I may've broken his nose. But that was the only swing I took at any of them. I swear."

Her expression grew serious. "Did you scare 'em?"

I hesitated a moment before finally admitting, "Maybe a little."

"Good." She smiled, her eyes dancing with mischief. "I was about to quit working and make some popcorn. Considering making it movie night with *Pretty Woman* again. Want to hang around for it?"

"Chick flick, huh?" I grimaced. "Can I talk you into, say, *Transformers? Fast and Furious?*"

Her eyes sparkled. "It's *Pretty Woman*. You can stay or go."

Heat radiated through my chest. "I'll stay."

★

I returned from my morning run, showered, and went to my closet. I had one last set of clothes, and that was it. Even if I broke down and did my laundry, I'd still be wearing the same crap I'd worn last week. And who wanted to do laundry every single week? I had no choice but to go to the mall. And if I didn't do it today, I'd have to do laundry very soon or wear something dirty.

By the time I made it to the main house, Emma had already dropped Scarlet off at school. And she was making me breakfast. Bacon. I grinned. "Smells great."

She jumped, then recomposed herself. "You scared me."

I chuckled. Startling people never got old. "Need some help?"

"Nope." She turned off the burner, then swung around for the spatula. "Just finishing up."

I snagged two plates from the cupboard and set them next to her as she bumped into me, dropping the spatula. My hands shot to her waist to steady her.

"Whoa." Watching a movie with Emma the night before had been nice. A little too nice. Touching her now only reminded me what I had missed while I'd been behaving like a total gentleman. The feel of her against my palms blew fuses in my brain. My hands had a mind of their own, one hand sliding around to her lower back, the other pulling her against me.

Her breath caught.

"This isn't as easy as I thought it'd be." Why was it so difficult to think about anything else with her so close?

"What's not easy?" Her voice was unsteady, the last syllable coming in higher than the rest.

"Being around you and keeping my hands to myself," I answered in a raspy voice.

She flattened her palms against my chest in a defensive gesture, then took a long, deep breath and lifted her chin. "It's probably just a moment of weakness. Like the kiss you said wouldn't happen again."

Her words were pushing me away, but her flushed cheeks and parted lips were begging me to do as I wanted. My veins thrummed with the desire to get her out of those jeans and nestle my hands into every curve of her body. If she didn't want that, she'd stop me. I prayed she wouldn't.

"Meant it at the time." I steered her backward until she bumped into the counter. I moved closer to her temple and got a whiff of her skin. Damn, she smelled good. Like spring flowers after a rain. "Now, not so much."

She licked her lips. "Listen, Liam..."

Her words died on her tongue when mine teased her ear lobe, my breath tickling her skin. A tiny moan slipped past her lips.

Slowly, my mouth kissed a path to her shoulder until I came to the strap of her tank top. I looped a thumb under it, along with her bra strap, and gently moved it off her shoulder. She shivered, her fingers trembling as they clutched the fabric of my shirt. Taking that as encouragement, I slipped a hand under her top.

Emma sucked in a lungful of air and laid a hand on my arm. "Don't," she whispered.

My breath whooshed out, and I touched my forehead against hers. "Why not?"

She chewed her lip. "Because we both know what happens next."

"We have a great time?" I shot her a lopsided grin.

"Yeah, until you leave." She straightened her top and skirted around me. "Breakfast is getting cold."

Yep, she'd stopped me. *Damn.* As she loaded up our plates with eggs and bacon, I made a serious effort not to think about where we could've gone if she'd been willing. *Down, boy.*

"I'm out of clothes. Will you go shopping with me?"

Her eyes stayed fixed on the plate as she pushed the eggs around with the fork. "I'm not so sure it's a good idea."

"You might be right." I waited a beat. "But I don't know the area. I can swear to stay in the friend zone, if that's what's holding you back. Please?"

She met my gaze. "Friend zone. You can't go back on your promise and excuse it with you 'thought so at the time.'"

"I'll treat you as if you're my sister." I held up a hand as if a bible were below it. "I swear."

Later that morning after Emma had a chance to

catch up on some work, we sifted through racks at the nearest mall. While I tried on shirts and pants, I behaved myself. This was no easy feat since I wanted more than anything to drag her into the dressing room with me. Anytime I felt the desire to seduce her rise up, I suppressed it. For one, I didn't want to get shot down again. And if I pursued her harder, she might think I was interested in a long-term relationship. I wasn't. And I didn't want to piss off Breanna.

We loaded up my loot from the mall, then picked up Scarlet on the way home. I went directly to my room to put all the crap away. Normally, right about now, we'd be getting ready for work, but neither of us had anywhere to go. Did she expect me to hang out with her and Scarlet this evening? I wanted to, but that was a hell of a temptation. I needed a distraction, another girl to take my mind off Emma.

Snatching up my keys, I headed out, stopping by the main house on impulse.

Emma was pouring steaming water into a mug. "Hey."

"Scarlet asleep?"

"Mm-hm." She tugged on the little tag attached to the string, then draped it over the side of the mug and squirted in some honey. "I can boil more water if you'd like some tea."

"Thanks, but I'm going out. Figured I'd check out that biker bar you tried talking me into that first night." And I needed to do that soon, because knowing we probably wouldn't be disturbed again until morning made me want to stay. I wondered if I made a move on Emma again if she'd say yes this time.

And what if she did? Breanna would make good on her promise if I hurt Emma. But even if Breanna never followed through, I still didn't want to do that to Emma.

"Guess I'll see you in the morning." I moved toward the front door. "'Night."

"Good night."

Once I was outside, I heard Emma throw the bolt lock. Ten minutes later, the Mercedes was rolling into the parking lot of Dirty Side Down. I smiled at the innocent biker slang on my way to the entrance, passing a sea of motorcycles — Harley's, Indians, and a few Victories.

After wrenching open the thick wooden door, I paused while my eyes adjusted to the dark. Swirls of smoke hung in the air, the only lighting coming from the neon signs and several lamps hanging low from the high ceiling. The scent of leather and dust wafted up my nose.

The place was busier than I expected for a Tuesday night. Bearded, tattooed guys in faded jeans and leather vests sprinkled the large room, some around the two pool tables, others seated on stools at the bar. A couple of women were wearing so little I half expected to see a dancing pole nearby.

I picked a stool in the corner where I could observe the crowd, hoping I hadn't made a mistake by venturing out of the Wagon Wheel and into a biker bar where I didn't know a soul or have any idea what kind of mess

I might get into. Taking on two or three guys and not getting my ass beat was in the realm of possibility. A whole bar full of guys was a different story.

As soon as I sat down, a woman with short, spiky hair and more than twice as many tattoos as I had slid a napkin in front of me.

"What can I get you?" Her smile was friendlier than I'd expected.

"Whatever you have on draft." I reached into my pocket for some cash when something brushed my thigh.

"Liam, you slumming?"

I laughed. Heather had been in the Wagon Wheel every night I'd been there. Couldn't help but notice glimpses of her butt cheeks under her itty bitty shorts and how her boobs were always exploding out of her top.

"So are you. Kiss on the lips?" I asked. The bartender reappeared with my beer and I glanced at Heather for confirmation.

"I thought you'd never ask." She slid her hips between my knees.

"The drink." I laughed, dodging her by moving my leg and maneuvering myself in the stool so she stood at my side. "You always order one with me."

"Honey, that's not the kiss on the lips I meant." Her mouth pulled up seductively. "Is that why you're always making me those things?"

The bartender rolled her eyes. "Do we look like we stock mango juice? Try again."

"Shot of Cuervo, please," Heather said, her gaze

staying on mine.

I tapped the twenty-dollar bill by my mug and the bartender swiped it off the bar, then halted. "You're Liam from the Wagon Wheel?"

Unsure if I should cop to it, I nodded slowly.

The bartender nudged the guy on the next stool over. "Hey, Mark, this is Liam, the guy who took on those douche bags last night." She set a shot glass in front of Heather and poured in the amber liquid.

Mark clasped my hand and slapped me on the shoulder with the other. "Del and Bobby think it's fun to lift their legs up and piss on everyone. Always love it when someone pisses back. Next drink's on me, brother." He returned to his drink, leaving me alone with Heather.

"Thanks for the drink." She downed it, skipping the salt and lime, then turned around. She lifted her elbows on the bar, her ample breasts straining against the tiny top. Under normal circumstances, I'd gladly steer her into the bathroom and give her what she obviously wanted. Although I enjoyed flirting with Heather, there was no part of me that actually wanted her.

I wanted Emma. I had no idea whether it was because I was living with her or because I'd already had a taste of her, but the very idea of being with anyone else felt like cheating.

Why those feelings were flooding me, I couldn't fathom. Emma wasn't my girlfriend. In fact, she'd shut me down more than once. So what did it matter if I spent some time with another girl? I should be able to take Heather home and do all the things to her that I'd been dreaming about doing with Emma.

But I couldn't.

Jesus, she'd gotten under my skin. Maybe once I got back to Hollywood, I'd be able to look at other girls without thinking of Emma.

Heather was eyeing me as if I was her next shot and she was going to swallow every drop.

"I should get going." I pushed off the bar, but Heather laid a hand on my arm.

"What's the rush? I don't bite, you know." One side of her mouth lifted. "Well, okay a little. But you might like it."

I was pretty sure I would—if not for Emma. Once I resumed my old life and Emma was just a memory, I might have a gig nearby at some point and look Heather up. She'd be fun. But not yet. "I have some work to catch up on."

"At the Wagon Wheel?" She raised a brow. "You're off duty."

"Just filling in there. I have another job." Which I needed to write songs for. I eased off the stool, backing away to make minimal physical contact with Heather.

"Give me a ride home?" she asked.

It was a trap. Had to be. She usually stuck around till midnight, and it was only ten now. Heather needed to know that my only offer was a ride. In my car, not on me.

I took both her hands in mine. "You're a beautiful girl, but I'm not available."

She tilted her eyes. "I overheard you saying you didn't have a girlfriend. Seeing Emma now or something?"

Releasing her hands, I stepped farther from the stool. "Emma and I are not involved. There's a loose end though I need to tie up. That won't happen until I'm back home. Sorry."

"Being a good boy, huh?" She closed the distance and laid a hand on my cheek. "Careful. Your tough-guy exterior is disintegrating before my eyes." She dropped her hand and whirled around. "Let's go. I'm starting a new job tomorrow and need my beauty rest."

After I dropped off Heather at her apartment a few blocks away, I drove from the curb as quickly as the car would go. Life in the spotlight had proved to me over and over how vicious rumors could be. They tended to be brutal even without fame. If anyone thought I'd stayed the night with Heather, Emma would probably hear about it. She might get hurt, and that wasn't an option. Especially with Breanna's threat looming over me.

On the drive to my rented room, all I thought about was getting Emma naked, feeling her firm thighs gripping my hips. Those images ignited a flood of words, so I killed the engine in front of Emma's place. I found the pad I kept in the console, and jotted down the lyrics before I forgot them.

It was well after midnight when I climbed out of my car and lumbered into my room.

CHAPTER SIXTEEN
★ *Emma* ★

When Liam finally emerged and came to the front for coffee, it was well after ten in the morning. I tried not to think about how late he'd been out or what he'd been doing. None of my business.

I glanced up from my work at the dining room table. He was wearing a gray tank that showed off his very nicely defined shoulders and one of the new jeans we'd bought together. Dark shadows covered his jaw, and his eyes were puffy from sleep. Yet he looked amazing. "Hey."

"Morning." He gave me a sexy half smile and poured himself some coffee.

"How was Dirty Side Down last night?" I wished I could shut my mouth. I didn't need to fish for information. I didn't want to know whatever he might have done at a seedy biker bar.

"I stopped by for a bit, then took off. Made a quick stop before coming home. Nothing too exciting."

"What, no fights?" I flashed him a flirty grin.

He shook his head. "Nah. Tryin' to stay out of trouble."

Abandoning my work for the moment, I sidled up

to him at the kitchen counter. "How's that working out for you?"

A long moment stretched by as his gaze spanned the length of my body. By the time his eyes met mine again, they smoldered. "Pretty good, I'd say."

The longer he stared at me, the more I wondered why I was holding back. Liam wasn't staying. We both knew that. But we couldn't deny the attraction between us. So what if we acted on it? We were both grown-ups of sound mind. So long as we both knew where we stood, who were we hurting?

"What are your plans today?" I asked, sliding my hands in my back pocket so I wouldn't be tempted to touch him.

He took a step toward me. "Was hoping to hang out with you a little."

I swallowed, my pulse hammering in my chest. "I have a couple more hours of work, but I'm free after that. What did you have in mind?"

"Nothing PG." He gave me a yummy lopsided smile as he inched closer and reached for my waist, his thumb stroking my skin. "You're driving me crazy," he rasped.

"Right." I laughed, my nerves alternating the tone of my voice from high to low. "And you're not driving me crazy. Not even a little bit."

Somehow he'd moved closer, and his thigh brushed my hip. My lungs refused to draw in air, my brain going on strike. My head screamed for him to step away so I wouldn't be dizzy anymore. But my body demanded to be heard, demanded satisfaction. I slipped a finger through his belt loop and yanked until our hips aligned and I could feel that he was just as affected as I was.

With his finger, he lifted my chin. "What are we gonna do about this?"

Good question. I knew what I *wanted* to do. But could I stay emotionally detached, or would I be devastated after he left? More likely, I'd be too busy hoping he would stay — and trying to tell myself he would — to think straight. And I'd probably sleep with him again in the meantime. After all that, yeah, I *would* be crushed.

I laced my fingers with his, reached up on my tiptoes, and brushed his lips with mine, then pushed his hands away as I sidestepped. "Nothing."

For the next couple of hours, I worked while Liam went for a jog then showered. We ran a couple of errands together, then picked up Scarlet on the way home.

While I did a few things around the house and started on dinner, Liam fixed the loose door hinge to my room and dismantled the shower head to remove the tiny rocks to improve the water flow. Later, he stayed with Scarlet while she drew pictures and watched cartoons. Liam was getting pretty good with Scarlet, even if he didn't think so.

In my entire life, I'd never known a happier day.

Thursday, Rocko called to say Duke had run into a complication from the surgery. An infection at the incision or something. Liam agreed to cover the weekend until Duke returned, though he qualified it by reminding Rocko he needed to be back in LA in a couple of weeks.

We worked together the next few days at the Wagon

Wheel, but we were all business. Liam was the perfect gentleman, bringing in the cases to restock behind the bar and any other heavy lifting. He opened doors for me, kept the men in line, and made the occasional joke. But he maintained a careful distance, avoiding any physical contact, and didn't flirt with me again.

Maybe he'd gotten over his infatuation or whatever it was. Believing that his feelings for me had limitations didn't stop me from liking him more with each passing day.

Del, Bobby, and Fritz came in regularly, as they always had, but they never crossed any lines.

I'd acquired two more bookkeeping clients, referred to me by the guy whose butt I'd saved. I only needed three or four more, and I'd be able to quit the bar. A few months up the road, I'd have enough in my car account for a down payment.

Soon, I'd be able to hang out with my kid all evening like most moms. After she went to bed, I'd put in another hour or two of work and go to sleep at a decent hour like a normal person. I just had to make it through the next few weeks.

But by then, Liam would be gone. Long before I replaced my car and quit tending bar, I'd be mending a broken heart. Originally Liam had said he had a month off, which gave me two more weeks at the most with him.

He was all kinds of bad for me. I knew that. He was impulsive, reckless, too quick to involve his fists, and worst of all, he couldn't commit to a woman.

On the other hand, since he'd arrived in town, he'd stood up for me against bullies and been nothing but honest. Well, except for the obvious, like what he did for work back in LA. But he'd been open about it being a secret instead of lying. Maybe someday, he'd trust me enough to tell me about his life — right about the time he realized he couldn't live without Scarlet and me.

Yeah, as if that was going to happen.

More than likely, I only had a few more days with Liam — if he didn't bail altogether and leave before Duke returned — and that would be it.

As much as I didn't want to admit it, I'd fallen for him. I'd fallen hard. But if Liam professed his undying love, how did I know he'd stick around till death do us part? And if he did, would that really be best for Scarlet and me?

As I sat at the dining room table Thursday afternoon — nearly two weeks since I'd met Liam — and as I re-added the numbers in the column, focus eluded me. The television blared from the living room, and every now and then, Scarlet's cheeks dimpled or Liam said something to her. But their interactions weren't what had me distracted. It was Liam and his sexy voice.

I glanced over my shoulder. Damn him for entertaining Scarlet and looking so good while he did it. Swiveling around in my chair, I returned to my files. But in my mind, all I saw were his wide shoulders and the way the thin fabric of his T-shirt fell over his muscular pecs. Yeah, he was pretty dreamy.

Something bumped against the back of my chair, and I jolted.

"Sorry. Didn't mean to disturb you."

"Yeah, right." I craned my neck to see him. "Wasn't getting much work done anyway."

"Scarlet's still absorbed in cartoons. Thinking about going running since I missed it this morning."

"Don't you ever skip a day?" I asked.

"I want to make sure I stick to my normal routine. Don't want to get too far off track while I'm here."

Getting off track... just another reminder that Scarlet and I weren't a part of his normal world. My heart contracted. "Well, I'll see you in a bit."

But Liam didn't move. I held his gaze and waited.

"What do you say about getting a babysitter later and doing something outside the house? Maybe go to a movie or something?"

My lids fluttered a brief moment while I digested his words and what they might mean. "Like... a date?"

"No. I mean, we agreed we wouldn't get involved, right? But I was thinking it might be nice to do grown-up things."

I tried to ignore the shiver of anticipation at the idea of doing *grown-up* things with Liam, only the two of us. I knew that wasn't what he meant though. Just getting out of the house with any adult was plenty exciting. And the opportunity to be around Liam might not come up again before he took off to LA. "We could drive into Reno and find a place that has karaoke on Thursday nights."

"Very funny." He held back a smile.

"Actually, I don't want to go far. On a school night, I won't have Lily for long, if she even agrees to it. Tonight's not one of her normal nights, and she has early morning college classes. If it's okay with you, we can go to the Wagon Wheel... as regular customers." I waited a beat and suppressed a giggle. "They have karaoke *there* too."

Liam slid a finger under my chin and sent me a crooked smile. "Sounds perfect."

Yep, going out alone with him tonight was a very bad idea. But in a bar where everyone knew us, the chances of getting into trouble were greatly diminished. It's not as if he'd make a move on me in front of everyone.

"Dinner first? Maybe around six?"

I swallowed and canted my head. "This is sounding more and more like a date."

He showed white teeth. "You wish."

★

Normally, I wore my hair straight since curling it could be labor-intensive. Putting effort toward those kinds of extras only took away from moments with my daughter. But tonight, I had a nondate with Liam, and I wanted to look *good*. He might as well know what he'd be missing once he returned to LA.

Okay, so in reality, he probably wouldn't give me a second thought once he was back home and surrounded by beautiful, scantily dressed women. But I had to at least try to make him remember me.

I curled my hair and wore a little extra makeup. After choosing a push-up bra and a top that dipped low in the front, I threw on my favorite jeans. I thought about wearing a miniskirt, but I didn't want him to think I was trying too hard. As I slipped on a pair of knee-length high-heeled boots, I heard the doorbell chime. By the time I made it to the living room, Liam had already let Lily in.

"Thanks so much for coming on such short notice." I gave Lily a quick hug. "I appreciate it."

Liam stood frozen, staring at me. "Wow. You look..."

"Too much?" I touched the low neckline of the top.

"Perfect," he finished. "You're unbelievable."

Yeah, he thought so now, while he was with me and no other girls were around to entice him. "Thank you. Let me say good night to Scarlet, then we can go."

I tracked down Scarlet in her room and gave her a kiss, promising to be home when she woke in the morning, then took a deep breath and headed to the living room to find Liam chatting it up with Lily. The poor girl looked hideously flustered, blushing and unable to meet his gaze.

"Ready?" I asked, stuffing my house key in one pocket and my ID and a few bills in the other.

He jerked his head toward the front door, and I threw Lily a smile over my shoulder. "See you by ten." That gave us four hours, long enough to make us both feel like we got some fun outside the house.

As Liam walked me to the passenger side of the Mercedes, I felt his fingertips on my lower back. He unlocked the door, opened it, and closed it for me after I climbed in.

My heart drummed so hard, I was half-afraid he'd hear it. For this not being a date, it sure seemed like one. But that didn't mean Liam felt the same. I sucked in a couple deep breaths and reminded myself that even if Liam wanted me in that way, he didn't want me enough to stay.

He slid behind the wheel and started the engine. "Where to?"

"Depends what you're in the mood for."

"Hamburgers?"

I lifted a shoulder. "Works for me. There's a nice restaurant in that shopping plaza where we got groceries the other day."

Liam nodded and pulled the Mercedes away from the curb.

CHAPTER SEVENTEEN
★ Liam ★

After I devoured my burger and she'd picked at her salad, we piled into the SUV and cruised into the parking lot of the Wagon Wheel.

"You're okay coming here on your day off?" I asked, putting the Mercedes in park.

"Only if you'll dance with me." She grinned wickedly and opened her door. I'd never seen her get out of the car that quickly. Probably because she didn't have a jacket or bag to take with her.

As soon as I opened the door into the bar, the blaring jukebox hit me. There were a few empty tables, but not many. Although some couples were taking advantage of the dance floor, they had a lot of room to move. Plenty of space to dazzle Emma with my two-step.

"C'mon." Emma yanked on my hand, leading me to the dance floor.

"Don't you want a drink first?"

"Yeah, but I'm sure Breanna will find us, eventually. I want to grab a table before they're all gone." She stopped at one in front of the stage. "You better be able to dance, my friend, or we're going home."

I chuckled. "I'll do my best."

"Wait. I'll be right back. Hold our table, would you?" She reached into her pocket and dug out a twenty dollar bill, then shoved it at me. "And would you order me a tequila sunrise?"

As she headed toward the restrooms, my gaze became glued to her ass. But this was not a date. I had to remember that.

"Something to drink?"

"Hey, Breanna." I looked up from my chair and gave her a smile. "Emma wants a tequila sunrise, but I'm driving so I'll have a... coke."

She narrowed her eyes. "What are you doing?"

"What do you mean?" I could feel wrinkles forming around my eyes. Why did Breanna look so pissed off? "I'm keeping my end of the bargain. What's your problem?"

"This" — she waved at me and the table in one long sweep — "looks suspiciously like a date."

I gave her a steely look. "It's not."

"Are you sure she knows that?"

"Positive." I was getting a little tired of Breanna's attitude. I hadn't made Emma cry, so she had no reason to grill me.

"You're seriously not going to call this a date?" Her jaw tightened. "*She did her hair.*"

"Would you lay off?" I pushed myself off the chair to tower over her and lowered my voice to a growl. "You read crap about me in a magazine, and you think you know me? You don't know anything."

Breanna laughed once. "Are you kidding? I've dated you a lot. You just had a different face each time." She spun and left me there, balling my hands into fists.

As soon as I spotted Emma heading toward me, memories of the past few moments of irritation practically went poof. Emma gave me a shy smile that made her seem so innocent as she took the chair next to me.

Breanna arrived and set two glasses in front of us. Without waiting for money, she pivoted and was gone before Emma had a chance to say hello. Emma stared after her.

"It's not you." I pushed the drink toward her. "She thinks this looks too similar to a date and that I'm going to end up hurting you."

"You will." Emma shrugged. "She's wasting her time trying to stop it."

My mouth dropped open. "How can you say that? I've done everything you asked. Mostly."

"I didn't say you'd hurt me on purpose. It's just who you are." She dipped her head toward my glass. "What are you drinking?"

Indignation rose up in me. And then I realized both Emma and Breanna were right. The girls who hung around Full Throttle, the groupies who came to all our shows, weren't usually looking for a relationship. They expected a bad boy who was going to take them on a wild ride. And that's exactly what they got. Breanna and Emma knew what they were getting, too, and I'd never tried to hide it. So how could I be mad at them?

"Hey." Her fingertips brushed my knuckles. "Don't

worry about it. Tonight, we're just two people getting out of the house for a while. Let's dance." She held my hand and coaxed me out on the dance floor.

I hadn't two-stepped in a couple of years, and I didn't want to mash anyone's toes. I paused before we joined them, taking a moment to mentally refresh my moves.

"You sure you can do this?" she challenged, her lips curving up.

"Might be a little rusty, but I think I'll manage." I slipped my hand under her arm until my fingers grazed her shoulder blade. She rested her palm on my shoulder and slid her other hand in mine. Beginning with my left, I moved forward as she stepped back. Quick-quick-slow-slow. Quick-quick-slow-slow.

Seeing I was about to run into another couple, I turned Emma, avoided them, then changed direction again. After a few more steps, I lifted my arm and twirled her.

Emma broke into a grin as she turned under our arms. "You're good, Liam."

We danced through the next song too. I held the two-step position while our bodies remained inches apart. She brushed up against me as she moved, and my body went ablaze with the urge to lead her to an out-of-the-way spot where Breanna couldn't see us.

I was barely touching her, yet I'd never been more aroused. If Emma drank more and got any friendlier, I didn't know what I'd do. Not like I'd take advantage and go for a drunk hookup, but how much temptation would I be able to withstand in one night before I succumbed?

After a much-needed break while she finished her

drink at the table, she dragged me off to dance again. By the time we made it back to the table, she glowed.

"Where'd you learn to two-step?" she asked, fanning herself with one hand while she used the other to lift her long hair off her neck.

"Two more?" Breanna asked as she rushed by.

"Yes, please," Emma called out as Breanna stopped at a nearby table.

I wasn't so sure a second drink was a good idea. We'd only been there forty-five minutes, and Emma wasn't a sumo wrestler. The alcohol would get to her way too fast.

"The summer after I graduated high school, I developed a huge crush on a girl who loved to dance."

"That was sweet of you to learn to dance for your girlfriend." The way Emma smiled at me, I guessed she was feeling that drink she'd just finished off.

"She wasn't my girlfriend until we started dancing together." I winked. "That's how I won her over."

"I bet you did." She gave me a flirty look.

Yep, the booze was kicking in. I prayed she would drink the next one painfully slowly. Seriously, I didn't need Emma getting tipsy and being cuter and harder to resist than she already was.

After three more drinks and two more hours, I decided that getting Emma away from alcohol and closer to coffee might be a pretty good idea. I opened my mouth to speak when the music abruptly slowed. She snaked her arms up around my neck and pressed her breasts against me. I only had to bend slightly and my mouth would capture hers.

Dear, God, if I didn't break away soon...

"I had a nice time tonight." She smiled dreamily.

I let my hands hang loosely at her waist, when what I really wanted to do was fold my arms around her and squeeze her closer. Encouraging her though could result in losing my last thread of willpower. "Yeah, me too."

At that, she snuggled closer and leaned her head on my shoulder. Sucking in a long, slow breath, I thought of scrubbing toilets, marketing meetings with the PR guys at my record label, and my parents' hateful divorce.

But even those thoughts couldn't kill my desire for Emma. I wanted to hear her whisper my name when I undressed her, listen to her sharp intake of air when I spent all night making up for the past two weeks of holding back. And then I wanted to wake up the next morning and do it all over again.

Worse, I wanted to tell her about my other life.

Who was I kidding? If Emma knew I was Saint Nick, the infamous bad boy, she'd change the locks on her door and make sure I never got close enough to influence Scarlet. The less she knew about me, the better off she was. When I left Gardnerville, Emma might remember me without a sour taste in her mouth.

But right now, we were dancing and Emma was wrapped around me like skin on a grape. The chance to be with her this way would never come again. Taking it any further was out of the question, but I could enjoy this moment while it was here.

I turned into her temple to get another whiff of cherries and vanilla from her hair, and the desire to keep her nearly overpowered me. I overlapped my hands behind her lower back, forcing her closer. She felt good against me. Right. I envisioned myself looking forward to coming home to her every day.

The desire to make that a reality had my heart racing. My addiction to her, my appetite for her, had me swallowing a ragged breath.

Before I'd become famous, I'd been with a few women. Since then, even more. And I'd never felt this way about any girl before, not even my first love. This thing with Emma was huge, powerful, and possibly the most dangerous thing to ever happen to me. She made me want to take care of her, make a real effort to be a good father to Scarlet, and give them everything they needed.

I'd let myself get too wrapped in Emma and her life. Her world, not mine. And someday when she realized who I really was, she might forgive me for hiding my other life, but she wouldn't want anything to do with me. Faith had been forgiving, but that was expected because we were family. Emma had made it very clear she didn't want any more drama in her life. My life was ripe with that crap.

The song ended, and I drank her in for a long moment before I let my hands fall to her hips and gently nudge her away. "We should get going. It's late, and Lily has an early class tomorrow."

She shook her head. "Right. Totally lost track. Let me go to the ladies' room and we can bail."

I returned to our table to get my keys and flagged Breanna. "We need to settle our tab."

She stopped right in front of me and stretched her shoulders back, her eyes turning to slits. "You mean *you* need to settle your tab. Like guys usually do on real dates."

I groaned. "Can you give it a rest? If it makes you happy, I can bully her into paying her share, though that would be ridiculous considering how much money I make."

"Whatever, Mr. Moneybags. It comes to fifty-five."

After swiping Emma's twenty from the table, I added three more then thrust the bills at Breanna. "Keep the change." Done with her attitude, I veered off and made my way to the small hallway where Emma would emerge shortly.

Moments later, I was unlocking the passenger side for her. As soon as she climbed in, I started to close the door but her arm shot out to stop it. She glanced up at me. "Thank you for a lovely night."

I couldn't help but smile. "You're welcome."

As soon as I pulled into the driveway of her house, I pivoted in my seat to find Emma had fallen asleep. Very carefully, I got out, rounded the hood, and opened her side. Sliding an arm behind her back and the other under her thighs, I lifted her out.

"Mmm..." Her eyes lifted halfway as she smiled. "You're so sweet."

"Yeah, that's me," I said dryly, negotiating the step onto the curb with her hundred pounds in my arms. "I'm sure you'll find lots of people who agree with you."

"It's true. People can decide who you are in their own minds, but it doesn't mean they're right. You can be labeled, categorized, classified, but you don't have to go along with it." She yawned as I took the last step onto the porch.

Emma was awfully philosophical for someone so tipsy. "Key?" I asked.

"Back pocket. Put me down."

She wobbled when her feet touched the ground, and my arms slipped around her.

"Whoops." She giggled as she reached into her back pocket, then held out a single key so close to my nose I smelled metal.

I backed up to keep myself from going cross-eyed and snatched the key. With one arm at her waist to keep her balanced, I unlocked the door. Despite the dim lights, I saw a head pop up from behind the couch. Lily.

"Emma spilled something on her top. We'll be right back." Steering Emma to the bedroom, I tried to shield her from Lily's view. She didn't need to see her boss drunk.

Once we were inside Emma's room, she closed the door and fell against me, sliding her arms around my neck. "One more dance."

"Uh..."

"You're worried I'm drunk. Well, I'm not." Her bottom lip jutted out.

"You don't want me, Em." I sidestepped, creating distance between us.

"Maybe I do."

"I'm not good for you. There are so many other guys who would be better."

She laughed once. "We all have some bad in us, Liam.

But some people are too full of themselves to see where they need work, while others are so fixated on their flaws that they can't see the good. You have to find the balance."

She almost sounded sober. But if she were in her right mind, she would've already asked about Scarlet and paid Lily. "Go change for bed. I'll be right back." I peeled her arms off me and disappeared out the door. After reaching into my pocket for cash, I separated four twenty-dollar bills from my wad of cash and handed them to Lily. I was probably overpaying her by a mile, but what the hell. "Keep the extra."

After escorting Lily to her car, I raced inside to check on Scarlet. Emma was already in the small room, stroking Scarlet's hair. Okay, so she wasn't that buzzed. I backed away, ready to make my escape when she spotted me. She tucked the blanket around Scarlet, then tiptoed out of the room. Once in the hallway, she closed the door behind her.

I shifted my weight, ready to flee. "I'm going to bed."

She sighed. "I scared you, huh? I guess the last thing you need is some drunk girl hanging all over you."

"No, that's not it." I ran my fingers over my short hair and relaxed against the doorframe that led to the living room. "It's just... we should call it a night. I had a great time with you though."

"Did you?" She tilted her head as she leaned against the other side of the door. Definitely sobering up. Being completely sound of mind didn't make her any safer from me. Because if she came onto me, giving in to her wouldn't be taking advantage, not if she wasn't drunk. I'd feel a lot less guilty doing something I wanted to do anyway.

I'd always been awful at lying, so I didn't attempt it as I allowed the corners of my mouth to pull up. "The best. It's been a while since I had that much fun."

"Really?" Her eyes danced, but by the way her nose wrinkled, I guessed she was skeptical. "A guy like you? I bet you had tons of fun before you ever met me."

Reaching up, I tugged on a lock of her silky hair, then said softly, "Yeah, but you *weren't* there."

Her eyes searched my face, and seconds passed. "The thing is, I almost believe you."

"Almost?" I'd been nothing but truthful to her since the moment I'd met her, and now, suddenly, my words weren't believable? It was a little insulting. I had a powerful urge to show her how much I enjoyed being with her. I wanted to show her a *lot* of things.

"I used to get caught up in guys like you, taking everything they said to heart. They acted as if I was the only girl in their world, and I fell for it every time." Emma blew air out in a whistle. "Then they'd go off to the next girl and do the same thing."

I adjusted my back against the doorframe, resisting the urge to prove to Emma that there was no other girl but her. "So... you think I'm a total player?" I would've been deeply offended at the implication, but her tone showed no malice. "I don't say things I don't mean."

"I'm getting that. But there's a difference between having deep feelings for only one girl and having feelings for many of them. I think you're in the second category. And when you say all those pretty things, you mean every word of it at the time. But then the next girl comes along, and all the others before her are forgotten. I'll be no different and, if I'm wise, I won't take anything you say seriously."

I pushed off the doorway and slid toward Emma until we were a breath away. She inhaled, her lips parting as I planted my fingers around the nape of her neck and bent to briefly brush my lips against her temple.

"The problem with that theory is I haven't been able to think about any other girl since I met you," I whispered into her ear. I released her and stepped back. "But my feelings for you don't change the facts. You can do better than me. You should wait for a guy who can commit to a life with you, be a father to your kid. Not waste all your amazingness on a guy who isn't going to stick around. Duke will be back any day now, and then I'll be gone."

The light died in her eyes as she focused on something behind me. "Of course you're leaving. That's always been the plan, right?" Then she met my gaze, her eyes void of emotion. "I appreciate the reminder." She turned, took the few short steps to her bedroom, and closed the door.

Though I felt dirty, I knew I deserved that. And she deserved so much better than me. I vowed to myself to not distract her from getting that. Somehow though, I didn't think it would be easy.

CHAPTER EIGHTEEN
★ *Emma* ★

I tried to close my heart to Liam. But that was impossible. When he'd said he had feelings for me, I believed him. And when he'd told me he hadn't thought of any other girl since he'd met me, I bought it hook, line, and sinker. I had no doubt Liam cared for me in his own way, but it still wasn't enough to make him stay.

The hole in my heart that had healed over after Kyle died was now ripped open, raw and bloody. I wanted to wish Liam away because then I could heal again. But I didn't want to miss out on a single minute I had left with him.

Liam drove me to work, as usual, Friday and Saturday. Though he was always sweet and helpful, he'd toned down the flirting. A part of me was grateful for that because when he laid on the charm, he was too much to resist. I was barely hanging on as it was.

When Sunday rolled around, Liam got a call from Rocko saying that he wouldn't be needed the following weekend. Duke was back, and tonight was Liam's last night at the Wagon Wheel.

As I worked the bar and Liam stood on stage,

butchering yet another of my favorite songs, I wondered if he'd leave come Monday or hang around a few more days. Was tonight all I had left? My stomach churned at the thought of standing by as he left and never seeing him again. My eyes stung, and I blinked the burn away as someone took the stool in front of me. I glanced up, ready to sling another drink.

"Cody, hi." I grinned. He and his girlfriend hadn't been in since early last summer. "Your usual?"

"Yeah, sounds good." He set his cell phone on the bar top.

I screwed the cap off the bottle and set it in front of Cody, then glanced around. "Where's Julia?"

Since I'd started working at the Wagon Wheel Saloon, I'd never seen one without the other. Cody was tall, dark, and gorgeous, definitely the hottest guy in Gardnerville — until Liam came along. Julie was blond, curvy, and quick to smile. And they were both fun and easy to talk to.

He glanced down at the napkin as I slid it in front of him. "Yeah... we broke up a few months ago, and she moved back to Colorado. Been throwing myself into work."

That explained why I hadn't seen either in ages. "Wow, uh, I'm so sorry."

"It was a surprise to me too. All that time with her, and I thought we both wanted the same thing. Turns out she was agreeable to getting married but gave a big thumbs-down to having kids." He scoffed.

"But you want it all?"

He shrugged. "Guess I'm old-fashioned."

No commitment phobias? No fear of being responsible for a kid? Cody was loved and respected by nearly everyone in town, he probably made good money as a veterinarian, and he had a great sense of humor. Not to mention good looks. He was pretty much perfect, and if Liam hadn't come into my life, I might've been interested in Cody.

"Wow, that guy can *not* sing. I'm rethinking my love for Led Zeppelin. Man, he must want everyone to suffer. I mean, why get up there and do that to us *on purpose*? And couldn't he have picked a shorter song?"

I snickered. "It's not voluntary."

He glanced over his shoulder at Liam. "He works here?"

I nodded, scanning the bar to see if anyone needed anything. A girl at the other end was slurping up the last of her drink, but I had a minute before I had to rush over. In fact, at the rate she'd sucked it down, it was probably better if I didn't serve her again right away. "Covering for Duke, but this is his last day."

"Rocko usually makes sure they can sing before he hires them." He grimaced.

"Duke had an emergency, and Liam was handy." In my peripheral vision, I saw someone push an empty glass forward. "Duty calls. Be back soon."

As I poured another scotch and soda, my thoughts doubled back to Cody. I felt bad for him. He'd invested two years into a relationship that ended up not being right for him. I should've been grateful to Liam for not wasting my time like that.

I noticed Liam making his way back behind the bar.

"Well, Julia's a fool to throw you away. Seriously."

"But *you* wouldn't throw me away?" Cody gave me a steady look.

I shrugged and found a bar towel to wipe down the area next to him. I needed to appear to be working. "If we were dating, probably not."

He mulled that over for a beat. "So, um, *you'd* date me?"

I froze. Oh, hell, Cody had taken that the wrong way. I wasn't in the market to date anyone right now. Liam had me so twisted up, I thought of only him. But even if I suddenly decided Liam was right for me, he'd already made it painfully clear that was never going to happen.

So why shouldn't I date someone else?

Maybe being with Cody would take my mind off Liam and remind me what was truly important in life. I'd always liked him. He'd had a girlfriend the whole time I'd known him, so I'd never seen him as anything more than a friend. But now that he was single, I realized he was just the kind of guy I needed.

I tilted my head as I considered his question. "I think I could stand it."

Just then, Liam slammed a cold mug under the beer spout. I glanced over to find him glaring. Okay, so that was a little bit awkward, him overhearing me accept a date with someone else. But hadn't he been the one who'd told me I should wait for a guy who'd appreciate all the amazingness I had to offer? Liam didn't want me, but he didn't want anyone else to have me either? That wasn't going to work for me.

Liam would leave soon, and it was going to hurt.

Until then, I refused to sit around and hope for Liam to realize he was an idiot. If we weren't going to be together, why pretend otherwise?

I scowled at Liam before returning my attention to Cody. "I work Friday, Saturday and Sunday, which leaves Monday through Thursday free. How about tomorrow?"

Cody beamed. "Pick you up at six?"

"Great." I plucked his cell off the bar and entered my phone number into his contacts, then handed it back. "Another beer?"

★

Liam gave me the cold shoulder the rest of the night. After he drove us home, he went straight to the garage and didn't come inside the house until morning. When I shuffled into the kitchen upon awakening, the only reason I knew he hadn't cleared out during the night was the fresh pot of coffee waiting for me.

When I went for a refill a few minutes later, I saw him through the kitchen window, wearing sweats as he sprinted down the driveway toward the garage. Even wet and breathing heavy after a run, he looked delicious.

I turned away from the window. I had a chance to go out with a great guy, and allowing Liam to distract me could blow the whole thing.

Thankfully, he didn't come to the main house all day, except when I'd gone to the office to drop off files. If not for the fork on the counter, I wouldn't have realized he'd been there.

When I'd begun making lunch, I texted him to let

him know when food would be ready. He'd texted back to say thanks and that he had things to do but he'd come up later and eat if I set it out. When I returned from picking up parsley and lemon for the tabbouleh, I noticed the lunch had been eaten and the container put in the dishwasher. He was obviously avoiding me, but that was a good thing if I was going to move on with my life.

Even knowing things were as they should be, frustration ripped through me. Deep down, I wanted him to fight for me.

After I'd picked up Scarlet from school and fixed dinner, I set it aside for Lily to feed Scarlet later — and for Liam to eat when he snuck in after I left. With everything set and Lily there early, I put on a slinky black dress and high heels. I was going out on a date with a guy who wanted the same things as I did. I was going to make the most of it.

Cody arrived on my doorstep right on time, carrying a bouquet bursting with blue irises and pink lilies.

"Thank you." I relieved him of the lovely flowers. "Come inside while I put them in a vase."

As soon as he stepped over the threshold, Scarlet darted over to us and scowled. "That's not Liam."

I licked my lips. Damn, I should have prepared better and anticipated Scarlet's inability to hold back. "No, sweetie, this is Cody. We're going to have dinner together. Lily, would you please find a vase for the flowers?"

Lily popped off the couch, snapping up the bouquet and disappearing into the kitchen.

"Why aren't you going out with Liam again?" Scarlet asked.

Wishing I'd never let Cody inside, I kneeled down to be eye level with her. "We'll talk about it in the morning." I dropped a kiss on her forehead and stood. "Love you bunches."

I strained my head toward the door, my eyes widening to hint at urgency. He got the idea, rushing out ahead of me.

"Sorry about that." Anxious to get away, I power walked toward the BMW parked in front. "You know how kids are."

He followed me to the passenger side, stopping beside the door without unlocking it. "Isn't Liam the bartender from last night?"

I took a deep breath and lifted my chin. Cody might as well know the truth. If things worked out between us, I didn't want to begin our future with lies. "He and I went out dancing last week, but only as friends. He's renting out the garage, though we're not involved. Scarlet just doesn't understand the difference."

"Fair enough." He hit the clicker and opened the passenger-side door for me.

I exhaled in relief, glad to have that out of the way. Now that Liam wasn't working at the bar, he'd leave soon, and there would be no chance of any more awkwardness from our nonrelationship.

My chest ached at the thought of him being out of my life.

Cody drove to Reno, and we ate dinner to a live

blues band. Afterward, while we sipped cappuccinos and enjoyed the music, he relayed anecdotes of his practice, and I regaled him with funny stories about Scarlet. It was nice. Relaxing.

Still, while I liked Cody and didn't regret spending time with him, I also knew it wasn't going to work between us. Using him to get my mind off Liam wasn't right, and I wouldn't want someone doing that to me. Once Liam left town and I'd had time to get over him, I hoped that having another relationship was in the realm of possibility. But not just yet.

When I'd swallowed my last sip from the warm mug, I checked the time on my cell. "We should probably get back. The babysitter has school tomorrow."

Cody was his usual amicable self on the drive back, but I sat stiff in my seat, wondering what I would do if he tried to kiss me good night. Would he walk me to my door?

By the time he pulled up in front of my house, I still hadn't figured out how to handle him, and then, before I knew it, he was already escorting me up the pathway to the porch.

The light switched on inside the house, and as soon as we hit the front steps, the door swung open. With the light behind him, Liam's eyes appeared dark and dangerous. "It's about time you got home."

"What are you doing?" I demanded, my jaw clenching. Why the hell was he showing up right when I arrived home with my date?

"I came up to get a snack."

"And how long have you been waiting there for me?" I peeked past him, then glanced over my shoulder to look for Lily's car. "Are you alone? Where's Lily?"

"When I was foraging for food earlier, she mentioned being worried about a test she had to prepare for. So I paid her, and she left. I've been with Scarlet ever since. Which is super easy since she always sleeps like a rock. But then you two arrived, slamming the car door and stomping loud enough to hear for blocks, so I came out to remind you to keep it down. You know how our neighbors hate it when we get noisy."

My hands rolled into fists at how he'd so skillfully used "always" as if he knew Scarlet so well and "our neighbors" as if he'd lived there a while. I didn't want to think about any underlying meaning to his comment about us being noisy enough for neighbors to hear.

I took a deep breath. "Oh. My. God. Get out. Go to your room."

"Go to my room?" He stepped out onto the porch and closed the door behind him, blocking me from entering. "What am I, five?"

"You're certainly acting like it." I shoved the ball of my hand into his shoulder. "Go away."

Liam opened his mouth, but Cody held up a hand. "You know what? I'm leaving." He turned to me. "I have no idea what's going on between you two, but when it's *really* over, I'd love to see you. Until then, I'm out." He held up both his palms and backed away, then jogged down the steps to his car.

"Get inside," I growled at Liam. "Right now."

Liam obeyed. Once he'd closed the door behind us, I whirled on him, my limbs trembling. "I can't believe you did that."

His mouth dropped open before he gathered himself and stalked toward me. "Did what? Stopped you from making a horrible mistake?"

"It's my life, Liam, which you've already made clear you don't want to be a part of. Deal with it, and try not to be a douche bag. I'm going to bed. You can let yourself out." I headed to my room, taking two steps before he grabbed my arm and yanked me around.

"Fine, but would you mind waiting until after I'm packed and gone before you parade your boyfriends right in front of me?"

I jerked my hand free, my lungs heaving in fury. "You told me to wait for a guy who'd appreciate me. Don't act all wounded because it happened so fast. I'm not going to pass up a great guy to save your feelings after you've already hurt mine." I raised my chin, sending him a steely stare. "And now, I'm going to bed. You should too."

When I moved to go, he snagged his arm around my waist. His other arm slipped behind my back, pressing me closer as he crushed his mouth against mine.

My head reeled as tingles of electricity licked at my fingers and toes, my middle pooling with heat. Drunk with the taste of him, I dived in, letting my burning need for him swallow me. With reckless abandon, my arms wound around his neck, and I shoved against him.

Liam growled softly against my mouth and pushed

back, smacking me into the wall. Sucking in ragged breaths, he trailed kisses along my jaw and temple.

More than anything, I wanted to tear his clothes off and drag him into my room. But I knew that wouldn't make him stay. I squeezed my eyes shut and gently nudged him away. "I'm not sure how productive this is, you know, since you're leaving."

He touched his forehead against mine. "Yeah. A decent guy would've left quietly and let you get on with your life. But I'm not decent. And that's why you can do so much better than me." He drew out a long breath and tunneled his fingers though his short hair. "You should go out with Cody again. Just, please, wait until I'm gone."

But he wasn't gone yet, and I still had a chance. I clamped onto his arm a moment. Then when I was sure he wasn't going anywhere yet, I laced my fingers through his. "I know you have some things to figure out on your own. But I don't want you to go."

He took a step back while keeping our fingers entwined. "Yeah, you do. You just don't realize it yet."

A long moment passed as emotion strangled me, rendering me unable to talk. Being speechless was probably for the best. Except that I wasn't that girl who held my feelings in check, afraid to get close. If Liam freaked out or got weird, then he wasn't worth loving after all.

"But I've already fallen for you," I uttered in a barely audible voice.

He shook his head and loosened his grasp on my

hand. "Em, I'm no good for you."

"Maybe you don't think so right now," I said, knowing he *was* good for me. Liam might be all kinds of things — impulsive, hot-tempered — but he was also protective and considerate. And regardless of his past indiscretions, he didn't lie to get what he wanted. Under all the flirting and fighting, he was a good man.

Only one thing made him wrong for me — something I would never compromise on — he had an aversion to commitments. Trying to sell myself to him was a waste of time because I couldn't force him to feel something that he didn't want to feel. Even if he saw things in me that he didn't want to live without, he had to want me bad enough to earn me.

I had to let him go.

Tears burned my eyes, but I held them back. He'd broken my heart into a million tiny pieces, but he didn't need to know that.

"I'm glad I met you." Stretching up on my tiptoes, I brushed a kiss to his cheek, then quietly disappeared into my room before he saw my wet lashes.

CHAPTER NINETEEN
★ *Liam* ★

After zipping up my duffel bag, I gathered up all the new clothes I'd bought with Emma and stuffed them in a kitchen bag I'd snagged from the main house. I slid the Mercedes key off my key ring, stuck it in my pocket, then loaded all my stuff into the Shelby.

I'd stayed overnight in hopes of getting some sleep before the long drive to Los Angeles, but all I'd gotten for my effort was scratchy lids and circles under my eyes. But what did I expect after getting only two hours of sleep?

Maybe once Gardnerville was behind me and I was in LA again, immersed in rabid fans and paparazzi, I'd forget about Emma. Of course I would. That was what I did. I banged chicks and moved on. Leaving women had always been easy, and Emma would be no different. Okay, so that wasn't the case at this very moment, but detachment would come later. Except for my family, I didn't care about anyone but myself. I was Saint Nick, infamous bad boy whose saving grace was his voice and lyrics. Beyond that, I wasn't much use to anyone.

I hadn't tried to kiss Emma again last night. After listening to her admit she'd fallen for me and that she was glad she'd met me, I knew I had to get out of there. Though she'd been dressed up for another guy, she looked beautiful with her blond hair falling over her shoulders, and I wanted to take her in my arms again and get my fill of her. But I was afraid if I touched her again, I wouldn't stop.

I couldn't do that to Emma, allow her to get in any deeper with me. It wasn't only about keeping promises but wanting her to be happy. Even if that meant being with Cody. Though the thought of her being with anyone else made me want to hunt him down and beat the crap out of him, I knew I had to set her free.

So I'd said good night and convinced myself to go to my own room.

And now I was leaving that room, never to return. I wouldn't see Emma ever again. Glancing up at the kitchen window, I took a big gulp of air and returned to the trunk of the Shelby. After checking to make sure I'd gotten everything, I closed the trunk and made my way to the driver's side. The sooner I left, the sooner she'd get on with her life.

With my fingers on the handle, I hesitated. Even if I was capable of leaving without saying good-bye, how much would it hurt Emma to bail on her? Besides, I had to see her one last time. And Scarlet.

I went around to the front, tapped on the door then let myself in. They sat at the dining room table, a plate of eggs and toast in front of each of them. God,

I was going to miss Scarlet's chubby cheeks and short attention span. She'd *really* grown on me.

I quietly slipped the Mercedes key on the little table by the front door and looked over Scarlet's shoulder at a drawing. "Oh, that's pretty. Unicorn?" The animal seemed a bit too hairy around the neck, but the horn protruding from its forehead pretty much nailed it.

"A fairy uni-lion."

And I'd miss all the crap she did that made absolutely no sense.

"Liam." Emma set her fork down and wiggled around to face me. "Did you want some breakfast? I have a few minutes before I have to drive Scarlet to school."

I shoved my hands in the pockets of my jeans. "Thanks, but I'll get something on my way out."

She returned to her eggs, head down so I couldn't read her. "All packed up?"

"Yeah." I nodded, suddenly incapable of forming any other words.

Emma rose from the chair and turned to Scarlet. "I'll be right back. We're going to step outside for a second."

"Wait." I bent over and scooped up Scarlet in a big hug. "I had a great time with you and your mom. I'll miss you."

"Love you." Scarlet snuggled against me, her tiny arms wrapping around my neck.

My throat thickened. It was like leaving Los Angeles and Xander all over again.

"Be good to your mom, huh?" I choked out and eased

her back into her booster seat, then walked toward the front door, not stopping until I reached the hood of the Shelby.

I turned to Emma. "I can only drive one car at a time, and I don't know when I'll be able to send for the Mercedes. Left the key on the little table. Cars don't do well if they sit too long, so if you could take it out now and then, I'd owe you one."

Her mouth parted as she eyed me. "Are you trying to give me your new car on the sly?"

My lip twitched. "Of course not."

Her eyes took on a steely glint. "Liam—"

"Shh." I brushed a finger across her cheek. "You need a car, and I have too many. I'd feel better knowing you and Scarlet were riding around in something safe and reliable. If it'll bother you to drive a brand new luxury car though, save it for emergencies."

She covered my hand with hers and closed her eyes. "Stay."

And ruin her chances with Pretty Boy? Though the concept was tempting, I didn't want to mess up her life that way. And when I bailed on her later, which I *would*, that bridge would already be burned. I couldn't do that to her.

"We both know I won't make it for the long haul. You deserve better."

"I deserve *you*." Her eyes shone with unshed tears, and I so badly wanted to take the pain away. "Stay. Please."

No matter how much I burned to keep her, I refused to give in and think only of myself, only to hurt her more up the road. I brushed my lips against hers, lingered a moment too long, then straightened. "I'm glad I met you too."

Using all my self-control, I commanded myself to get inside the Shelby. I started the engine, then passed the gate and screeched down the street. But speed wasn't enough. Probably never would be. I was leaving Gardnerville and Emma, and I'd never return. And, damn it, my entire body screamed to turn the car around and beg her to pack their things and drive home with me.

But I'd never ask that of either of them. They needed stability which I couldn't provide, and in the end, she'd leave me anyway once she realized I was Nick Black. If I didn't abandon her first.

I'd have to get over her, damn it. I would. No woman had ever been able to hold my attention for long. Emma would be no different.

I needed to get home and hide until I my goatee grew back, and I'd wear hats until my hair got a little longer. I couldn't risk pictures of me this way getting out and Emma seeing them. She could never figure out I was Nick Black.

I didn't care about my last paycheck, but I'd left my address blank on the forms I'd filled out for Rocko. The last thing I wanted was anyone poking around to find an address in order to mail it. Someone might learn something I didn't want them to know — then tell Emma.

She needed to be free of me, and knowing who I really was and seeing me on the cover of rags would be a constant reminder of me. Not the way for her to be free. I'd make a super-quick stop at the bar to give Rocko my sister's address, and then I was out of there.

As the Wagon Wheel neared, I slowed. I'd get in and get out. No chatting it up with Rocko or anyone else, and I sure as hell didn't need any alcohol fueling my emotions. But, damn, a drink would go a long way to dull the ache burning its way to the innermost part of my soul.

I turned in, parked, and stalked through the door on my way to the bar. I claimed a stool in the corner against the wall that afforded a view of the whole place. My eyes immediately focused on Heather giggling with a friend. As usual, she wasn't wearing much — a spaghetti-strap tank and shorts so tiny I could almost see her ass.

"What can I get you?" The sandy-haired bartender slid a napkin toward me.

"Is Rocko around?"

"Yep. Should be reappearing any minute. Something to drink while you're waiting?"

"Thanks, but I'd better not." The last thing I needed was to get a buzz on and be unable to drive.

He moved onto the next customer. I felt rude not introducing myself, but then that might open the door to an actual conversation and possibly delay me.

When I scanned the bar for Rocko, I met Heather's gaze. Without taking her eyes off me, she said something to her friend then strutted over.

"Buy me a shot?" She gave me a bedroom smile that promised a reward for my generosity.

I shrugged, waved to the bartender, and pointed at Heather, then held up one finger. I whipped out a ten and placed it on the bar.

"Aren't you having anything?" she asked.

"I'm leaving in a minute."

"Yeah? Me too. Sure you don't want to ignore that loose end and join me?" She leaned forward, giving me a better view of her breasts, her hip bumping my thigh.

Now more than ever, Heather could be the perfect way to get my mind off Emma. But the idea disintegrated in my head as quickly as it had formed. Sure, she was willing. That's all I'd ever required of any girl. But Emma would find out, and she might be crushed.

Besides, after being with Emma and falling for her, I needed more than physical gratification. Though I'd never slept with Emma, the little I'd done with her had been more fulfilling than all the sex I'd ever had.

Damn, she'd ruined me for any other woman.

"Under different circumstances, I'd probably take you up on that. Chalk it up to bad timing." I nudged her aside and deserted the stool in search of Rocko. On the way to his office, I spotted him talking to the bouncer near the restrooms.

It took about thirty seconds to say good-bye and hand him a piece of paper with Faith's address before I bolted toward the exit. Unfortunately, before I got out of the restroom hallway, I bumped into Breanna, and my whole body went rigid. She was the last person I wanted to talk to right now.

"I saw that." She wagged a finger at me. "I'm not sure whether to be impressed you're walking away from the easiest girl in Gardnerville or pissed that you bought her a drink and let her practically grind on you."

I scoffed. "Emma and I aren't together. Technically, I'm free to do whoever I want."

She scowled at me. "You can't be blind to how Emma feels about you."

Remorse crept up my throat like acid, and I stared at my toes. "Yeah, well, she's out of my life now. Already said good-bye. No harm, no foul."

"No harm? You seriously think Emma's okay with you leaving?" Breanna glared at me, and I flinched. "I warned you not to hurt her."

"And I'm keeping my promise. You see this?" I waved my keys. "Going back to LA. This is me not hurting her."

Breanna scoffed. "You make it all sound so noble, but I know better."

I pinched the bridge of my nose. "I can't stay and let her think it might work and then it doesn't. She's better off if I leave." Silence stretched, and then I met Breanna's gaze.

"Oh, my God. You're *in love* with her." She looked genuinely surprised. Like I wasn't capable of truly loving anyone.

Irritation consumed me, and I steadied my racing pulse. "What does it matter? Love always turns to hate anyway. May as well quit while I'm ahead."

"Once you find it, you cherish it. If you love your partner and treat each other with respect, it can last a lifetime. It's something you work at every day." She nudged my bicep with an index finger. "And in return, a lasting, committed relationship can bring you a lot of happiness."

"You sound like a greeting card." I gave her a smug smile. "And that philosophy worked for you, huh?"

Breanna lifted her chin. "I haven't met anyone I could have that with. But you have, and you're throwing it all away."

"I'd rather her remember me this way, before she hates me."

"You think she's not going to hate you for leaving?" The way she looked at me, I thought I might've grown an eye on my forehead.

I blew out a breath. "I'm not good for Emma."

Breanna gave me the stink-eye. "And if she disagrees?"

"Obviously she's crazy and shouldn't be making her own decisions." I snorted. "Look, my world would slowly drain her, kill her spirit. She's not tough enough for that."

Her eyes turned to steel. "Is that the excuse you're using to slither away? Because if you think Emma's weak, try looking in the mirror," she hissed. "That girl has more strength than both of us together." Breanna straightened, her eyes darkening. "She had that baby by herself, all alone in that hospital, without asking her family for help. Then she pulled herself up and made a life for herself."

Breanna's eyes were pooling, and I felt like an ass. "Doesn't change the fact that she can do better than me," I said.

She laughed once, looking me up and down. "You keep saying that, and you know what? You're right. She can do better than a guy too immature to understand how badly he's screwing up. Stay the hell away from her," she growled before turning on her heel and marching off.

While avoiding eye contact with anyone else, I high-tailed it to my car. I had to get away fast, before I changed my mind.

CHAPTER TWENTY
★ *Liam* ★

When I drove through the gates of my house in the Hollywood Hills, takeout food on the passenger seat, the grounds were deserted. The paparazzi had apparently long since given up and had no idea when to expect me. Good. I'd have some moments of peace for a while... until I needed to eat again.

But if I left the house, the paparazzi would see I had a new look. If pictures of me clean-shaven ever got to Emma, she'd figure out who I was. Nothing to be done about the length of my hair, but I could regrow my goatee. I had a week before rehearsal with the rest of Full Throttle for our second CD. That should be enough time to get something going.

And plenty of time home alone to regret leaving Emma. I scrubbed my hands over my face, my elbows resting on the steering wheel. I had to get through this.

God, should I have stayed with her? I rid myself of the thought as I killed the engine, closed the garage door, and slipped into my house. After dropping my duffel bag in the foyer, I fished through the kitchen junk drawer for a pencil and snatched up a pad of paper from the counter. I collapsed onto the couch and began scrawling the words that rushed into my head.

Showed up at the bar all beaten and worn. Only thing left of me was doubt and scorn. You saw something else, saw what I could be, and my mental shackles began to break free. But I can't take the chance that I might stumble, to leave you in my wake to cry or crumble.

With each word I scrawled on the page, the letters etched into my heart. The words wouldn't have hurt so much if they weren't so true. I sucked in a deep breath and began the chorus.

I'm still not worth your tears, or wasting your good years, on a man who won't be there. If I could, I would, I swear.

The lyrics didn't exactly say badass. I sounded defeated, pathetic. The record label probably wouldn't go for it since being a rebel was how I'd built my reputation. My bandmates would think I'd lost my mind, gone soft over a girl. But when it came to creating music, I'd never worried about pleasing others. I'd always followed my passion, and that wasn't going to change anytime soon.

If I didn't record it with Full Throttle, I'd do it on my own one day. Unless I came to my senses first. I'd probably get over Emma soon enough and wonder why I thought I'd ever want to settle down with her. The song would probably end up in the trash.

I jotted down a few more lines, then tossed the pad and pencil on the coffee table. After a few rounds pacing through the living room, I returned to the couch and reread the lines before plucking up the pencil and scribbling down another verse.

Moonlight peeked through the drapes by the time I set the pencil down. Now that the song was finished, I wanted nothing to do with it. It only made me think of Emma. I crumpled it into a tight ball then launched it the several yards into the dining room. It bounced off the wall, hit the floor, and rolled toward me. On my way to the kitchen later, I'd pick it up and make sure it made it into the trash.

Without the song to obsess over, I had nothing to do but think about Emma and how much I missed her. My soul was broken, shattered, and I swallowed back nausea. I wasn't ready to meet up with the band yet, and I couldn't leave the house with no facial hair anyway. I wanted to see Xander, but it was past his bedtime and Faith probably wouldn't let me see him anyway.

I wouldn't know for sure unless I asked.

I retrieved my cell from my pocket and texted her. *Back in town. What r u guys doing tmrrw?*

Seconds later, the reply came. *Seeing u :-)*

My breath rushed out of my lungs as a weight lifted off me. I should've known that Faith wouldn't cut me out of her life for long. From now on, I'd do my best to never again give my sister a reason to get so pissed off at me. *Will text you when I wake up.*

I wasn't sure if that was going to happen since I doubted I'd ever fall asleep. Too wired and unable to stop thinking of Emma and the way she'd looked at me when she'd asked me to stay.

Maybe I should've closed the deal with her, gotten

her out of my system. Knowing she thought I was a douche bag for sleeping with her then bailing would curb my desire to run back to Nevada and grovel at her feet. But there was no memory of her naked and moving beneath me. No words of love to hold onto. Just the memory of the hurt in her eyes as I'd driven away. And the ache in my chest from missing her.

★

The earth around me trembled, and I opened my eyes. Another earthquake? Normally, anytime the earth moved, I opened my eyes only long enough to make sure the roof hadn't collapsed. Then I went back to sleep. And after such a long night of tossing and turning, I could use the extra rest.

"Uncle Liam, wake up."

My eyes popped open, and my mouth widened into a huge grin. No earthquake after all. Just a three-year-old monkey jumping on my bed. I sat up and hugged him. "Hey, buddy. Missed you."

"You weren't answering my calls or texts." Faith stood beside the bed, looming over me. "I'd already told Xander he was seeing you today, and he couldn't wait anymore. So we decided to come to you."

I flashed my sister a smile. "Good to see you."

"Wow." Faith frowned, tapping an index finger against her lips. "I'm trying to decide which way you look best." She ran a hand over my head, then flicked a finger over my jaw. "And shaved. What the hell happened?"

"Didn't want anyone to recognize me."

She scooted onto the bed. "Did it work?"

"Yeah. But now I can't leave the house until my goatee grows back. If pictures of me like this get out, I won't be able to do it again."

"Do what? Run away and hide?" She lifted one brow, then her face softened. "I was worried about you."

"I'm fine." If she tried to pry into what I'd been up to the past few weeks, I might not be so fine. I didn't want to talk about Emma, and Faith would never stop probing if she thought there was something to know. I shifted to Xander to change the subject. "What did you want to do today, buddy?"

Three hours later, we'd played Go Fish, watched cartoons until my eyes glazed over, and dipped into the frozen meals since almost everything else in my fridge had expired.

"We should get going. I'd already made plans for later today before you texted me."

Dread burned like fire in the pit of my stomach at the idea of having nothing to distract me from thoughts of Emma. "Yeah, okay."

She swiped up her purse from the coffee table. "I'll come back tonight and do some grocery shopping on the way so you have healthy stuff to eat until you come out of hiding."

"You're the best." I ruffled Xander's head before they shuffled out the door.

And then I was alone again. God, I had to pull myself out of this funk. I wasn't going to have Emma, ever. I needed to reconcile myself to that fact and move on.

But that didn't mean there weren't other ways to make

her life easier so I wouldn't worry about her and Scarlet. I picked up my cell and called my business manager.

"Are you back now?" No greeting, which was typical of Aidan. He wasn't a people person, but he sure did take care of business. "Got a pileup of crap here."

"Yeah, come over tomorrow, and we'll go through it. For now, I want you to buy a house. Not just put in an offer. I want you to get that house, even if you have to pay double what it's worth. And be discreet. I don't want the tenant knowing the buyer is me. If we pay cash, we can probably do a superfast escrow."

"It's your money," he growled. "Give me the address."

★

First thing the next morning, I texted each of my bandmates to let them know I was back in town and tweaking the songs for our next album. I told them I wasn't leaving my house for another week, so if they wanted to see me, they'd have to make the trip. Theo took me up on it, and since my appointment with Aidan wasn't until later that afternoon, I agreed.

After checking the peephole to make sure the paparazzi hadn't passed through the gate, I opened the door, and Theo strutted through the foyer in his usual jeans and T-shirt. We knuckle-bumped fists.

"Hey, man." After sliding his sunglasses off his blond head, he set them on the coffee table before dropping onto the sofa.

"Make yourself comfortable." I chuckled.

"So where've you been?"

I shrugged. "Had to get away for a bit."

Theo raised his brows. "You were totally MIA. Where did you go? You know, in case I ever want to disappear."

"If you ever need to do that, call me and I'll tell you how it's done. In the meantime, none of your business." I curled up my lip and tossed a well-used pad of paper at him. "Songs. Haven't put them in the computer yet."

"Right, rehearsals start next week." He flipped through the first few sheets, then his gaze shot to mine. "Hey, we're going into the studio in a couple months to record, right? "Cause I'm getting low on cash."

Theo tended to live for the moment, but he wasn't an idiot or overly extravagant. "But we made so much off our sales and the tour. How could all that money be gone already?" Keeping my ear alert for his reply, I darted into the office for another pad of paper, then returned to find him still rifling through the sheets of lyrics.

"These are great." He flipped another page and scanned the next one. "Can't wait to lay down some beats."

"Hold on." I flattened my palm across the sheet, covering up my scrawl. "What happened to all your money?" The last thing I wanted was the IRS coming down on any of us because Theo didn't pay his taxes. Drunken brawls were one thing. Not paying the government was something else entirely.

Theo's brows lowered as he leaned back and lifted his feet onto the coffee table. "I have no idea. One minute I was rollin' in it. The next thing I knew, most of it was gone."

I claimed the other end of the couch, bringing one leg up

so I could nudge him with my shoe if I needed to. "There has to be some trail. Didn't you check your bank statements?"

His head swayed back and forth. "Hate dealing with that stuff. There's a reason I'm a musician and not an accountant."

I understood that all too well. Still, some things had to be done whether I liked it or not. "So, you don't keep track of your money?"

"No." He scratched his blond chin stubble. "I just make more so I don't have to worry about running out. I have plenty of other ways to spend my free time."

Since I hadn't been a shining example of how to live my life, I didn't feel I had the right to lecture him. "But unless you're blowing it all, you should still have a ton." I shoved him with the toe of my shoe. "Maybe a professional should sort it out for you."

"I don't know. Don't like anyone up in my business."

"Yeah, neither do I. But I have the balls to log into my bank account and see what's going on. If you won't do that, then you need to hire someone who will." I'd vouch for Emma, but she was four hundred miles away in Nevada. "I don't know of anyone around here who could do that. I can ask Aidan though."

"What, you got someone out of town you trust? I'll pay extra for him to come out here."

"*She* would probably charge two or three hundred per hour, plus travel expenses. For that kind of money, wouldn't you rather spend a little quality time with your bank statements?"

He grimaced. "Not really."

"Well, she already has a job and a kid, so you'd have to spring for a sitter. But that's only if Emma said yes."

"If you think I can trust her, set it up."

Hell, no. As soon as I heard Emma's voice, I'd be making plans to see her again. I scrolled through my contacts on my cell and jotted her number down on a fresh piece of paper. "You can depend on her, but leave me out of it." I thrust the sheet at him. "She only knows me as Liam, not the singer of Full Throttle. Don't give her any information on me. None. You refer to me as Nick Black or say anything else, and I'm going to beat your ass."

He mimed zipping his lips. I knew he could keep a secret. But could he keep his hands off my girl? With me out of the picture, Emma was free to love whomever she wished. Theo had a way of making women fall for him, and it never ended well for the girl. Not that I had room to criticize. But at least I was upfront and conscientious about their feelings. Theo was downright oblivious to his effect on women. I saw it in my sister Faith every time she looked at him.

"One last thing." I took a deep breath, met his gaze, and spoke very clearly. "You try anything with Emma or if I find out you didn't do right by her, I'm coming after you. Got it?" Theo tended to go for wilder girls without kids, but who knew when his tastes might change? At some point, he'd grow up and have a real relationship. I just didn't want it to be with Emma. Or Faith. "She's sorting out your mess, if she's up for it, and that's it."

Theo held up a hand. "Look, if I had an itch to scratch

and wanted to date an accountant nerd, it wouldn't be one with baby baggage who you're obviously in love with."

After a moment, I closed my mouth and regained control of my body. "I'm not in love with her."

He rolled his eyes. "Yeah, sure, pal."

I wasn't. And I'd prove it the next time some hot chick came on to me and I forgot all about Emma. Losing interest in her was bound to happen. It was the way I was built.

★

After Aidan left later that day, all the guys showed up on my doorstep — at Theo's insistence. Apparently, he'd been so excited about the new lyrics, he couldn't wait to try them out. He brought a sweet little redhead with him who didn't look a day over eighteen. She sipped on a beer and looked up at him adoringly while I marveled at his cluelessness. He was going to break the poor girl's heart because, as usual, he had more charm than perception. The fact that this schoolgirl was drinking proved my point. I often doubted he'd ever grow up and settle down. Never really cared what he did though. Until today.

Caleb sat in the corner and leafed though my lyrics, aloof as ever, his straight light brown hair forming a curtain around his face. And alone. Because no girl was ever good enough for him. The days he slummed, he usually used the girl then ignored her mercilessly. His snobby attitude had always bothered me on some level, but I'd let it slide because he was such a talented bassist.

He had a wicked sense of business too, and his instincts had been good for the band.

As always, Sebastian was drunk. He'd ambled through the living room, his dark curly hair in desperate need of a trim, and gone straight to my fridge for a beer. Who needed girls when you were too drunk to do anything with them? I didn't have to wonder why he hadn't made it to this year's Most Beautiful People list. He'd more likely be confused with the guys on Duck Dynasty. I itched to tell him to clean himself up, but I didn't think he'd hear me through the alcohol fog.

And these were my bandmates, the guys I'd be working so closely with the next few months. Discontent infected my heart and drained into my brain.

What was I thinking to let the band come over so soon? I should've waited, maybe until my hair grew out and I felt like myself again. I missed the old me, the one who didn't have much of a conscience. I missed Nick Black who didn't mind if Theo charmed his way through life and missed out on a meaningful relationship. I missed that part of me who always blew off how Caleb treated everyone with disdain except us, the old me who turned a blind eye to Sebastian's drinking and the risk he posed every time he got into his car.

But the old me would probably never be seen again, regardless how long I grew my hair. Why hadn't the band's indiscretions bothered me before? Damn Emma and her lofty morals rubbing off on me.

Damn myself for wanting to deserve her.

As the other guys set up in my home studio, I knew

giving them what they wanted wasn't happening anytime soon. I stood my guitar against the wall and addressed the redhead. "Sweetheart, you got ID on you?"

Red's head snapped toward me, her fingers splayed over her chest, lips parted. If she was legal, I shouldn't have a problem with her being here with Theo — so long as she wasn't drinking. Hell, I'd been with groupies that young. But now, it no longer felt right. If she really was eighteen, that was only fourteen years away from Scarlet's age. And how would Emma feel if it was her daughter hanging onto some drummer who was only looking to get laid? The girl might not have been mine or Emma's kid, but she was somebody's daughter.

And she still hadn't offered me her ID. "You're not even legal. Jesus, Theo, what's the matter with you?"

His eyes grew wide, bouncing between me and the girl. "She said she was eighteen."

"Eighteen. Not twenty-one. Yet you gave her alcohol." I reached into my pocket, handed the girl a fifty, then led her toward the door. "Take a cab home. Don't come back until you're twenty-one."

After I finished seeing the girl out, I returned to the studio. As soon as the door opened, the murmurs stopped and everyone's eyes shot to me. *Here we go...*

"What the hell was that?" Theo rubbed the back of his neck. "Not like I was going to do anything with her once I realized how old she was."

I took a deep breath. "Do I really need to explain why it's such a bad idea for a seventeen-year-old girl to drink around guys with our reputation? It'd be a PR nightmare. Not even Violet could put a spin on that one." Violet might have been young, but she'd inherited Aiden's business sense. Except his daughter was far more ruthless. If she couldn't fix it, nobody could.

Theo exhaled, avoiding my eyes, and I knew he got it. But I wasn't done yet. "If you want to rob the cradle, do that on your own time." I shook my head. "And I don't know about you, but the brawls and public drunkenness are getting old. I'd better not see any headlines about the band's bad behavior. "

"Since when are you the scruples police?" Sebastian slurred before taking another pull of his beer.

Without waiting for Theo's reaction, I took a deep breath and turned on my best friend. "Sebastian, you're going into rehab, and you're not coming back until you're clean."

Caleb cast me a perplexed glance. "Sebastian doesn't have time for a full rehab program. We have to work on our songs and make sure they're great before we start recording."

"Then I'll have the label rearrange our schedule so Sebastian has some extra time." I ran a hand through my hair, knowing I was bluffing and hoping like hell the studio would cooperate. If not, maybe Aiden could smooth things over. "Outlaw Dogs can move ahead of us. Our albums are releasing at the same time, so it shouldn't matter who goes first. There's no shortage of bands waiting to record."

"Who the hell made you God?" Sebastian's fists tightened at his sides. "You can't tell us what to do."

My shoulders went rigid, and I hated myself for what I was about to do. But I'd known Sebastian since high school. He and Theo were my closest friends. I'd hate myself even more if anything happened to either of them because I hadn't had the balls to speak up.

"Actually, I can. I own the rights to the name Full Throttle." I met their gazes, one by one. "I write most of the songs, and I'm the front man. Sorry, but if you guys don't play it my way, you'll have to find yourself another gig."

"What the hell you gonna do without a lead guitar?" Sebastian sneered, using the end of the beer bottle as a pointer.

I gave a careless shrug. "I won't be without one, because I'll get a temporary guy. If you can't stay sober, he'll become permanent." I scanned the room, my shoulders stretching back. My eyes landed on Caleb, expecting him to turn on me too. "Any more questions?"

"Hope you know what you're doing, man." Caleb glanced at the other two who were disbanding so fast I half suspected a crew was filming porn outside and the guys didn't want to miss the money shot.

As Sebastian moved toward the door, I hurried over and blocked his way out. "Dude, you're my best friend," I said.

He gave me a half laugh. "Not anymore."

In my peripheral vision, Theo slipped past me and out the door. Damn. "Why not? Because a true friend would let you start drinking first thing in the morning, maybe kill an entire family with your car by the end of the day?" I attempted to hook an arm around his shoulder but he dodged me. "I want my best friend back without worrying every day if he's going to get into a horrible accident. When you're out of rehab, you'll have your spot back. Until then, Full Throttle won't be the same without you."

Sebastian's eyes darkened, his face a mask of cold fury. "Get the hell out of my way."

"Let 'em go, Nick." Caleb held the door open, and Sebastian stormed out.

I flipped around, preparing myself for a battle with Caleb. We'd been tied together by our involvement in Full Throttle, but we'd never been close. I wondered if he would become more distant now that I'd practically broken up the band. "You're pissed at me too, I suppose?"

"Nah." He shook his head. "It was a bit of a surprise at first, but I think you did the right thing. The label will understand, and we'll make it work. Sebastian needed to hear that. They both did. I don't envy you though. You're not going to be very popular for a while."

Yeah, but I was getting used to being disliked — by Breanna for abandoning Emma, and now my friends. The temptation to hit the liquor cabinet and drown out the fact that I'd driven everyone away weighed heavily on me. But I was afraid if I got wasted, I'd drunk-dial Emma. I'd have to deal with the mess I'd made with a clear head. Just great.

CHAPTER TWENTY-ONE

★ Emma ★

Crap, I'd poured in rum by mistake, and now I had to start the vodka tonic all over again. Damn Liam for making me want him and then bailing on me. My stomach took an unpleasant turn.

Even if he had stayed, he wouldn't have made a life with Scarlet and me. He'd said over and over he didn't want to be a father. It had been lose-lose for me from the beginning, no matter how I might've played it.

I dabbed the sweat off my forehead and glanced over to find Breanna already at the bar to collect her order. I still had three more to make. "Sorry. Need another minute."

"So..." Breanna scrunched up her nose as I attempted to make the drinks again. "How are you doing with Liam gone?"

I flinched, then concentrated harder on the Long Island iced teas. Didn't want to mess those up. "I don't know. Just trying to get through each day, I guess. I miss him."

There was a long pause like she was trying to decide what to say. "What if you knew he'd taken Heather home the night he went to Dirty Side Down? Knowing he was with another woman, would that make you miss him less?"

He'd taken Heather home that night? A dull ache ignited in my heart, growing with each second until it reached my very core. "How do you know that?" I asked in a small voice.

"I heard one of the Smith Construction guys talking about how he'd seen them leave the bar together and how Liam was lucky he'd gotten to *tap that* before he took off." Breanna grimaced. "Men can be such dogs."

No wonder he'd been so determined to get away from me. What did he need me for when he'd already gotten what he'd wanted from Heather? For all I knew, he'd gotten more of her on his way out of town. After I'd practically thrown myself at him and admitted to falling for him, who would blame him for getting the hell out while he could?

I shouldn't have been surprised that yet another man had disappointed me. It was my life story. Still, learning that Liam had taken up with Heather cut me deeply. Suddenly my entire body slowed, and moving became difficult.

How could I want him after he'd so easily discarded me for Heather? But this new development was exactly what I needed to help me get over him. He'd done me a huge favor. Maybe it wouldn't take decades for the ache in my heart to subside. Maybe just years. Lucky me.

Tears burned the back of my throat as I set the finished drinks on the tray. "In a way, this is better. Now I know beyond any doubt that he left because he didn't love me. I have to accept that."

"He obviously cared about you. But it doesn't matter how a guy feels if he can't rise to the occasion and man up." Breanna picked up the tray and softened her voice. "I'm so sorry he did that."

"Me too," I muttered, but Breanna had already disappeared into the crowd.

A few minutes later, she showed up again with a tray full of dirty glasses. "Something else is bothering you." She snuck peeks at me while she unloaded the tray. "Want to talk about it? I need three more ice teas, so you have another minute or two to spill it before I have to run."

I plucked up the two liquor bottles in each hand and poured them into three glasses, one after the other. Now wasn't the best time to tell her, but when would be? I was leaving town tomorrow, and I didn't want Breanna to find out after the fact.

"I got a strange offer today to sort out financial stuff for someone. The money's fantastic, childcare is paid for, and I can drive out with Scarlet and Lily. While I'm there, I can return Liam's car to him. After we fly back first class, I'll have the rest of the cash for a down payment on my new car. Too good to pass up."

"LA, huh?" Breanna chewed on that for several seconds. "So how did this guy hear about you?"

"Liam. The client is the drummer for Full Throttle." I pushed the shot glasses toward her. "Maybe they're friends or something."

She scowled. "That's *if* he's got friends."

"You don't like him very much, do you?" I sighed, knowing I shouldn't like him either.

"Not particularly," she said slowly, moving the glasses to her tray. "So why are you stressed about the job?"

"I'm excited about it, actually. That's not what's freaking me out." I popped a straw into each glass. "I want to see my parents while I'm there, but I'm terrified."

Breanna reached out a hand to give mine a gentle squeeze. "They're going to be thrilled to see you."

My throat constricted. "I hope so."

"I *know* so." She gave me a comforting smile. "When are you leaving?"

I swallowed and sucked in a deep breath. "Tomorrow."

Her brows shot up. "Want me to go with you? I could ask Marianne to cover me here."

My forehead crinkled, and I wondered how many new wrinkles I'd get over the next few days. Maybe even earn an ulcer? "I think this is something I have to do on my own."

"I'm here if you need me." She gave me another smile before picking up her tray and turning on her heel.

The idea of seeing Liam when I delivered his car was a bit nerve-racking too. He'd only been gone a few days, and I was every bit in love with him as when he'd left. Heather or no Heather, I didn't figure my feelings would change anytime soon.

★

I was in Los Angeles less than a day and had already figured out Theo's problem. Someone had gotten hold of his bank info and was having ball at his expense. Judging by the sheer number of electronic debits, ranging from tampons to women's shoes and wrinkle cream, he'd been being hosed for a while.

In the end, Theo had no clue which day he'd been in what town, and it was impossible for me to tell if the brewery in Ohio had been visited by him while he'd been on tour or if it was more fraud. After I compared each debit with his tour stops, I filed a dispute for the most recent fraudulent debits, then had the bank give him a temporary credit and cancel his ATM card. For the next five to seven days, until Theo received the new card, I wouldn't have to worry about anyone stealing from him.

Before I left, I reconciled his account, filed receipts and gave him a few tips on managing his money. Not the forensic accounting I'd expected, but it felt good to help him sort things out. And at two-fifty an hour, I'd earned over three thousand dollars.

As I collected my adding machine and brief case, Theo folded my hand into both of his. "I don't know how to thank you for everything you've done."

I flashed him an easy grin. "A check would be nice."

Theo bent down for a pen and began recording my info into the check register, just as I'd taught him. I suppressed a proud smile. A moment later, he tore out the check and thrust it toward me. "So you're coming back once a month?"

"I guess." I wrinkled my nose. "You sure you don't want to hire someone locally? You'll be paying me for a whole day, as well as all my travel expenses. I'm ripping you off if it ends up being only several hours of work."

He nudged my shoulder with his knuckles, then pressed his mouth into a grim line. "But you're the only one I trust."

All-expense-paid trip to sunny California once a month? No problem. "See you in a month then." After slipping his check into my briefcase, I turned to go.

Lily and Scarlet weren't expecting me at the hotel for a couple more hours, but it was too late to do anything touristy. I spun around to Theo as he opened the door. "How's Liam?"

"Uh... we kind of had a falling out." He averted his gaze. "I think."

"You two aren't friends anymore?"

"I'm not sure, actually." Theo groaned and rolled his eyes. "It's possible you're the only one he hasn't alienated."

If only he knew. Since Theo seemed inclined to spill his guts, I gave in to the urge and clung to any thread that led to Liam. "What did he do?"

"Fell off the radar for weeks and wouldn't answer his phone. When he came back, he was all high and mighty, started telling me how to live my life."

High and mighty? "He suddenly has morals and expects you to have them, too?"

Theo scowled. "Exactly. It was extremely annoying."

I bit my lip to keep from smiling. Knowing that Liam wouldn't be getting into as much trouble, possibly be a positive influence on his nephew, put me at ease. But I reminded myself that he hadn't changed enough to want to be with me. And it didn't undo the night he'd spent with Heather.

★

I sucked down more soda, hoping to calm my nerves. In a few minutes, we'd arrive in Oxnard at the house I'd grown up in. I half hoped my parents would be out and I'd have a whole month before the opportunity came around to try again. Except I was dying to see them. The closer I got to my old neighborhood, the more it hit me how much I'd missed them.

Lily's head popped into my peripheral vision when she moved forward from where she sat with Scarlet in the back. "Are you okay?"

"Yeah, I have to pee," I lied. Nerves could be contagious, and I didn't want Lily stressed out like me. "You guys will stay in the car until I know it's okay for you to come inside?"

"Sure." Lily disappeared from my view.

A mall whizzed by, the asphalt lot filled with cars. That hadn't been there before. They'd added another movie theater too, but I would've bet anything that my parents had never been inside it. My dad hated crowds, and my mother always used to complain about the unsanitary conditions of public places.

I smiled to myself as I recognized my old high school, its beige stone walls behind high, chain-link fences. Thankfully, some things hadn't changed.

My fingers trembled on the steering wheel. Only a couple more blocks.

Moments later, I pulled up in front of the neighbor's house. My mom was out front with her back to us, and I couldn't see her hair beyond the huge, straw hat. Her jean-clad knees were buried in dirt, a gloved hand gripped a trowel, and her other hand patted the soil.

My heart thumped louder. I checked my hair and makeup in the mirror, took a deep breath, then pivoted in my seat to see Scarlet. "I'll be back in a couple of minutes, sweetie. Hang on."

I opened the driver's-side door of Liam's Mercedes, set a boot flat on the street and then the other boot. After dusting off my jeans, I straightened my blouse and filled my lungs with air. My mom didn't glance behind her as I walked the narrow concrete pathway toward the front porch. Before the steps, I stopped only three feet from her profile.

She hadn't changed. Her chin-length blond hair was gathered at the nape of her neck under the straw hat.

I took a deep breath. "Mom?"

She froze, and her hand shook against the trowel which was partially obscured by dirt.

"It's Emma." My voice broke on the last syllable. She released the trowel, pushed off the ground, and turned, her lip quivering. I choked on a sob and closed the distance, my arms wrapping around her. "I've missed you so much."

She embraced me, her cheek pressing against mine, and she held me as if she was afraid to let me go or I might disappear again. Her shoulders vibrated against mine as she whispered, "My baby. You're here."

The tension drained out of me as I basked in her familiar scent of soap and candles, tears dripping onto my mother's shirt.

After what seemed minutes, she loosened her hold. "Let me have a look at you," she said softly. My arms dropped, but I found her hand. As she eased away, I saw her wet lashes. "You look so beautiful, sweetheart."

"So do you." I kissed her leathery cheek and whispered, "I'm sorry. I'm so so sorry."

"I'll have none of that." She wiped her eyes with the back of her hand. "We'll not spoil a minute of this by drudging up the past. Besides, I'm the one who should be apologizing."

What? "But I'm the one who left."

She closed her hands over mine. "I never believed you did that out of spite. You were *driven* away. Because we didn't have the sense to do right by you."

"Mom," I choked out, my face crumpling. I wasn't sure if I could hold it together.

"No more talk of the past." She ran a hand down my hair. "Let's go get your father."

The screen door slammed shut. "Everything okay, honey?"

My dad looked almost the same, tall, lean, and straight, except with a little more gray in his sandy-blond hair. He'd always looked like he belonged in a library, his glasses hanging too low on the bridge of his nose, the remaining strands of hair mussed. He was staring as though he didn't recognize me. Had I changed that much? Or would he not forgive me as easily as my mom had?

"Well, don't stand there with your mouth hanging open," my mom teased. "Say hello to your daughter."

Still, he didn't move. I climbed the steps, stopped in front of him, and took his hand. "Hi, Dad." My heart pounded as I held my breath.

His chin twitched, and his eyes pooled before he yanked me into a hug and dropped a kiss on the top of my head. "So many things I'd do differently," he whispered hoarsely.

"Me too." Sniffing back a sob, I remembered Lily and Scarlet. Careful not to unwind my arm from my dad's waist, afraid to let him go just yet, I twisted around to my mom. I reached out, grabbed her hand. "There's someone I want you to meet."

CHAPTER TWENTY-TWO
★ *Liam* ★

It had been three weeks since I'd left Emma in Nevada. Not knowing if she was all right drove me crazy. Getting a good night's sleep wasn't getting any easier, and I frequently squelched the burning need to text Theo about her, see if they ever got together on his money situation. But I didn't want to take a chance that he might slip and she'd find out I'd checked up on her.

Emma needed to think I didn't care so she could move on. She was a survivor; I knew that. But I still obsessed over whether she'd gone out with Pretty Boy again, how many dates they'd been on, or if she'd slept with him yet. Not a place my mind should go, but I went there anyway. And it just about tore me in two.

I hadn't been with any girls since Emma. Every girl I'd met just wasn't her. My feelings would change though—I was sure of it—and when they did, I'd be glad I hadn't called her and put her through the yo-yo grind.

We'd held auditions for a replacement lead guitar and unanimously voted in Brett, a down-to-earth guy who obviously spent a lot of time at the gym. After Violet set him up with a photographer and his shirtless pictures hit the Internet, he could barely keep up with all the comments and direct messages on Twitter and Instagram.

Brett, Caleb, and Theo had been over to my house nearly every day to work on the songs for our next album. We were laying down some wicked beats, and I was proud of our progress. Not only for the music we were creating, but that I no longer lived a life where I did things that made me feel guilty or risked Faith being disappointed in me.

Theo hadn't gotten into any brawls that I knew of, and he hadn't brought over any girls. But he'd been a little distant, which I assumed meant that he still thought I'd been an ass for interfering in their personal lives. I missed the way it used to be, the camaraderie. No doubt he resented me for calling him on his bad behavior and ousting Sebastian. What was I supposed to do, crawl back to them and apologize for expecting them to be better?

I tossed the pad of paper down in disgust. Jesus, I was turning into my sister.

I missed Sebastian, and not a day went by that I didn't worry about him. A part of me regretted cutting him loose. I mean, he was either going to dig himself out of the hole or he wasn't. That was *his* decision. Still, I lived in fear that if he had his place in the band again, he'd never realize he was an alcoholic and eventually end up in jail for manslaughter. Or end up dead.

I abandoned the sofa and my lyrics, fixed myself a bowl of cereal, and sat at the table. My phone dinged, signaling a new text. As I spooned another bite of cereal into my mouth, I glanced over at my phone.

I got a notice that my house has been sold. Did you buy it?

Crap. It was Emma. My stomach flipped. *Why would you think it was me?*

Because you wouldn't take your share of the tips. Because you drove me around for weeks and wouldn't let me give you gas money. Because you left me a brand new luxury car to drive. Because the mysterious new owner reduced my rent by $300. You didn't answer my question.

Busted. *Yes, I bought it.*

I sat still, incapable of eating my cereal as I waited for her reply. Emma wasn't one to appreciate charity. She was going to be pissed.

Why? she asked simply.

I took a deep breath and turned on speech-to-text. *Because you have plumbing problems which are likely caused by old galvanized pipe. Because I saw water stains on the ceiling inside, and every time I returned from a run and looked up, I noticed five layers of roofing.* I paused a moment before adding the last bit. *Because I want you and Scarlet safe, and I knew the property managers I hired would maintain the house properly.*

I clicked send and waited. A full minute passed and nothing came, so I forced myself to set the phone down before filling the spoon again with milk and cereal. As I swallowed a second bite, my phone dinged again.

Thank you.

You're welcome, I fired back. And now that her question had been answered, that was it. I couldn't encourage anything more, not if she was going to get on with her life. But as I resumed my breakfast, I held the hope that she wasn't finished with me yet.

And thank you for sending Theo my way.

So he'd followed through. Good for him. *That worked out, huh?*

Yes. I left your car with him and flew back. I hope that's ok. And I'll be returning once a month to monitor his finances.

Yeah, thanks. I resisted the urge to invite more conversation though I itched to tell her to call me next time she was in the area. I clenched my jaw, pissed at myself for letting the conversation get as far as it had. *I picked it up. Thanks for driving it back.*

Sure. Thanks for the referral.

You're welcome.

I waited, hoping she'd say something else, but expecting nothing. Emma wasn't going to chase me, because I hadn't given her a reason to. I was the one who'd left. She'd reached out, and I'd shut her down. That was it. My gut wrenched when the phone's silence confirmed I was right.

I dropped the spoon into the bowl and pushed it away. Rubbing my temples, I tried to un-know that Emma would be in town, only a few miles from me, every month. So accessible. I could keep myself occupied with work to avoid running into her on a temporary basis. But month after month?

The front door creaked open, and I sprang from the chair to see who it was. Other than my sister and the band, people didn't usually come into my house without knocking.

"Liam?"

What the hell was Sebastian doing at my house? I had assumed he'd be off getting drunk somewhere. I entered the foyer with caution, in case he'd showed up to try to beat my ass. "What's going on?"

Sebastian had cut off all the overgrown, unhealthy waves, and he'd shaved. Yet he still looked like hell. Dark circles showed in contrast against pale skin that had been olive in his healthier days. His shoulders drooped, and his hands shook as he brought a bottle of water to his lips. He chugged some, then glanced away a moment before answering. "Rough few days. After I left here, I got an earful from Caleb. He pissed me off pretty good. So I figured I'd go a week without a beer, you know, to show you idiots that I could do it."

My respect for Caleb was steadily climbing. I jerked my head toward the living room and led the way. "How did that turn out for you?"

"Not so good." He lowered to the overstuffed chair. "You were right about everything. Theo needs to quit acting like a child, and I need to quit drinking." He regarded his knees for a long moment. "I can't do this on my own."

I patted him on the shoulder. "How can I help?"

"Found a good facility with an impressive success rate. I'd drive myself, but once the withdrawals get rough and the urge to get drunk wins out, having access to a car is probably a bad idea. I'd appreciate a ride."

The staff had to have a way of ensuring that anyone on the program couldn't drive off and lose their hard-won progress. But if Sebastian wanted me to drive him,

I was more than happy to spend a couple of hours with my old friend.

★

After dropping Sebastian off at rehab, I pulled up to my gate to find Theo's Ferrari in my driveway, parked behind Caleb's black Jag and Brett's Jeep. I slid my roadster into the garage and slipped into the house.

Theo sat on the sofa with a blonde who, surprisingly, looked like she was in her early twenties. Seemed a little old for him; probably a relative or something. Certainly not someone he wanted to bag.

Through the window that overlooked the deck, Brett was surrounded by pretty girls. I assumed since they'd brought guests that this visit wasn't a rehearsal. Social call? Coming to hang out with the guy who'd threatened to cut them out? Unlikely.

A sick feeling percolated, spreading like roots and embedding in my gut. Had my bandmates come to tell me they were striking out on their own? Sure, I could get another drummer and bassist or lead guitar. But I didn't want to. I wanted Brett and Theo. And, yeah, I wanted Caleb — who happened to be making his way to me.

"Heard from Sebastian?" I asked.

"He called me earlier before stopping by to see you." Caleb shifted his weight and held my gaze. "You know, I've been trying to get his ass into rehab for months. Guess he just needed to hear it from his best friend." He gave me a nod, then he strolled through the french doors to where Brett grinned at the crowd of girls.

Just a few feet from me, Theo bent closer to the blonde and his lips moved. Then he headed toward me.

"Uh... What's going on?" I asked. "Got the feeling you guys were pissed at me."

"Maybe. Doesn't mean we *should* be."

I wasn't sure what he meant by that.

"Sebastian stopped by earlier today. Wasn't looking so hot. He said you were right, and we needed to stop being jackasses." Theo rolled his eyes. "Caleb and I got together and agreed there was a lot to what you said. Maybe threatening us wasn't the best way to go." He punched me hard in the shoulder. "But you were right to say something. It's strange but... I'm kind of relieved."

My brows raised. "How so?"

"For one, I don't have to worry anymore about landing in jail." He tunneled his fingers through his shaggy blond hair. "God, you and Sebastian have infected me."

I hadn't expected that. "So you and I are good?"

"We're better than good, man." He slapped me on the back, then slung an arm around my shoulder. "Fights or no fights, I'll always be badder than you."

I chuckled. "Is that so?"

"Yep. We brought you a peace offering." He wiggled his eyebrows, then steered me toward the window. "Let me show you. Check out the scenery, dude. Pick anyone you want."

Out on the deck near my oversized spa, I counted six girls stripped down to very tiny bikinis. They were all smokin' hot, ranging from dark skinned to light, curly hair to straight, slim to voluptuous. "You brought them for *me*? Why so many?"

"You've changed so much the past few weeks I had no idea what you might be in the mood for."

I was in the mood for a little Emma, not a perfect stranger. God, did I used to sleep with just anyone this way? "Where'd you get 'em?"

"Some of her model friends, all very excited to meet the great Nick Black." Theo grinned, his eyes darting to the girl he'd left on the couch. "It's the least we could do."

Struggling to muster up joy from someplace inside me, I smiled. "Great."

"I'll invite them inside to meet you."

I inwardly sighed. "Plenty of towels in the trunk by the spa."

Two hours later, the speakers blasted Ylvis's "What Does the Fox Say," making me regret spending so much money on the state-of-the-art sound system. Three of the six girls were gyrating in front of the TV. The other three were talking me up.

Before I'd met Emma, I wouldn't have thought twice about taking any one of them to my room, maybe even two or three. But no matter which pretty girl was speaking to me, I only saw Emma. *What the hell did she do to me?*

I had to make it stop, whatever it took. I'd never be able to give Emma what she needed, so what was stopping me from delivering to someone else whose needs were so much simpler? I only had to pick one.

The closest girl to me had strawberry blond hair,

freckles on her cute, upturned nose, and eyes as blue as the sky at twilight. She'd do.

"Follow me," I whispered, then I turned and headed toward my bedroom, knowing she would be right behind me.

★

The next morning, the sun peeked through the curtains, and I lay on my back, still contemplating the ceiling.

I was so screwed.

I'd had a beautiful, scantily dressed girl in my bedroom last night. She'd stripped off her blouse to expose a purple lace bra and flat tummy. She'd rubbed up against me and tried to peel my shirt off, and still Emma's image swam before me.

I'd captured the girl's wrist to stop her. "Sorry. It's not you, I swear."

She pouted. "Obviously, it *is* me, or you'd already be naked."

"Any other time, and we'd be there, trust me."

The girl swiped her blouse up from the floor and pulled it over her head. "So why aren't we?"

I hesitated, scrubbing my hands over my face. If I didn't give this chick something, who knew what rumors would run rampant? I decided on the truth. "I can't stop thinking about this girl I met."

"The great Nick Black in love? Your fans will be very sorry to hear that." She turned to let herself out.

"I'm not in love," I insisted.

She shrugged, then twisted back to leave, halting when her hand covered the doorknob. "Whatever. If you care about her so much that you can't be with other girls, then you should be with *her*."

I'd stayed in my room for another hour after she'd left. Theo and Brett had come to check on me, but I pretended to be asleep to avoid them probing into my love life. A few minutes later, the music stopped and the front door closed. Soon after, motors revved and the gate hummed open.

There would be questions from the guys later, I was sure of it. I so wasn't looking forward to being grilled. For now, I had to get through the day without jumping into my car and driving straight to Gardnerville.

After I dragged my ass out of bed, I threw on some sweats and checked my e-mail in the office. My copies of the house documents had arrived in my inbox. I scanned the PDF quickly for anything that stood out as inaccurate, then printed them out. I gathered the stack and took it to the living room coffee table to examine more closely later.

I strode to my gym to run on the treadmill. I preferred running on the streets but hated it when the paparazzi followed me. What was so interesting about watching me run?

Sweat trickled down my chest after running nearly four miles, and I looked up to see Faith standing in the doorway. I wasn't in the mood for company. "Hey, what's up? Xander here, too?"

"Nah, he's at home with Mom. By the way, why haven't you called her since you've been back?"

Because I was afraid she'd use her sixth sense against me and pry into my love life. "Been busy."

"Uh-huh." She widened her stance, tilting her head up.

Oh, goodie. Faith was in the mood to be judgy. What else was new? Worse, her scowl said there would probably be some kind of lecture involved. Might as well get it over with. Or maybe I could delay it... I managed a bright smile then stepped off the treadmill and grabbed a fresh towel to sop up the sweat. "You know better than to show up without my nephew. What's wrong with you?"

"Got a call from Aidan this morning."

Which meant everyone, not just Faith, was butting into my life. Fantastic. I brushed past her on my way to the kitchen for a cold drink. "And?"

"Says you've been acting weird."

I stopped to lift a brow at her. "For instance?"

"Let's see... First, you disappeared for weeks." She held up a finger as she listed off my offenses. "Then you returned but barely talked to anyone, and when you finally got together with the guys to rehearse, you fired Sebastian and threatened Theo. And apparently, according to what Theo told Aidan..." She stuck out a fourth finger. "You're no longer interested in women."

No way would I reply to that last one. Faith knew better. I resumed my trip to the fridge and procured a soda. "Thirsty?"

"No, thanks," she called out from the living room.

As I popped the top and took a swig, I headed her way. She was staring down at the escrow papers. My bad for leaving them out, and I was about to pay for that.

She glanced up at me. "You bought a house in Gardnerville?"

"Uh..." Why was I so reluctant to cop to it? Because I didn't want her to know about Emma. "Sort of."

"Do you plan on moving there?"

"Of course not."

"Vacation home?"

And expose Emma to my bad self? "No way."

"Rental?" She sifted through the papers, stopping at one, then looking up at me. "Appraisal says it's worth fifty thousand *less* than what you paid. Why would you overpay for a house in Gardnerville if you're not going to use it?"

I knew my sister well enough to know that she wouldn't stop until she had all the answers. "I wanted Emma to pay less rent to help her get ahead. And the place wasn't maintained properly. If I'm her landlord, I can make sure the roof gets redone and the leaks are fixed." I turned on the TV and sat on the other end of the couch, pretending to be absorbed in the channel guide and hoping that explanation would satisfy her.

"This Emma chick must be special."

"Yeah, she's, uh, kind of amazing."

"Amazing, huh?" One side of her mouth curled up. "As in you slept with her and want to sleep with her again one day?"

Oh, here we go. There was no stopping my sister now. "Yeah, I liked her, okay? But, no, I never slept with her." I brushed Faith off with a wave of my hand, then turned down the volume on the TV. "I'm not right for her."

Her eyes turned to slits. "Why not?"

The inquisition would never end. I groaned. "Because Emma's good. She cares about people and always tries to do the right thing. We're too different."

"You bought her house, Liam, overpaid and everything so she wouldn't have to fork out as much rent. Same Emma who's working with Theo? Which means you got her a bookkeeping gig too. Looks to me like you do lots of things right."

I squirmed on the couch. Why hadn't I just finished my workout and told her I had somewhere to be? "But I do too many other things wrong."

Her hand shot out toward my head to whack me and I glared. "Yeah, you mess up," she said. "We all do. Guess what? We're human. What matters most is how you handle it after the fact. Do you own up and take responsibility for what you did, or do you slither away and decide that being a decent person is too much work?"

Well, when she put it that way... "Yeah, but if I'm screwing up all the time, she'll get tired of it."

"Little brother, she may not see it that way. No sane woman expects her man to be perfect. That only happens in movies and romance novels. In real life, they just want more good from their guy than bad. And if the good is really good, and if you own up when you need to, the bad is so much less bad."

"So you're saying —"

"We all mess up, but you have to focus on the good."

Emma had said something similar the night we'd gone out dancing. Something about all of us having some bad inside us. And that we had to find the balance. But even if Emma wanted me, despite her being way too good for me, I wasn't a death-till-we-part kind of guy. "Plus she's got a four-year-old daughter to worry about, and I screw up too often to do right by a kid."

"Do you get along with the little girl?" Faith asked.

I grinned, remembering her dimples. "She's adorable."

"Saying you can't do right by her is stupid. You may be Xander's uncle, but you're the only dad figure he's ever known."

"That's different. He's blood. I'm not built for the long haul for just anyone. I can't try and then fail. Can't do that to Scarlet or disrespect Emma that way."

"Disrespect her?" Faith's mouth dropped open. When she closed her mouth and leveled me with a stare, I knew I was about to plunge into the kind of hell only mothers and sisters could inflict. "You have this thing about not disrespecting women. You've beat up guys over it." She paused for dramatic effect, and I cringed over what else she had in store for me. "You're such a hypocrite."

My head snapped around. "What?"

"Sweet little college girl comes up to you, and all she wants is attention from the rock star she's been crushing on. And you have no problem giving her what she wants."

"Oh, c'mon. That's not the same thing." What the hell was Faith playing at?

"You just go with it, even if it's obvious the girl has no respect for herself." She pressed her lips together before continuing. "If you were going to do right by one of your groupies, you'd give her an autograph or a backstage pass or something, have a nice conversation so she feels good about herself, then let her leave with her dignity intact."

I didn't like where this was going. Dropping my chin, I ground my teeth and hoped she'd be done with me soon. But Faith showed no mercy.

"Let me put it this way: Once she puts her clothes back on and she's leaving your hotel room, how much respect do you have for her then?"

I couldn't look at Faith, just kept my head down. "Okay, you made your point. Are we done yet?"

"No. What was that crap you were slinging about not being made for the long haul?"

I redistributed my weight to my other leg, my fingers twitching at my sides. "Relationships don't work out—as our parents and Xander's dad have proved. And... I don't know if I've got it in me to stay with any one person that long. Not only that, I'm not ready to be Scarlet's father."

Faith blew out a breath, shaking her head. "Mom and Dad weren't right for each other. They only got married because she was pregnant with me. As for my own marriage, we both know I can't pick 'em. From the very beginning, it wasn't right with Xander's father." She waved an index finger at me. "You, on the other hand, have this Emma girl that you think is pretty great and who is obviously good for you, and you're walking away."

I let my forehead drop into my palms. "Come back when you're not lecturing me nonstop, huh?"

She reached into her pocket and pulled out a paper, then carefully unfolded it. "I picked this up off the floor the other day." She laid it on the counter in front of me. "These lyrics are beautiful yet disturbing. Explains a lot, I guess. But I want you to know I think it's all a load of crap. You *are* good enough for this Emma chick, and there's absolutely no reason why you can't have a long, healthy relationship with her."

It was the lyrics to the song I'd written as soon as I'd arrived from Gardnerville. I shook my head at Faith. "But what if it doesn't work out? I can't hurt her that way."

Faith flicked me in the ear, then sighed. "What would you do if Emma showed up here?"

"She won't. I gave her my real name. She won't connect that to Nick Black unless she really digs, which she's probably not going to do because I didn't give her a reason to." I leaned forward to get Faith's attention. "Don't be tracking her down and calling her. If you happen to run into her while she's here working with Theo, promise me you won't tell her who I am. Once she knows, seeing me on TV or in the papers will only make things harder for her."

Faith reached up and cupped my cheeks. "When did you decide it's easier to do without the things you love than fight for what you want?" She released me and turned to leave. "I promise Emma won't hear it from me. By the way, I'm leaving town tomorrow. Want to keep an eye on Xander for a couple of days?"

CHAPTER TWENTY-THREE
★ *Emma* ★

I wiped down the bar, counting the minutes until I could go home and snuggle up to Scarlet. She was all I had these days. Well, except my parents once a month. But day-to-day, Scarlet was my whole world as my broken heart mended.

Not that it was mending. I missed Liam now more than ever. But if he came back to me, did I really want him? Liam had chosen Heather over me, then left Scarlet and me behind. And when I'd texted him a couple of weeks ago, his lackluster replies and following silence had hurt me more than his leaving.

I was done with him. I had to be.

Theo had referred a couple of other clients to me, but they were in LA. Career-wise, it made sense to move there. Living closer to my parents made a lot of sense too. The only problem was being that close to Liam, but what were the chances I'd run into him in a city that big?

Hearing the squeak of vinyl, I whipped around to see who had taken a stool. An extremely pretty girl offered me a smile. She was so lean, she made me feel clunky and awkward. Even her dark hair was delicate and feminine, cut into a long pixie. She rested her elbows on the bar, chin in her palms as she followed me with her eyes. There was something eerily familiar about her.

I smiled back and slid a napkin in front of her. "Something to drink?"

She blinked. "Oh, right. This is a bar." She bit her lip and scanned the liquor shelf behind me. "How about a ginger ale?"

I poured the soda, dropped in a straw, then set the glass on the napkin. "What brings you here?"

"You." She gave me a sheepish grin. "I was curious what kept Liam here so long."

Was she his girlfriend? I swallowed back the nausea rolling in. "But he's home now?"

Her lip curved up. "Yes. We talked, and things are better. I mean, he's more like the old Liam, you know? Before he changed. He used to be so sweet. Turns out this was a good trip for him."

Oh, my God. Tears threatened, but I refused to let them fall. "I'm happy you two reconciled."

"Yeah, it's great. Still hasn't seen our parents, but I don't think he can hold out much longer."

Was she referring to her in-laws? Or *his* in-laws. Wait. Were they even married? "So he's doing okay?"

"Yes and no." She pursed her lips. "I think he misses you."

Crap, was I the other woman? And how could she be so calm about it? I held my laced fingers in front of myself to keep from twitching. "He never told me about you. Nothing really happened between us anyway. I don't have a claim on him, I swear."

A groove appeared between her brows. "Why would I care if you were with him? And anything you two might've done is TMI. Seriously." She grimaced. "No details, please."

I scanned the bar, hoping no one else needed a drink. "So... you guys have an open relationship?"

"Open relationship?" She looked as baffled as I was. "What?"

"You know, allowed to date other people." I wasn't sure I wanted to know the answer, yet couldn't help needing to ask.

"What the—" She sprang off the stool. "He never mentioned me, did he? My name is Faith."

I shook my head. "No. He never told me about his other life."

"Ew! I'm his *sister*, Emma, not his girlfriend." She danced around in a circle shuddering. "Gross."

"Sorry. I didn't know. He never told me what he does for work or where he lives or anything." Monumentally relieved Liam wasn't dating her, I bit my lip to keep from laughing and ended up snorting. "I just assumed—"

"Stop." She waved it away, shutting her eyes shut in horror. "Let's move on. Please."

Gladly. I tried to remain unaffected as I wiped down the bar next to her. "So he doesn't have a wife or girlfriend back home?" Not that it mattered, since he didn't want me anyway. When she didn't answer, I glanced up at her.

She returned to her place on the barstool. "No, he doesn't. He's in love with *you*."

Stunned, I sucked in a breath, then did my best to shake it off. Back to reality, I forced a laugh. "If he loved me, he'd be with me. He's not. He doesn't."

"Well, I didn't say my brother was smart." She reached out for my wrist when I was about to back away. "He's afraid to take the leap. His whole life, all he's seen is bad relationships. It's all he knows."

"Doesn't change anything for me. He still left."

"And the fact that he bought you a house doesn't mean anything to you either?"

"He bought *himself* a house. It's not in my name." Usually, I was desperate to hear anything about Liam, but if I'd known how painful it would be, I would've walked away from Faith the moment she mentioned his name.

"He could've bought any house, but he bought *that* one, to take care of you."

I turned away, unable to listen to Faith, not willing to allow myself to hope. "I still pay rent."

Faith moaned. "But he hasn't been with any other girl since before he disappeared."

"You can't know that unless you've been with him every minute of every day." Not that it would make a difference to me anyway. He'd made his choice, and I wasn't it.

"No. But I know Liam. And I don't think you should write him off yet."

I bit my bottom lip, measuring my next words, then I met her eyes. "Too late. I already have."

I pivoted and made my way to the other end of the bar and whispered in Duke's ear to take over service to the pretty, dark-haired girl. While I helped other customers, I avoided glancing her way. When I checked for her a few minutes later, she was gone.

By eleven, the evening had worn on me. Bartending had never been my life-long dream, but most of the time I'd been content knowing that I was closer to my goals every day. Until Liam came along. Now I found myself counting the hours until I closed Sunday nights, until I was with Scarlet again. She didn't completely fill the void, but being around her helped.

I had to get past this. I needed to make good on my words to Faith and write Liam off.

"Hey, sweetie, can I get four shots of Jack and two pitchers?" Breanna called out from the other end of the bar.

I faked a smile and headed toward the bottle of Jack. "Sure."

"Emma, could I get vodka tonic?" Heather bellied up to the bar.

I stiffened and reminded myself to be friendly. "Let me just finish this draft, and I'll be right with you."

As I positioned the pitcher under the spout and lifted the lever, I snuck a peek at Heather. As usual, she was a guy magnet in a short dress with her long hair cascading over her shoulders.

Her gaze wandered to Duke at the other end of the bar, and she sighed. "I miss Liam."

"I bet you do," I muttered, wishing I hadn't opened my mouth.

Her eyes went catlike as she sized me up. "What's that supposed to mean?"

I had to remind myself that, although she'd been with more than a few guys, she was still only twenty-one and naïve in many ways. "You hooked up with Liam. Not surprised you'd want more."

She scrunched up her nose, then suddenly her eyes widened. "Oh, my God. You're the loose end."

I blinked. "What?"

"Never mind." She scooted closer, crowding Breanna, and lowered her voice. "Listen, I never slept with Liam, never even kissed him. Not that I didn't try *really* hard. I mean, what girl wouldn't want him? He gave me a ride home once, but he was very clear about not being available. And anytime I saw him, he was always alone, never with a girl."

My stomach lurched, and I struggled to breathe in air. My entire basis for writing off Liam had been blown out of the water. How the hell was I going to get over him now?

CHAPTER TWENTY-FOUR

★ *Liam* ★

Caleb had requested a short break to check out a music institute where he could learn more about producing and arranging music — which could mean I'd have to audition a bassist to replace him. I was so not looking forward to losing another band member. While he did a tour of the school, which I secretly hoped he'd hate, I drove the two hours to San Diego. Figuring that Faith had already briefed my mom on my love life, I didn't see a reason to continue avoiding her.

I always loved visiting my mom. But even though I'd grown up and left home, a part of me always dreaded seeing my stepfather. We'd never really gotten along. I knew he was all bark and no bite, but the bark still grated on my nerves. Mostly because I always walked away from him feeling unwanted.

After I endured the scolding for disappearing without informing anyone, my mom chilled and we chatted about the upcoming CD, my plans for touring, and finally, Xander. But she didn't pry into my love life. She was probably waiting for me to open up, but I didn't feel like it. I was exhausted from days of spending long hours in rehearsal and then dealing with traffic during the drive to see them. I wasn't in the mood to be pressured.

During a lull in our conversation, she excused herself to finish up some of the side dishes. "Why don't you help Carl with the grill?"

Though spending time with my stepdad was the last thing I wanted to do, I obeyed and slipped through the french doors to the grill out back.

"Grab the steaks," he ordered without even looking at me.

Technically, he was retired from the service, but he still treated me like he was in the military and I was his recruit. I bristled. "You could ask nicely."

He spared me a glance, irritation making his features appear even harsher. "Just go get the damn steaks, son."

My fingertips curled into my palms. I was twenty-four, full grown, yet he still managed to make me feel like a twelve-year-old. "And don't call me that. You're not my dad."

His hands stilled and he set the bag of charcoal to the side of the grill. He pivoted slowly and stretched up to his full height. He was a big man, broad and muscular. He easily intimated anyone, even a guy like me who'd proved he could take care of himself.

Fighting the urge to shrink back, I lifted my chin and stood my ground. "You're not my dad," I repeated.

His already-ruddy complexion deepened. "That's what I get after sixteen years of puttin' up with all your horseshit?"

I shifted my weight uncomfortably. Instinct told me I'd taken on the wrong battle. But I had no intention of backing down. I angled to the side, making myself a smaller target. "Apparently."

His eyes slanted into slits. "That piece o' shit gets to slap your mother around then abandon his two children, and he still rates higher than the guy who picked up the pieces? Did you know that your mother was so twitchy after he left, I met her a year later and it still took me two years to get her to give me a chance?" Carl ran his thick fingers through what was left of his red hair, then he scoffed. "Yeah, that's some dad you got there."

My dad had beat my mom? "Still doesn't make you my dad," I growled.

He nodded slowly, never breaking eye contact with me. "When you were thirteen and broke your arm, I picked you up from school and took you to the hospital. I held your hand while they set the bone."

He took a step forward, but the lines on his face had smoothed out and I didn't understand why he wasn't already trying to beat the crap out of me. I'd never spoken up until now. Why wasn't he freaking out?

"I taught you how to drive because your mom was too nervous to get in a car with you behind the wheel. I did everything a father would do." He drew in a long, deep breath and seconds ticked by. Then he met by gaze again, steady, pleading. "Spent a lot of time talkin' to men, not sharin' my feelings. So I'm not good with words, and maybe... maybe I didn't always say the right thing. But to me, whether we share DNA or not, you've always been my son."

He might as well have punched me in the gut with all the wind he'd just knocked out of me. I twisted away, unable to look at him. My head reeled. All this time, I'd thought he didn't want me around, that I was in his way. Turns out, his real crime was being a crappy communicator.

True, he didn't always use the right words, but he was right about one thing. He'd *shown* me he loved me. Like when he'd given me the sex talk on my fourteenth birthday and when he'd taken me camping the next summer even though my mom and Faith refused to go with us. He'd proved his love when he'd taught me how to shoot a rifle, and he'd been the one to take me to jujitsu lessons three times a week and cheer me on at tournaments.

He'd also taught me to respect women, to protect them. He'd taught me how to take pride in work, taught me to be on time and accountable. I'd thrown a lot of his lessons out the window once Full Throttle had begun to make a name for itself. But he'd given me enough of a foundation that I had eventually come back around.

I whirled around and marched up to Carl, then drew him into a big bear hug. "I'm sorry for being an ass. Thanks for being such a great dad and putting up with all my crap."

"Yeah, okay." He coughed and slapped me on the back, then shoved me away. "Now get the hell out of here and fetch me those steaks."

I laughed and did as I was told.

After we'd eaten and I helped my mom clean up, I sat at the dining room table to reply to a text. Carl passed by, and I glanced up in time to see him drop a kiss on his wife's cheek and then pat her on the rump. He strolled off, and she gazed after him adoringly.

Holy crap. My mom and stepdad were still in love after over fifteen years of marriage. How had I never noticed that? I'd seen so many marriages fall apart, but had never noticed the ones that had held together. Some relationships, the right ones, endured.

As rough as it had been for Emma, she'd still been brave enough to try one more time. I'd had my heart crushed when I'd been seventeen and, afraid to get hurt again, I'd turned off my emotions. But where had that gotten me? Not happy and not Emma, that was for sure. Yes, relationships were hard and breakups were messy. Yet I wanted to try again with Emma. Damn it, I wanted her. And Scarlet. More than ever. And if I put in the effort and ended up being half the father Carl had been to me, I'd do okay. I knew who to ask for advice if I ran into any serious problems.

If Emma still wanted me and we decided to do this thing, and if I screwed up now and then along the way, maybe she'd stick it out with me. It was worth a shot. *They* were worth a shot.

The other day, I'd finally broken down and asked Theo how Emma was working out. He'd mentioned she was mulling over the idea of relocating to LA since she now had two more clients in the area. When I'd first met her, I'd been sure that this wasn't the place for her, that the city would devour her. I'd been so wrong. Emma was one of the toughest people I'd ever met. If anyone could survive in LA, it was her.

"Thinking about that girl, sweetheart?" my mom asked, jolting me out of my thoughts.

Oh, here we go. "Maybe."

She skirted around a chair to get to me, kissed the top of my head, then cupped my face. "Stop torturing yourself and go get her, silly boy."

My thoughts exactly. I couldn't predict the future, but I could try every day for the rest of my life to make Emma and Scarlet happy, to make their lives better.

But what if it was too late and she was already involved with some guy like Pretty Boy and I'd lost my chance with her forever? On the other hand, what if she wasn't dating anyone? What if she was waiting for me to stop being an idiot?

Emma had asked me to stay, and she didn't say things she didn't mean. She'd had strong feelings for me at the time. I hoped she still did. She might have already given up on me and moved on, but I wouldn't know unless I tried.

I covered my mom's hands with mine. "I think I will."

Finding Theo's number, I tapped the call button. "Yeah, it's me. When's Emma coming back into town to work for you?"

"She'll be here Monday night," he answered. "Why?"

"Tell her Nick Black is performing at a local club. Offer her tickets."

"What about the rest of the band?"

"This late notice, not sure Aidan has time to set up a paying gig. Didn't think you and the guys would want to do a freebie."

"You're my friend. If you need to do this, I'm in. I'll get Brett and Caleb on board and get back to you."

"Thanks, man."

"Glad to see you're finally growing some balls, bro."

"What?"

"I'm not blind. You wouldn't have warned me to keep my hands off Emma if you didn't care about her. And, uh, you were kind of annoying at first, but I think things turned out pretty good. I'm thinking she might be part of the reason."

"Yeah, well, I hope she cooperates." I hung up with Theo and dialed the number to the Wagon Wheel. It was early enough in the evening that I might catch Breanna when she wasn't swamped. "Hi, can I talk to Breanna?"

"Who should I tell her is calling?" I recognized Rocko's voice.

If I gave my real name, Emma might get wind of it. "Nick Black of Full Throttle."

"You don't want to give me your real name, then just say so, jerkface. Hold on."

I chuckled as I waited. About a minute later, Breanna came on the line. "Hi, honey, so good to hear from you," she said in a syrupy sweet voice.

"Cut the crap, Breanna. I need a favor."

"That attitude doesn't work for me," she chirped.

This was starting off all wrong. Breanna wasn't going to make it easy on me, and I wasn't sure I deserved her help. But I needed it. I'd have to work at her from a different angle. "Can you keep a secret?"

"I don't know," she said wryly. "Can I?"

Obviously she could or else Emma would've already found out about me. "Theo's going to offer Emma two tickets to a Full Throttle gig here in LA. I want you to make sure she shows up."

"That's gonna be hard to do from here."

"Not if you come with her."

"That's so generous of you to offer me an all-expense-paid trip to LA," she cooed. "And you're flying me first class? I'm honored."

I grinned. A part of me loved Breanna protecting Emma so fiercely and how she wasn't taking any crap from me. "I'll make sure you get two seats on the same flight. All you have to do is figure out how to get Emma to invite you along."

"One question. Are you doing all this because you want to be with Emma?"

Hell, I was hoping Breanna wouldn't go there. What if I told her the truth and then she refused to help because she still hated me? On the other hand, if Breanna thought my intentions weren't honorable, she'd likely refuse to help me. Either way, I could be screwed. My only choice was to go with the truth and cross my fingers.

"No." I waited a beat, hoping and praying Beanna would be onboard. "I want her *and* Scarlet."

I heard a tiny intake of air. I hoped that was a good sign.

CHAPTER TWENTY-FIVE
★ *Emma* ★

The limo slowed as we drove by the front of the club. I peered through the tinted glass. "Are all those people waiting to get in? We'll be in line forever."

Our driver, Sol, a beefy guy with arms the size of my waist, eyed me through his rearview mirror. "Leave that to me."

Breanna bumped my shoulder as she gazed out my window. "Nick Black brings a crowd at full price. With a free concert, what did you expect?"

"You look gorgeous, by the way," I said. Her long dark hair fell in soft waves over her shoulders, and she wore a daring low-cut tank top, snug jeans, and high heels.

"Maybe so, but tonight, you'll be the most beautiful woman in the whole place." Breanna kissed me on the cheek. Not sure what was up with that, but I didn't have time to ask. Sol had turned the limo around and was pulling up right in front of the entrance. It was a dark brick building, guarded by a tall, wide, bald guy with an earpiece.

"Wait here." Sol climbed out, leaving us parked

illegally as he strode up to the bouncer at the door.

After Sol flipped a thumb at us, another guy dashed over to my side and opened the door. Breanna nudged me, and I scrambled out. We were ushered ahead of everyone in line, past the velvet ropes, through the door, and down a short hallway. Inside, my eyes adjusted to the dim lighting as we weaved past round, cloth-covered tables to a seat right in front of the stage.

"Nice table," Breanna commented as she claimed a chair. "That was so sweet of Theo to set this up."

"Yes, it was." I'd been a Full Throttle fan since the first time I'd heard them, even bought their CD. Hell, I frequently sang their songs for karaoke. Nick's voice had a rich, deep timber that soothed yet excited, and made him perfect for singing rock. But did they sound as good live? I hoped so. Either way, being treated like a VIP was kind of nice.

"Something to drink?" A waiter handed us each a menu. Instead of rushing off, he waited patiently while I decided what I wanted.

"A glass of your house wine, please." Assuming this place worked the same way as The Wagon Wheel, I fished out a twenty from my purse and handed it to him.

He waved a palm. "I'm under very strict orders to give you anything you want on the band."

"Thank you so much," Breanna said with a smile, before she eyed me. "Wow, you're conveniently connected."

"I guess." I hoped Theo wasn't trying to soften me up for something. He wasn't a bad guy, and he was plenty good-looking. He just wasn't my type. Then again, I had a feeling no one would be my type so long as Liam was alive.

But I couldn't think about him right now. I was out with my best friend at a trendy night club and being treated as royalty. I intended to have fun tonight if it killed me.

Music blared from the speakers as guys set up equipment on the stage, and the place got louder as more people crowded in. Breanna and I laughed and talked while we ate, and by the time we finished our meals, the place buzzed with energy.

When the waiter took away our plates, the house music lowered as a heavyset man with shoulder-length brown hair took the stage and adjusted the microphone. "Good evening, and thank you all for coming. Without further delay, it is my honor to present" — he waited two seconds before shouting — "Full Throttle!"

The crowd applauded, some girls screamed. The lights dimmed as four guys replaced the man on stage. They took their positions, instruments ready, and the light over the singer dimmed a little more, drowning his features in darkness. He seemed leaner than in the magazines and taller. And something about the way he moved seemed strangely familiar. He dragged the guitar strap over his shoulder, letting the guitar hang effortlessly against his hip, and then he raised the microphone.

Though I couldn't see his face, tingles spread over my neck and shoulders at the sight of Nick Black in the flesh.

The lead guitarist hit the first chord, and I recognized the tune almost immediately. The same song Liam had butchered his second week of karaoke at the Wagon Wheel. Liam... he wasn't for me, I reminded myself. I needed to get him out of my head.

When the song ended, and the last chord played, the audience shouted and stomped their feet. When the applause died, Nick Black bent toward the microphone and cleared his throat.

"Last month, I took off. Got rid of the hair, shaved off my goatee, and got in my car without telling anyone where I was going. Hell, I didn't even know where I was going."

That voice...

The lights gradually brightened until I saw Nick's face. *Liam's* face!

I sucked in a shaky breath, and my gaze shot to Breanna—who had practically invited herself along as soon as I'd told her about Theo's offer. I'd figured she was a big fan, but now I wondered if she'd had another reason for coming.

"Close your mouth, sweetie." Breanna tapped under my chin.

"You knew about Liam?"

"Yes." She covered my hand with her own. "Just listen."

That wouldn't be easy since the only thing running through my head was that Nick Black had worked the bar with me, driven me home, danced with me, held me, kissed me, and played with my daughter. I had totally wanted Liam, but never, in a million years would I have ever dated Nick Black, the guy I'd read about, the guy who had almost daily escapades on TMZ.

Yet somehow, when I looked at the man onstage,

I didn't see Nick Black. I saw Liam, the guy who had stood up for me, protected me, and taken care of me, the guy who'd colored with Scarlet and made her giggle. And I didn't want to miss a single word that came from his mouth.

"The plan was to pass through the small town and move on," Liam continued. "Ended up tending bar and getting to know this amazing woman and her daughter. Spent some weeks there, and I fell a little bit more in love with them every day." He paused to scan the audience, and his eyes landed on me.

My mouth parted and I hugged myself, trying to dial down the adrenaline roaring through my limbs.

"I'm guessing every one of you here has heard more than one juicy thing about me, something that makes me every kind of wrong for any decent girl."

A few girls in the crowd yelled.

"I'll be the first to admit that most of what you read about me is true. So naturally, when I met this girl, I didn't want her to know who I really was. Being around her gave me a chance to be someone else, and I liked who I was when I was with her. Before I knew it, my time was up, and I left. I was all packed and standing beside my car ready to go, and she asked me to stay. But I didn't. What was one more mistake on top of so many others?" He flashed the audience that sexy smile.

My eyes misted, and I wondered what rehashing history mattered. Why the hell was I here, and had Liam orchestrated this whole thing?

"So I arrived in LA to an empty home, and all I thought

about was her. I didn't do anything about it. I mean, why would anyone want to do something that might make them happy, right? So I moped around the house, accomplishing very little. But I did write this song."

He strummed a few notes on his guitar, then the bass joined in and the drums. Liam brought the microphone closer and began to sing. "Showed up at the bar all beaten and worn..."

As he sang, I turned to Breanna. "What the hell is going on?"

"Wait and see." She patted my hand. Okay, so she wasn't going to cough up anything.

Liam finished the chorus and went into the next verse.

"I thought I could do it, stay disconnected, but the longer I knew you, the more I expected. You gave me that look, and I wanted to stay. You whispered my name, and I pushed you away. So take this chance, and find someone new, 'cause I can't believe, I'm the best you can do."

My breath froze in my lungs, my chest squeezing as he went into the chorus.

"I'm not worth your tears, or wasting your good years, on a man who won't be there. If I could, I would, I swear. Take this chance, find someone new. Someone who will always come through. 'Cause I can't believe I'm the best you can do."

He did the chorus one more time, and the audience clapped while tears trickled down my cheek.

So that's why he'd left? Nick Black didn't think he

was worth my tears? The fact that he'd sung this for me in front of everyone only proved that he was. But why sing *those* words for me? Had he brought me here just to tell me I needed to move on?

After the weeks of crying for him, I hadn't allowed myself to hope. Because if I did and I was disappointed again, recovering would be even harder.

"Without all the hair, no one recognized me. I actually behaved myself. Sort of." Liam gave the audience a lopsided smile. "Figured I was doing her a favor by letting her get on with her life. Then I got home, and I realized... all that crap I was doing before I met her, that wasn't me. The person that I was with her, the man who was there for her, that's the *real* me. That's the kind of person I want to be."

I took a couple deep breaths, trying to loosen my constricting throat.

"Emma," his eyes found me again. "I'm in love with you. You're the first girl I've ever said that to, and you'll be the last."

He removed the microphone from the stand, tugged it loose, and jumped off the stage, taking it with him. He stopped right in front of my table and dropped to his knees. My stomach did a somersault.

"I know I have no right to hope for anything from you, especially forgiveness. But I'm going to ask anyway because, more than anything, I want you and Scarlet in my life. And I'm hoping when I ask you the same question you asked me when I was leaving, you'll give me a different answer." Liam took my free hand and pressed it against his heart. "Emma, will you please stay?"

I swallowed, unable to speak and afraid to move for fear that my jellylike legs might not support me. My heart was telling me to say yes. My head was too jumbled to give me any advice. The crowd roared, and cameras exploded into what seemed a million different lights, but I barely noticed any of it as he gently slid his hands behind my neck and pulled me to him. His mouth covered mine, and for a moment, I lost myself in the kiss.

Much too soon, he withdrew. "Was that a yes?"

My gaze drifted to the crowd, all eyes on us, and it hit me how life would be if I were in a relationship with the singer of Full Throttle. Messy. Crazy. Hectic. I'd be in the spotlight by his side. But I didn't care about any of that so long as we had our special moments in private, just as we did before. And if he really loved me, that's all I needed.

I reached over to the microphone and switched it off. "What specifically are you offering?"

He laid his palms on my cheeks. "An exclusive relationship. A commitment. A promise for more." He searched my eyes. "Ah, hell, Emma. I've been miserable without you." He leaned in and whispered in my ear, "I know I need to earn your trust first. Right now, I just want to be with you for as long as you're willing."

My insides warmed. Liam was offering exactly what I wanted. What was I waiting for? I clicked the microphone back on.

"What do you say, Em? Will you stay?"

"No," I said. The audience hissed, and Liam's face

fell. I slid my arms around his neck. "*We'll* stay."

"Let's get out of here." Liam rested his forehead against mine a moment, then relieved me of the microphone. "Thank you, everyone, for sharing this moment with me. Have a great night." He passed it to the nearest body, draped his arm around my shoulder, and led me toward the exit. I braked and glanced over my shoulder for Breanna. "I can't leave her."

"She's not expecting to ride with us. Who do you think helped set this up?" His eyes focused on the exit. "C'mon."

I waved to her, and she blew me a kiss. Then I let Liam steer me outside.

Moments later, I was seated beside Liam, and the limo was easing onto the street. When I turned toward him, he brushed his knuckles against my cheeks and gazed into my eyes.

"I don't deserve you, but I don't care anymore. I'm going to work hard every day to be the man you want, and maybe you'll never change your mind."

"You're *already* the man I want. Just as you are." I twisted and slung my leg over to straddle him. I felt his warm hands at my waist as I bent to taste his lips. As soon as our mouths touched, he crushed me against him, his tongue searching, teasing, and I melted against him. Heat flared in my belly, and when his lips wandered to my neck, shivers danced along my spine.

I groaned, knowing I couldn't stay out with Liam all night. "I have to go back to the hotel. I don't want Scarlet waking up and me not there. I know you have a perfectly good house but there's plenty of room at the hotel. I have adjoining rooms. We'll have one of them all to ourselves."

His jaw went slack. "Emma Taylor, are you inviting me to stay the night in your hotel room?"

"Absolutely." I kissed him on the nose.

"It's scandalous." Liam grinned but faltered a moment later. "We have to stop by my house to check on something though." His gaze darted away. "I, uh, got a puppy who's stuck in a crate and probably dying to pee right now. Adorable yellow lab. Scarlet's going to love him."

"You bought my daughter a puppy?" After I'd asked him not to?

He pressed his palms to my cheeks, looking into my eyes. "I bought *myself* a puppy... for Scarlet to play with."

He'd worked out a way to do as I'd asked, while still giving Scarlet what she wanted? "I love you, Liam. So much."

His brows shot up. "Yeah?"

"Yeah." I grinned and planted my hands behind his head and kissed him, softer this time. My insides heated, and all I wanted was to get to get him alone. Which could be very soon since the limo had just braked. I peered through the window to see we'd pulled up in front of a huge house and the gate was already opening. "Actually... Lily's not expecting me back at the hotel right away, so we have some time. You let the puppy out to pee, we'll play with him for a bit, then he goes right back into the crate. You and I have some business to take care of."

"Sure am lookin' forward to that." His mouth curled up in that sexy way.

I dropped a chaste kiss on his forehead before

climbing off him and reaching for the handle. "Let's go meet our new puppy."

The End

★

If you enjoyed Liam and Emma's story, please recommend The Runaway Rock Star to friends, reader's groups and discussion boards or show your love by reviewing it on Amazon, GoodReads or your own site. Thank you!

★

Books in the Rock Star Kisses series:

The Runaway Rock Star

BOOK ONE

The Baby and the Rock Star

BOOK TWO

Tempting the Rock Star

BOOK THREE

THE ROCK STAR KISSES SERIES

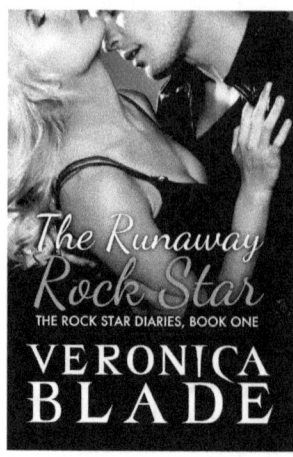

An infamous bad-boy rocker falls for a small-town girl who has no idea who he is. Considering his reputation, that's probably a good thing.

He's working hard to get his life back on track after three years of alcohol-induced oblivion. She can't forget their one wild night together—that he doesn't remember.

Book Three 'Tempting the Rock Star'

coming soon!

★

To receive updates, pre-order discount alerts or news on upcoming releases, please visit VeronicaBlade.com and sign up for Veronica's newsletter.

More Titles by Veronica Blade

Should a woman who's unable to forget her first love give "happily ever after" one more try?

When good-girl Maddie switches places with her famous bad-girl twin Jackie, she has some pretty high stilettos to fill.

When Hunter realizes he botched the annulment of his marriage to his longtime friend, he must decide if she and their marriage are worth fighting for.

A micro trilogy including Single-Handed, Singled Out (book two) & Single-minded (book three).

SHAPES OF AUTUMN SERIES

Thrown to the Wolves:
The Legend of Hannah & Eli (prequel)

My Wolf's Bane (book one)

Wolves at the Door
(book two)

Dead Wolf Walking
(book three)

The Dark Wolf (book four)

Lord of the Wolves (book five)

Different species. Mortal enemies. It'll never work, but they'll die trying.

Free e-Book Offer

For a limited time, *Thrown To The Wolves: The Legend of Hannah & Eli (Shapes of Autumn Prequel)* is available for free from my website.

Find out more at VeronicaBlade.com

More Titles by Veronica Blade

A newbie witch enlists help from the scrumptious school bad-boy to make her life and death choice between two battling covens.

The witch queen must make the impossible choice between abandoning the throne and her people, or spending eternity with the man she loves.

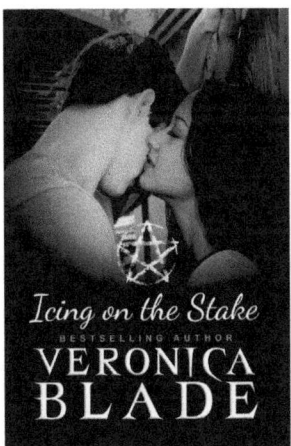

Sofia lays her hard-won anonymity on the line by saving the most popular boy in school. Worse, she's been exposed to the vampire hunters who attacked him.

A Cinderella who spends her nights as a wolf. A prince with a taste for blood.

About Veronica Blade

Veronica Blade lives near Carson City, Nevada with her husband and furbabies but also spends a lot of time in southern California. She writes sweet romances to live vicariously through her characters. Except her heroes and heroines lead far more interesting lives—and they are always way hotter.

★

You can visit Veronica Blade on Facebook, check out her website at VeronicaBlade.com or follow her on Twitter @VeronicaBlade. You can even e-mail her at veronica@ veronicablade.com. She loves hearing from readers!